I know who owns the diary. The script is a little smoother, but I recognize the fat, curly letters even before I see the name written at the bottom. She used to write it on all my folders. It made my stuff look like it belonged to her. I never minded. I thought it made *me* look like hers. Like I belonged to her.

But I haven't spoken to Tessa Waye since sixth grade, and I seriously doubt she's trying to reconnect now. This doesn't make any sense, and I don't know why I turn another page, but I do and there it is: a single yellow Post-it Note pasted across some random Wednesday morning's entry. It says:

FIND ME.

ND ME FIND ME FIND ME FIND ME FIND ME
FIND ME FIND ME FIND ME FIND ME FIND M
ND ME FIND ME FIND ME FIND ME FIND ME
FIND ME FIND ME FIND ME FIND ME FIND M
ND ME FIND ME FIND ME FIND ME FIND ME
FIND ME FIND ME FIND ME FIND ME FIND M
ND ME FIND ME FIND ME FIND ME FIND ME
FIND ME FIND ME FIND ME FIND ME FIND M
ND ME FIND ME FIND ME FIND ME FIND ME
FIND ME FIND ME FIND ME FIND ME FIND M

ND ME **FIND** ME FIND ME FIND ME FIND ME

FIND ME FIND ME FIND ME FIND ME FIND M
ND ME FIND ME FIND ME FIND ME FIND ME
FIND ME FIND ME FIND ME FIND ME FIND M
ND ME FIND ME FIND ME FIND ME FIND ME
FIND ME FIND ME FIND ME FIND ME FIND M
ND ME FIND ME FIND ME FIND ME FIND ME
FIND ME FIND ME FIND ME FIND ME FIND M

ND ME FIND ME FIND ME FIND **ME** FIND ME

FIND ME FIND ME FIND ME FIND ME FIND M
ND ME FIND ME FIND ME FIND ME FIND ME
FIND ME FIND ME FIND ME FIND ME FIND M
ND ME FIND ME FIND ME FIND ME FIND ME

FIND ME FIND ME **ROMILY BERNARD** FIND M

ND ME FIND ME FIND ME FIND ME FIND ME
FIND ME FIND ME FIND ME FIND ME FIND M
ND ME FIND ME FIND ME FIND ME FIND ME

FIND ME FIND ME FIND **HARPER TEEN** FIND M
An Imprint of HarperCollinsPublishers

ND ME FIND ME FIND ME FIND ME FIND ME
FIND ME FIND ME FIND ME FIND ME FIND M
ND ME FIND ME FIND ME FIND ME FIND ME
FIND ME FIND ME FIND ME FIND ME FIND M

HarperTeen is an imprint of HarperCollins Publishers.

For information address HarperCollins Children's Books, a division of HarperCollins Publishers, 195 Broadway, New York, NY 10007.
www.epicreads.com

ISBN 978-0-06-222904-5

Typography by Joel Tippie
18 19 20 CG/LSCH 10 9 8 7 6 5 4 3 2
❖
First paperback edition, 2014

For Tony, who believed

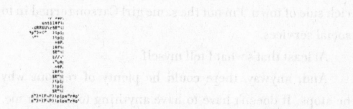

I'm halfway through the remote computer's firewall when Detective Carson parks on the other side of our street. This isn't usually a time I like to be interrupted—actually, when I'm hacking, I *never* like to be interrupted—but because he makes my feet hit the floor so I'm ready to run, because he makes my heart thump bass lines in my ears, because it's him and he's back and I'm scared, I take a few minutes. I sit in the dark, watch the unmarked police car idle, and tell myself it'll be okay.

After all, I'm prepared. I wired my foster parents' security cameras to route the front yard video feed through my computer. I can see everything—the blacked-out sedan, the shadowy streetscape, the neighbors' darkened houses—without leaving my desk. For a full five minutes, there's nothing. No movement. No anything. This should be all kinds of uninteresting, but my palms still go slick.

It's stupid to be scared. He can't touch me now. Not when I have this shiny new life. My foster parents belong in a Disney movie. My sister and I live with them on the rich side of town. I'm not the same girl Carson turned in to social services.

At least that's what I tell myself.

And, anyway, there could be plenty of reasons why he stops. It doesn't have to have anything to do with me. He could stop because he's been assigned to this area. Or because he lives nearby.

Or because he's watching you. In my head, I smother the words, but they still squirm.

He doesn't know. He doesn't know. He doesn't know. I flick my eyes to the lines of computer code running across my monitor but can't concentrate. I have to keep repeating keystrokes.

My dad's been gone for ten months and you'd think Carson would take a hint, but he's told everyone he thinks Lily and I are his last links to tracking down our drug-dealer father. He might actually be right, and that's what really scares me. Because if my dad does return, if he does see a policeman outside our new house, he'll think I've turned narc. It'll ruin everything.

Well, everything that's left.

It's so damn little I almost laugh. Then I hear the car door slam, and my heart rides up my throat with spurs.

He's never gotten out before. I jerk around to better face the monitor. It's definitely Carson. I recognize his lanky build, the way his shoulders crouch underneath his Members Only jacket. He's killed the sedan's engine, but it's okay. Really. He's just lingering by the curb.

It's fine.

Until he starts moving toward the house.

I nearly overturn my chair. The wheels screech backward, and my bare feet slap the floor. I'm standing now. Ready.

But I don't know what I'm ready to do. If I go downstairs, I'll have to use the windows to track him, and he might see the movement.

But staying here's no good. The security cameras only watch the front. The rear and side yards are blind, which means I'm blind. I'll have to wait for his moves, his decisions.

No way that's going to happen.

I grab my baseball bat—the one I keep next to my bed, the one everyone thinks I have because I just *love* me some sports—and go to my bedroom door.

And I can't get my feet to move any farther.

This isn't how moments like these are supposed to go. My hands shouldn't be shaking. I shouldn't be Wick Tate, the girl I am. I should be the sister Lily deserves.

And I'm going to be. But the two feet of space between my body and the door might as well be two miles for all the good it's doing me. I'm afraid. People like me were meant to stay behind computers. It's where we belong.

I wrench the door open anyway. In the hallway, there's only blackened silence, but the curtains drift like they've just been brushed, and somewhere downstairs, something creaks.

It ignites static inside my head, like my brain's been suddenly tuned to a television channel filled with snow.

Adrenaline, I think, forcing one foot in front of the other. *I'm kicking into panic mode, but it can be controlled.*

And it will *be controlled.* I hoist the bat onto one shoulder and start for the stairway, making it almost to the top step before I realize I'm not alone. There's a shadow sliding along the wall, inching up from downstairs. For a heartbeat, I think I might faint.

It's Carson. He's already here. I've let Lily down. I've—

The shadow creeps closer, and my sister's face floats out of the dark. "Wick?"

"Jesus, Lily!"

Lily steps forward, drawing close enough so I can see how she's eyeing the baseball bat. "What are you doing?"

"We have a visitor." Weird how my voice sounds flat and confident when my insides are churning and liquid. I push past her, telling myself I'm fine, and maybe I am. Maybe I just needed to see the last person I have left to lose.

I hustle down the stairs, one hand skimming the wall. "Stay put."

But, of course, she doesn't. Lily trails me so closely her toes brush my heels.

"What kind of visitor?"

I can barely hear her, but I know what she's really getting at. Lily's hoping it isn't what I think, that there's some pleasant explanation to all this. It's a fantasy I can't afford. Actually, it's a fantasy neither of us can afford.

I round on her. "Lil, it's five thirty in the morning. What do *you* think Carson's here for?"

Even though it quivers, Lily's chin lifts. "Maybe he's here because he knows about your hacking."

He couldn't. "He doesn't."

"How can you be sure?"

"Because I am." *Mostly.*

Below us, a dark shape sweeps past the windows. It hesitates near the front door, and we watch something arch through the air.

It's an arm. A *hand.* Carson's checking the window lock.

Lily grabs me, and for a second, she looks far younger than eleven. "Wick, we have to wake up Bren and Todd."

No way. No how. Our foster parents would have a flying duck fit. Bren and Todd have no clue any of this is going on, and I prefer it that way. They don't need to know about my little computer habits. They don't need to know there's a hollow-faced policeman coming by only at night. They already know enough—anything more and they might turn me in to the cops, and Lily over to the state.

Not going to happen.

And why would anyone believe me anyway? Todd would want a confrontation with the detective. I'd be dragged out to give my version, and Carson would have some sort of lie to explain everything away—police always do—and then I'm left looking like the lying juvenile delinquent everyone already thinks I am.

"Wick!" Lily's fingers dig in harder, and I shake her off. "Call them," she whispers, and there's a simmering hysteria in her voice I haven't heard since the day the police came for our dad.

"Go back upstairs."

"Call them." Lily repeats the words like a prayer, but they're really a conjuring spell. My sister wants to summon some mythical parents to protect us, some powerful adults to make all the nightmares vanish. I don't really blame her. It's tough to feel safe when all you have is me.

"You don't have to do this anymore, Wick."

If I don't, who will? Bren? Todd? I know Lily wants them to fix everything, but why should they?

Just because someone should protect you doesn't mean they will. I almost say it, but I swallow the words. That's not something I want Lily to know.

Even if I'm pretty sure she already does.

Lily plucks at my elbow. "He wouldn't dare break in."

And my brain agrees with her, but the rest of me . . . the rest of me believes he would dare. Cops don't have to be careful with people like us. We're the enemy. Lily and I may have a fancy new life, but maybe he knows what's still inside us, and that's what makes me raise my bat. "You know as well as I do that they're not always the good guys."

Through the window, we watch Carson twist to the

right. He hovers for a moment, like he heard something, and then strides across the front of the house.

Where's he going now? Confused, I press a little closer to the window, half expecting him to jump into my field of vision, horror-movie-style.

I creep another inch closer and see the last of his shadow as he turns the corner of the house.

What's he doing? There's nothing around there except—the back door! I spin on my heel, my chest funneling shut. *Did we lock it?*

I seize Lily's hand and drag her down the hallway, dodging Bren's yoga gear and Todd's line of penny loafers. I can barely see, but we move pretty quickly in the dark. We're good at it. We've had practice.

We just haven't practiced enough.

Carson passes the sunroom's tall windows before we've even reached the end of the hall. He's on the rear steps, under the yellow porch light, by the time my feet hit the kitchen tile. I skid to a halt, and Lily shrinks into my hip. There's no sound except for our breathing: too loud and too harsh.

Outside, Carson presses one gloved hand to the window, shielding his eyes to look inside, and in the dark, my gasp is strangled.

He won't be able to see anything. He won't know we're here. My brain repeats this, but my body creeps closer to the wall.

Carson's hand seizes the door handle. The metal click-clicks. He's testing the lock, and it's holding. Thank God.

I sag in relief until I hear him laugh. Low and curdled, it sounds like it surfaced from some deep, dark place inside him.

Lily cringes. "Are you sure he's only looking for Dad?"

"Yes."

No.

She makes some impossibly small whimper, an animal sound, and I'm afraid he'll hear it. He can't. I *know* he can't. But when Carson tenses up, when his head tilts so his deep-set eyes slide into blackened hollows, I wrap one arm around my sister's thin shoulders.

I pull her closer and closer until I feel our bones meet through our skin. We stand in the dark, and we watch him smile.

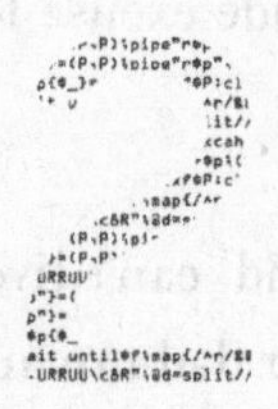

"Wick, police officers are supposed to be good."

Sure they are, I think. And parents are there when you need them, your teachers care what happens to you, and someday your prince will come. But Lily knows all those lies, so I don't say a word. My sister is vibrating in the dim light. Anything more and she'll splinter.

"Well, yeah, usually they are," I say.

But this one isn't. The unspoken words hang between us, suspended with strobe lights.

We stand in Bren's kitchen long after Carson's left. All around us, shadows are draining down the walls. In my panic, I didn't realize how close we were to dawn.

"Why was he really here, Wick?"

"I already told you." I rub my eyes until colors erupt in starbursts. "He wants Dad."

"But Dad's not here."

Yeah, exactly, so where does that leave you? It leaves me with the hacking. He must know about my . . . extracurricular activities. My chest shrinks around the thought. I don't answer Lily. I could. I even have a ready-made excuse for just such an occasion.

Actually, I have several.

Consider these my top three desert island, can't-live-without-'em picks: Carson's here because our dad ran and Carson thinks we're helping him stay on the run. Carson's here because our dad ran and we're now Carson's last connection to him. Carson's here because he's looking for any loose ends he can further unravel.

They're all very tidy little excuses, but I can't seem to say any of them because there's a tiny, nagging sensation eating up my insides. It's very small, but it has teeth and claws.

Lily's stiff, like the same thing eating me might be eating her, too. And when she turns to face me, I know it is. There's accusation in her eyes.

"He must know. You have to stop hacking."

"He doesn't know, and I'm not hurting anyone." Lily glares at me, and I roll my eyes. I refuse to feel guilty about this. The spiky knot blooming in my throat is not regret. The tightening in my gut is not worry.

It's anger.

"I'm not hurting anyone who doesn't deserve to be hurt," I amend.

And I'm pretty sure that's true. No, I *am* sure that's true. I run online investigations. I specialize in cheating husbands. Yes, it's hacking, but it's not hacking to crash servers or set loose viruses.

And yeah, sure, I do it for a price. I charge for invading some guy's privacy, for looking through his bank records or email files. But Lily and I need the money, and these women—my customers—need answers. I make sure they really know who they love. I make sure no one ends up like my mom did. Every single one of my customers begs for help, thanks me when I finish. I've said "you're welcome" so many times, the words taste bitter.

I'm Robin Hood with Kool-Aid-colored hair—a hero—but Lily's looking at me like I'm some sort of villain, like I would twirl my mustache while tying busty girls to train tracks, like I let her down.

"We have Bren and Todd now, Wick."

"Oh yeah?" Oddly, analyzing the situation calms me. I look at Lily and feel stronger. "For how long? Dad's been gone for almost a year and the last three homes didn't keep us past a couple of months. We have to look out for ourselves."

"But what about—?" Lily waves one hand at the door, unable to bring herself to say Carson's name.

"Don't worry. I'll take care of it." She ought to know I'm full of shit, but Lily relaxes like she believes every word. You'd think it would make me feel proud.

She flings herself into me and we hug. Hard. "Lil, if I

get enough money, it won't matter when they throw us out. We'll be able to go anywhere. I know you hate the hacking, but the money will keep us safe."

"*If* we need it."

"*When* we need it."

Upstairs, a shower cuts on, and a woman starts singing about how the hills are alive with the sound of music.

For God's sake, Bren. I run one hand over my face. No one has a right to be that happy without serious meds being involved. It's just annoying for the rest of us.

Usually, I would get Lily to agree with me, but she's already gone. I can hear her dashing across the upstairs hallway, making for her bedroom. She knows the game. When Bren comes to wake us up, Lily will need to look like nothing happened. *I'll* need to look like nothing happened.

Except I feel so shaky, I know I'll never pull it off. I'm not in the mood for sunny. In fact, I'm not in the mood for any of this. I need space. So I shove my feet into my battered Converse sneakers—the only things left from my wardrobe Bren didn't pitch into the garbage—and bang through the front door.

It would be a pretty excellent exit too if I didn't nearly trip and fall on my face. Something tangled up my feet. I twist and see a small, brown package sitting on the top step.

It's addressed to me.

It wasn't here last night.

But Carson was. The idea pops sweat between my

shoulder blades. I start to walk away, but that won't work. Bren will only find it and then there will be questions and I'll have to come up with answers and I don't have the energy.

The package is the size of a paperback novel. I could fit it in my messenger bag, throw it away later.

Because I definitely shouldn't open it.

Because he definitely has to be playing some game with me.

But if I don't, I'll look scared. Worse, I'll *know* I'm scared.

Scared enough to go back inside? I look at the house, think about explaining it to Lily, think about explaining it to Bren.

Yeah, never mind. I hook two fingers into the wrapping's edges and rip. The result is a pretty big letdown. Carson's left me a water-stained book.

Well, okay then. I rub my thumb along the frayed binding, irritation pinching all my insides like mosquitoes are eating me alive. Is Carson trying to make friends? Not freaking likely. So what's his angle? I can't figure it out, and instead of feeling relieved, I feel foolish.

And worried.

And even though I know I'm alone, I cut a quick glance up and down the street. Nothing. No one. I'm safe. But I still want to run.

There has to be something I'm missing here. There has to be a point I'm not understanding. I pick at a pear-shaped stain on the book's corner.

Maybe there's a message. I open the cover, and amusement temporarily overrides my confusion. This isn't a book. It's a diary. *Well, whatever.*

I didn't think people did this sort of thing anymore. I've never been attracted to the idea myself. I mean, why would you want to publish all your secrets? Why would you want to write down everything that scares you?

It's like making a map of your weaknesses. It's not smart. But all that aside, why would someone send it to me? Then I flip to the next page, and my stomach rocks to one side, settles upside down.

I know who owns the diary. The script is a little smoother, but I recognize the fat, curly letters even before I see the name written at the bottom. She used to write it on all my folders. It made my stuff look like it belonged to her. I never minded. I thought it made *me* look like hers. Like I belonged to her.

But I haven't spoken to Tessa Waye since sixth grade, and I seriously doubt she's trying to reconnect now. This doesn't make any sense, and I don't know why I turn another page, but I do and there it is: a single yellow Post-it Note pasted across some random Wednesday morning's entry. It says:

FIND ME.

He said if I told anyone, he'd kill me. I believe him.

—Page 49 of Tessa Waye's diary

Find me? There's a flickering under my scalp, a tingling along my spine. The annoying mosquitoes have grown into spiders. They're crawling across my skin. *What the hell is this?*

I turn the Post-it Note over like there's going to be some better explanation on the other side, and naturally, there isn't. There's just *Find me* in slanting black letters. The handwriting doesn't match Tessa's. The two words are stabbed across the paper.

"Morning!"

The voice makes my feet stutter against the sidewalk. It's another jogger, and no matter how perky his greeting, the dude looks miserable. He slogs down our street, his tennis shoes trailing heavily along the asphalt.

"Morning!" It's a half-assed response, and that won't work. My voice sounds scraped and scared instead of bright and perky. A tone like that could draw a round of "Are you okay, little girl?"

So I summon up a thousand-watt smile, but it ends up not mattering. The guy's halfway up the hill now.

I glare at his back, hating him for noticing me. It happens a lot now. I blame Bren. In my old clothes and my old life, no one noticed me. Now I'm on the rich side of town, wearing Abercrombie. I'm all . . . approachable.

Damn it all.

Above me, the pink sky is marbled with clouds. It's going to be another gorgeous day. Lots of sunshine. Probably a breeze. Other than the diary, there's no sign of Detective Carson, and even better than that, there's no sign of my dad.

It ought to make me feel loads better. But I don't. *Find me* clings to me with spiderweb strings. I can't wipe it away. I start to close the diary, and a dirty fifty-dollar bill falls on my sneakers.

I usually take a small payment up front before beginning a job, but that's via an online wire transfer. I don't take personal deliveries on *any* of my work, and I sure as hell don't find people in the real world. I do cyberspace. I'm kind of specific.

I'm also supposed to be a secret.

There are only three people who know about me, and none of them would make contact like this. That means . . .

Someone *else* knows.

Any other student might look weird showing up at school at seven in the morning, but I've been taking computer courses every semester since freshman year, so I don't look any weirder than usual when I edge through the gym's side door. Homeroom doesn't start for another hour and a half, so I have plenty of time and minimal witnesses. Exactly the way I like it.

I stop by my locker, trading my history book for my math notes, before heading to the computer lab. Mrs. Lowe leaves the classroom open in case her students need to use the equipment for one of her assignments. She should know better. Really, I mean, anyone could walk in here and start using the computers for their own purposes.

People like me, for instance.

I push open the door, anticipating a stretch of isolation, and realize it's *so* not going to happen. I'm not alone. In my haze, I missed seeing Griff, my lab partner. He looks up, and his eyes kind of . . . flicker. I don't know how to describe it, but I know he's surprised.

Maybe it's my hair. I'm a natural blonde, the kind of pale yellow that belongs to princesses in fairy tales, Barbie dolls, and my dad. So I dye it. Frequently. I changed the color to dark red yesterday afternoon, picked the shade because it would make me look like a graphic novel character. I thought the superhero red looked awesome. I guess Griff doesn't agree.

I don't care—*I don't*—but my ears still go all hot. These days, I keep wishing I were someone else even though I kind of am. My new life is crammed on top of me, pinching like it will never, ever fit. I hate how stupid I feel. Maybe my mom felt like that too. Maybe that's why she jumped. Makes me wonder if she had the right idea.

She didn't, of course—I'd never leave Lily like she left us—but the running-away part I get. She was escaping my dad. It was her salvation, but it made our lives worse.

"You're here early." Griff's smile feels like a kick to my stomach. He straightens—so he can see me better—and I have to fight the urge to squirm. I don't know why he pays attention to me. It makes me nervous.

"Yeah, pretty early." I start to say more, mention something about my upcoming English project, anything that won't keep me standing here like a total dork with my mouth hanging open, but I don't. This is kind of a problem I have with Griff. He has the weirdest bottle-green eyes. They're very clear, and they make me feel very . . . muddy.

I clear my throat. "I actually got up on time."

"Me too." Griff returns to concentrating on his notepad. He's drawing again—actually he's always drawing and I want to ask about it, but I chicken out.

You'd think we would be friends. Until I went into the foster system, I lived two streets away from him, but we're nothing alike. Griff moves pretty easily through school.

He's funny, gets along with everyone, and has even been known to save bullied band geeks. If I stood up to one of Matthew Bradford's roid rages, I'd be a smear on the gym floor. Griff never hesitated. Part of me really admires him for it. . . . Part of me is jealous he can pull it off.

I weave through the scattered chairs, heading for the computer workstation closest to the rear. Lauren Cross, my best friend, would say it's my favorite, but probably because it's her favorite too.

Back here, there's a little more room for my stuff, and I can lean against the concrete walls. If anyone asks, I say it's because I like to sleep through the lectures. But honestly, I just like it better. It's almost as good as being invisible.

I have a few things for my biology class I should do, but I'm not in the mood to mess with any of them. Carson is branded on my brain.

He's after our dad. And I say have at it, buddy. Party on. Unless . . . unless he knows about me. Could I have made a mistake? Could it have led Carson to me?

I don't think he left Tessa's diary—I don't think he even noticed it was there. Doesn't mean the detective isn't keeping tabs, though, and if he wants a closer look at me, I should get a closer look at him. Email would be a good starting point. I don't remember if he had a BlackBerry, but they're easy enough to break into if he did.

In fact, I'd love to start now. The want is bad enough to make my teeth ache, but I don't dare try anything at school. The availability of hardware is attractive, but not enough to chance the administration's spyware. I'm not willing to risk it.

Yet.

A few Google searches never hurt anyone, though, and I spend almost forty minutes scrolling through online newspaper articles that mention Carson. His picture is on the police department's website, and there's a blurb commending him for his superior level of community involvement.

Community involvement? Is that what we're calling it now? Carson's grinning like a jackass, and I'm sure it's supposed to be charming, but all I see is the skull behind the smile.

Outside the classroom, the noise level is swelling. Windows line the front half of the computer lab, and I can see more students dragging in from the parking lot. Their voices are unusually low, humming like wasps.

Well, except for one.

Jenna Maxwell is crying.

Sobbing, actually.

This is unusual for a lot of reasons. Mostly because Jenna is never unhappy. She has the proportions of a Bratz doll and the temperament of a pit viper. She's president of our class, heads up the Beta Club, and enjoys watching nerds get tossed into Dumpsters.

As one of those nerds, I'm pretty interested in anything that would make Jenna cry. Part of me really hopes her convertible's been keyed, but I would also settle for an STD.

Jenna briefly disappears into a pack of girls, and I slide my eyes back to the computer screen. Something's definitely up. There's too much hugging going on.

"Amazing," Griff says, stretching his arms behind his head. "I didn't think she was programmed to cry."

"Yeah, it makes her look almost lifelike." The words shoot out of my mouth before they can be swallowed, and I envision them writhing around on the table in front of me.

Shit. I cut my gaze to Griff. He'll look at me the same disappointed way Bren and Todd do. The same way everyone does.

Except he doesn't.

Our eyes touch, and one side of his mouth slants up in what might very well be a smile. It makes my insides grow two pounds heavier, and suddenly, I don't know what to say. I should look away, but I don't.

Actually, I don't think I can.

Griff has a smile that can charm teachers, but never cheerleaders. I spent all last year kinda sorta maybe wanting him to give me that smile. Then he did, and I had no idea what to do.

Apparently, I still don't.

Griff returns to studying the cluster of girls. "I always thought they were frenemies. I guess she really was close to Tessa."

Was? I sit up a little, pressing my shoulders into the plastic chair. "What do you mean?"

Griff takes so long to answer I don't think he's going to

respond, but finally he says, "You don't know?"

"Know what?"

"Tessa jumped off a building."

The room narrows and narrows until it's sleek and long. I focus on Griff, who looks embarrassed, like he's afraid I'll cry.

Most people get that way when they're talking to me about jumpers. They stare at me, but they can only think about my mom.

"Tessa jumped off a building?" I repeat it carefully, because the words in my head are so loud I worry they'll spew from my mouth: *Find me. Find me. Find. Me.*

"Yeah, it was early yesterday." Griff passes one ink-stained hand across his face. It does nothing to loosen his gritted expression. He shakes his head like Tessa's news is a bone he's choking on.

I concentrate on the computer keys, but all I can think of is the diary curled up in my bag, pressing against my leg. You can barely see the bulge, but the edges are blooming razor blades.

"There has to be some sort of mistake."

"That's not what Jenna's saying." Griff reaches into his pocket, pulls out his cell. After briefly fiddling with the keypad, he shows me the screen. It's Jenna Maxwell's Facebook page. "She says Tessa committed suicide."

He says I'm his. His forever.

—Page 18 of Tessa Waye's diary

Suicide.

At first, I'm gaping because I can't believe it, and, then I'm gaping because I'm struggling to breathe.

Suicide? No way.

"No. You're wrong—*she's* wrong. There has to be some mistake."

"Wick, I'm really sorry. I didn't think. Please. Sit down."

Sit down? I'm not—I glance down. Blink. *Well, look at that. I* am *standing.*

I'm also making a scene. Across the computer lab, Mrs. Lowe's homeroom students are trickling in. Gazes slide in our direction.

Find me.

But I can't. I'm too late. Poor Tessa.

"Wick?" Griff edges close. Too close.

Well, shit, now I really can't breathe. I need to get out of here. I need to focus. Why would Tessa commit suicide? And why the hell would someone leave me her diary?

"Wick!" Griff's long fingers circle my wrist. The touch burns me straight to my bones. "Are you okay?"

What? I look at him and regret it. I recognize the expression twisting up his features. Griff thinks, because he knows about my mom, he knows about me. He thinks he understands—that he gets me.

He *so* doesn't. I'm not even sure I do.

"What's going on here?" Mrs. Lowe—red-eyed and rumpled—elbows her way through the students now staring at us. She takes one look at me and grabs my sleeve. "Miss Tate, are you sick?"

No, but I'm going to be if you don't move. The woman's breath reeks of coffee. As much as I love caffeine, I almost gag.

"It's my fault." Griff eases himself in between us, and for a moment, all I can see is how his shoulder blades press through his faded polo. "I told her about Tessa."

The teacher's eyelids squeeze shut like she's making a birthday wish. "You poor thing. I guess you would've found out sooner or later. Principal Matthews didn't want to break it to everyone like this, but Miss Maxwell's already told half the school. Here. Sit down." She pushes me into my seat, pins me with one hand. "You look horrible."

Gee, thanks. "I'm—"

"You look like you're about to have a panic attack."

"No, she's just . . ." Griff trails off, which is far better for him than he realizes. If he had agreed with Mrs. Lowe, he'd be waving good-bye with a stump.

"Is it a panic attack, dear?" Our teacher peers into my face again, and for the first time, I notice how her makeup is smeared from tears. "Do you need a paper bag?"

Seriously? I stare at her and try to formulate some sort of response. Yes, I was kind of hyperventilating. No, I'm not having a panic—

Wait a minute.

"Yes, ma'am." I rub my breastbone like my chest is shrinking and try to look ill. "Yes, I am. I think I'm going to be sick."

Mrs. Lowe nods like this stuff is totally normal, like it's just another day in the Wick Tate Neighborhood. It kind of makes me hate her.

"Do you want to go to the nurse?" she asks.

Hell yes, I do. The nurse, the moon, the ninth circle of hell, I don't care where I go as long as I'm away from the feeling of Griff's hands and everyone else's stares. I need space, and the nurse's office will have to do.

I shove myself up, stabbing both palms into the desk-top. Mrs. Lowe steps back, but Griff gets closer, and heat swallows my neck.

"I'll go with you."

The hell you will. I jerk my elbow away, not realizing until now he was holding it—he was holding *me*. "I'm fine."

"You look like you're going to faint."

"I'm fine," I repeat, amazed the sentence can even make it out of my mouth. My teeth are clenched. "I just need to go to the nurse's office. She'll know what to do."

I don't wait for them to agree. I push my way past them, even though Griff reaches for me like he doesn't want me to go, and Mrs. Lowe is screeching about a hall pass. I shoulder my bag and run for the door.

In the hallway, everyone's pairing off, clumping into groups so they can hug and cry.

Not a single person notices as I weave past. I've never been more grateful.

Nurse Smith's office is near the front of the school, part of the campus I carefully avoid because of its close proximity to the principal's office. And the attendance office. And the counselors' office.

You can probably see the theme here. I'm not a big fan of authority figures, and they're not a big fan of me, either. But even though I'm not very familiar with this side of the school, it's easy to find the glass door to Nurse Smith's office, because it's crawling with people.

Good God, they've brought in reinforcements.

Counselors, from the well-adjusted look of them. It's almost enough to make me turn around, but Nurse Smith sees me first. "Wicket?"

Great. We've never met, but the nurse knows me on sight. My charming reputation must precede me.

Nurse Smith presses one hand to my forehead. "You look pale, Wicket. Are you about to be sick?"

No . . . well . . . maybe. I haven't decided yet. There's a migraine starting to bloom behind my left eye.

"Sick to my stomach," I say.

One of the counselors comes forward. She's wearing a man's dress shirt and looks like she purchases cat food in bulk. "The principal said we could start working with the students. Does she need one of us?"

"No," I announce, a little loudly for someone who's supposed to be nauseous, but whatever.

Nurse Smith waves off the other woman and steers me into a chair by her desk. "Sit here. I'll get you a wet washcloth."

Yeah, sure, fine. I rub my temples while the five counselors watch with interest. They look primed and ready to save the world, one hysterical student at a time.

"Wicket," Nurse Smith says. "Breathe in through your nose and out through your mouth. Don't think about the nausea. Find your center."

Great. Give the woman some glasses and a notebook and she could be Dr. Norcut, the psychiatrist Bren sends me to. I suck air in through my nose, count to five (get bored by three), and blow everything out my mouth.

"Now." The nurse sits down in the chair next to me, hands me the washcloth. "Tell me what happened."

I spend a minute wiping and re-wiping my face, because if she makes me answer, I don't actually know what I'll say. I mean, where do I begin? Eleven years ago when my dad started cooking meth in our garage? Four years ago when they found my mom at the bottom of a building? Or does it just go back to this morning, when I found out someone knows about my hacking and left me Tessa's diary?

I shake my head like I have no idea, but behind my eyes, *Find me* glows.

Nurse Smith shifts closer. She pats my hand, but her fingers just end up bouncing off my knotted fists. "Did you know Tessa?"

I nod, but it feels like a lie. This shouldn't hurt like it does. Even though we were in the same grade, Tessa and I haven't spoken in years. She is . . . *was* popular. I'm not. She was from a prominent family, and I'm not. It sounds like a stupid divide some after-school special could fix, but it isn't. Even if her father hadn't decided my dad was dangerous and I was trash, we still wouldn't be friends. She would have left me.

Another reason it's pathetic I still miss her.

"Wick," Nurse Smith continues. "The police ruled it a suicide, and we were going to break it to the students with the help of counselors, but . . ." She pans both hands apart in a helpless gesture. "It sort of got away from us. I'm so sorry you're upset. Did you know Tessa well? Did you notice changes in her?"

"Nothing was any different," I manage. In fact, Tessa

and I were exactly like we'd been for the past five years.

"Did she tell you anything about how she was feeling?"

"No . . . nothing like that." But she used to. We used to tell each other everything, but even before Tessa's death, I was the only one who remembered that.

Nurse Smith goes quiet, and for a long moment, we just watch the counselors prepare their grief management booklets and business cards.

"You're hurting pretty badly, aren't you, dear?"

I have no idea what to say, but I sneak a look at her anyway. Nurse Smith takes it as an agreement. Her eyes go all crinkly.

"Honey, you got a lot going on."

You have no idea. I stuff a growl down my throat. Nurse Smith doesn't have a clue, and that's the point. It means I'm doing well at keeping my hacking secret. No one knows.

Right?

"Maybe you should take some time off."

Not a bad thought. I keep staring at the floor. This is all I can really concentrate on anyway, but from the sound of it, Nurse Smith is heading somewhere good with this time-off stuff.

Even if I'm not looking at her, I can feel her worry. It's in the way she touches my shoulder, in the way her voice rounds and softens. She feels sorry for me and I don't want any part of it, but then, suddenly, I see the pity as a way to escape.

"Of course this would upset you. It's totally understandable after . . . well, you know . . . your mama and all."

There's another pause. She wants me to spill, but I won't. I focus on where her white sneakers meet the floor and think maybe I won't have to. For once, there's no reason for me to lie.

My dad taught me this trick. People hate silence. They will, almost always, fill it up. If you remember that, their need can become your leverage. It's another angle you can work.

So right now I will say nothing, and the nurse will fill up the gap with something. I just have to hope it's something I want.

Nurse Smith's hand slows . . . pauses between my shoulder blades. "Would you like to go home?"

Bingo.

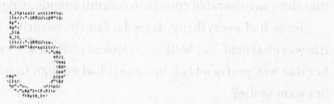

It's a trick I've learned over the years.

I stay perfect on the outside so no one knows

I'm rotten underneath.

—Page 22 of Tessa Waye's diary

Of course, the downside to everyone thinking you're a basket case is they don't like to leave you alone. I can't just walk myself home, even though that's how I got to school. Nurse Smith says she's going to go get Todd.

"Go get him?"

"Yes, he arrived with the other counselors." She hands me a Dixie cup of tap water. "I'll let him know you need to leave. He's been with the principal, trying to help us decide how to handle everything, but I'm sure he'll take you home right away."

Nurse Smith disappears, leaving me to sip my water like a good little girl. I still can't believe Tessa's gone. Even though we hadn't spoken in years, even though her parents made it clear we could no longer be friends, the knowledge that she was miserable enough to commit suicide stings.

Tessa had everything: friends, family, security. Her life was charmed. . . . Well . . . it looked charmed. I know her dad was pretty awful, but was it bad enough to make her want to die?

I don't end up with much time to obsess. Todd shows up in less than five minutes, and Nurse Smith is right behind him, melty as microwaved Play-Doh.

"We really appreciate all that you've done, Mr. Callaway," she gushes. "Getting all these counselors here, helping us prepare the outreach efforts—"

Todd waves away her compliments. "Please, just call me Todd. I was glad to do it. I know a bunch of these kids from church. It was important for me to be able to support them through this tragedy."

"That's so wonderful. My Krista was in your youth group class last fall, and she had nothing but nice things to say about you."

Todd nods absently, his eyes trained on me. "I'm really sorry this happened, Wick. When the principal called me about Tessa this morning, I came to find you, but Lily said you'd already left. What can I do to help?"

I have no idea what to say to that, so I shrug.

"Fair enough; let's go."

Nurse Smith pushes paperwork across her desk and shows him where to sign. "It's so wonderful to deal with a father who understands his child's needs."

"The advantage of owning your own company." Todd smiles shyly. "When you're married to the boss, no one will give you crap about going to get your kid."

His kid? It makes me cross even as something inside me pricks to life. I ignore the wiggly, happy feeling. It's only a matter of time before Bren and Todd decide I don't match their perfect-life decor. It's kind of hard to tell your neighbors how well your foster kid is doing when she has meltdowns at school.

Signing me out takes the longest ten minutes of my life, and once we're ready to go, I get up so quickly, the room tilts. My worst migraines always begin like this. My edges feel frayed.

In this case, I'm glad. It makes me look that much sicker when Todd opens the passenger door of his black Range Rover. I'm not in the mood for explanations, and I'm *really* not in the mood to visit the shrink they got me. Todd and Bren are big believers in the power of counselors and self-help books. I guess they figure the family that goes to therapy together stays together.

Norcut was Bren's idea. She's supposed to be some sort of industry leader in dealing with at-risk children, and her schedule is supposed to have a three-month waiting period, but every time Lily or I twitch, Bren speed-dials the woman, and we get a same-day appointment. Maybe since I'm supposed to be sick, I'll get out of it.

"Wicket?"

Or maybe not. I stifle a sigh. Todd always uses my full name. I hate that. It's Wick, people. It's what you light to set stuff on fire. "Yeah?"

"Is there anything I can do?"

Find me. I put one hand to my mouth, and I'm not sure what I'm holding back, but thankfully, Todd doesn't say anything else.

At the school's entrance, we turn left, but my body still expects for us to make a right, still expects to turn toward the poorer part of town. I don't know if I'll ever get over how weird it is to live where my old neighbors come to work. The woman who was two doors down from us cleans Bren's best friend's house. The guys who lived behind us detail Todd's SUV every Saturday. None of them talk to me anymore.

I don't blame them.

You'd think I'd fit in better. With Bren and Todd's money, I look just like my classmates now, but I spent too much time on the outside to feel like I belong. Peachtree City is a planned community. Nothing grew up organically, because everything has its proper place . . . except for us.

People like Lily and me aren't part of that plan, and now all I want to do is punch holes in everything so the hypocrisy shines through—like our neighbor who rushed over right after social services dropped us off. I recognized her name from the newspaper's blog. She wanted us shipped to some at-risk youth camp . . . until Bren and Todd stepped in. Now the woman wants to be friends. I don't know how Todd and Bren put up with it. Maybe, deep down, it's because they're just like the rest of them.

We drive the whole way home in silence. At first, I think it's a good thing, but then I begin obsessing about why the hell Tessa's diary ended up with me and who could know about my hacking. I start wishing Todd would just say something—anything—that might drown out the *Find me*.

But I don't think it could silence all the whys.

At home, Todd unlocks the side door for us and ushers me inside. The house is blissfully quiet and smells like lemons. Bren must have been cleaning before she went downtown. Either all the singing put her in the mood or Tessa's suicide gave her anxiety.

"Thanks for taking me home."

"Of course." Todd shoots me a funny look, like he doesn't understand why I'd think he *wouldn't*. It must be nice to still believe in people, to think they really do care about each other. That version of the world is so weird to me that it might as well be Strawberry Shortcake Land. Then I realize some people are actually living that life. They just aren't me.

I start to shuffle past him. "Are you going back to my school? Won't they need your help?"

"No, I'll stay put. You shouldn't be alone right now. I can work from here. Principal Matthews wanted some input on how to improve the counseling program. I'll use today to pull together some notes."

Mr. Matthews wants help? Briefly, I'm surprised and then . . . I get it. I've investigated every set of foster parents we've had. Mrs. Peterson had crazy credit card debt. The Beards cheated on their taxes. Basically, everyone had some "problem."

Except for Bren and Todd.

They were married three years ago after meeting through an online dating service. Bren describes it as a whirlwind romance, but Todd said he just knew she was the right one. Their record is spotless . . . except for when Todd's little brother died when they were just kids.

It was awful. Tore his family apart. For his parents, it became a reason to die. For Todd, it became a reason to live. He says it's what brought him to his true calling: counseling. He lived through hell, and now he teaches other people how to do it.

My foster parents own a successful consulting firm, but Todd's happiest on Tuesday and Thursday nights, when he does counseling, and on Sundays, when he works with his church's youth groups.

In other words, it makes perfect sense that Mr. Matthews would want his help. He's living proof that good things really can crawl out of bad.

I reach for the banister. "I still don't feel very well. I'm going to go lie down."

"I didn't know you and Tessa were friends."

I pause. There are a lot of responses I could give here. The trick is deciding which one. I turn slowly toward Todd. "We were pretty close."

Once. Before her dad decided I was the wrong kind of friend. Before Tessa went on to become prom queen and I went on to become . . . me. We hadn't spoken in five years, but I actually feel closer to her now. Tessa carried something very dark inside her, probably the same something my mom carried. I wish I could have fixed it. I wish I could have fixed it for them both.

Except now isn't the time for that stuff. I look at Todd and think maybe I shouldn't have said anything. My admission should cue another round of softening, a set of stupid clichés, or, God forbid, a hug, but Todd doesn't move.

"If, you know, you ever start to feel like that, Wicket, you know . . . you could always talk to me."

Oh my God, cue the cheesy background music, we're having A Moment. Todd's eyes are Disney-animal huge. It's like looking at Bambi, and I have no idea what to say. You know, I've always gotten the feeling it was more Bren who was into the whole fostering thing. She's the one who's said over and over how much she wanted kids and could never have them, but now Todd's trying so hard it makes me rethink it.

"No, I'm good." It's the truth . . . as much as I know it. This is more honest than I meant to be, but the words bubble up anyway. Maybe that's why Todd likes counseling. He compels the truth to rise. It's like his superpower.

Too bad I don't believe in heroes, super or otherwise.

Todd braces one hand against the banister, sunlight winking off his wedding band. "You sure you're okay?"

I'm always okay. I freeze a smile. "I'm fine, Todd."

And I really mean it. Because I'm always okay, even when I'm not.

Upstairs, someone put the baseball bat back on my bed. For a second I think it must've been Bren, but Bren would've tossed the bat in the closet or put it up on a shelf. Lily's the only one who would leave it within easy reach, and the realization is a brief, painful pulse.

I drop my messenger bag on the floor and sit down heavily next to it. My head is really starting to thump. If I were smart, I'd power through the pain and use the day off from school to finish up my current job. I'm almost done with the target's financials. A little more digging and I'll be through.

But I'd rather look through Tessa's diary, and I'll be honest, that's kind of weird for me. On the one hand, invading privacy is my thing. On the other hand, I do that for jobs, and this is not a job. I haven't accepted it. I don't want it.

I open the diary anyway.

The first entry is from six months ago, and Tessa has doodled her name up and down the margin. I skim the top few paragraphs and it feels . . . odd. Not that there's anything really odd about what Tessa wrote—it's mostly about how miserable she felt at home—it's just uncomfortable looking at her personal thoughts.

She never meant for anyone to know about how she cheated on her history quiz and was embarrassed at having grown too tall to be a flyer in cheerleading. All this was supposed to stay private.

Plus, looking through it seems pointless. There's a whole chunk of pages ripped out from the middle and a few close to the end. From what's left, you can tell Tessa was upset, but she doesn't seem like someone who was ready to take her life. I flip closer to the end, and at the top of page fifty-four, I see two short sentences that make my insides free-fall:

I think I've found a solution. It's three stories up and has no one watching the fire escape.

I slap the diary shut. Tessa was a jumper and I knew that . . . so why am I about to cry?

Because my mom jumped too, and the second I think about *her* I can't put the memory away. Suddenly, I'm choking and I'm crying and I'm *done*. It's been four years and I still can't get past it. Maybe I'm not supposed to.

I shove the diary into my bag. This isn't about saving or finding Tessa. It's about saving me. I can't do this. I'll take some time off instead, lie low for a while.

It's not great timing, since my, um, business doesn't really advertise. I work by word of mouth. One woman gives my info to another woman who gives it to another woman. It doesn't sound like it would work, but it does. I have a waiting list, and now it's going to have to wait a little longer.

This diary crap has hit way too close to home. Even if Tessa hadn't committed suicide, I would have to regroup, take time. We need the money, but we also need me to stay out of jail.

Find me.

Dammit. I need to think about something other than that . . . except there are only two questions left:

How did someone know about my hacking?

And who left Tessa's diary?

Neither one is good. I wipe tears from my cheeks, trying to ignore the pain behind my eyes. Inside my messenger bag, my cell buzzes. I immediately think of Lily and plunge my hand into the inside pocket. The diary grabs my fingers instead. I shove it aside and find my phone.

I have a new text.

R U OK?

My heart does a little flip. Not Lily. It's Griff. For a second, I'm confused. How did he get my number? Then I remember he asked for it last semester when we were working on a project together.

He's checking up on me. Another example of the nice-guy stuff he does and another example of why I should continue to avoid him. I don't deserve nice.

I fiddle with the buttons for a minute, trying to think

of a response. *Am I okay? Of course I am. Does he think this is the first time I've gone to pieces?*

I put the phone down, determined to ignore him, but my hand drifts to my elbow, where I can still feel his fingers on my skin.

I wiggle my mouse, and the desktop leaps to life. There's a picture of Lily and me as my background. Dad took this almost two weeks before the police tried to take him, and I haven't seen Lily's smile look the same since.

And it's another reason to keep moving. I'll ignore the text, finish my work, get all this behind me. Sooner I do, the sooner I get paid.

I log into my Gmail account, thinking I could send my current customer some of the new updates on her boyfriend. My current target is shockingly clean. If all men were like this, I wouldn't be in business, but it will be nice to send good news for once.

There are three new messages in my in-box. The first is from a customer I finished up last week, confirming her wire transfer. Great. I open up another window and double-check the transfer number she included in the email. The money's there, and everything looks legit. Even better.

I spend another moment transferring the funds into a separate account. I'm still kind of learning the finances thing. I never had much practice until now. Dad was in charge of everything. Norcut says that was probably why my mom jumped. She thought she'd never get control of her life again, and suicide was the only choice she had left that didn't involve him.

I think it's nice that Norcut has an explanation for everything. Ever since that little comment, I've been pouring coffee into her office orchids. We'll see if she can explain why they all die.

The second email is from my current customer. Now she wants me to check the boyfriend's work history too. If I had to bet, there's nothing to be found there, either, but the lady's way paranoid. She wants the full workup. She also wants to say thank you.

I close the email before I have time to read it, but the words "grateful" and "feel safer" stick to me. I get more thank-yous than anyone—including me—would ever guess, but I try never to read them. Because even though Lily and I need the money, and even though these women need answers, I still believe that only the vilest, rottenest of people would make their living from hacking. Maybe I deserve everything I've gotten from life. Maybe it's cosmic payback for invading people's privacy.

I send the woman an updated quote, including instructions to send another transfer with the new payment amount. Then I click on the third email. I don't recognize the address, and there's no subject. It's just four little words, but they make my insides go cold:

`Will you do it?`

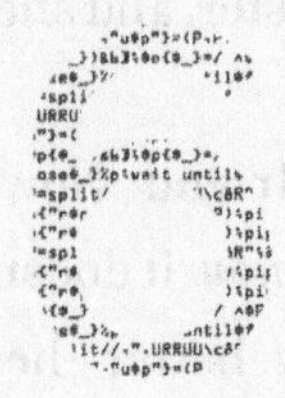

He understands things by cutting them apart.

—Page 21 of Tessa Waye's diary

What. The. Hell? How did this person even *find me*? Only three people in the entire world know about my hacking.

The first? Lily.

The second? Lauren.

The third? My dad's best friend and partner, Joe.

Is that too many? It must be. Someone must have told. Someone must have slipped up. Panic rises in me like a tsunami, and I think I'm going to drown.

Or I could get a grip. The thought emerges in Technicolor and makes me sit up straight.

Right. Get a grip. Think this through. Get a plan like I did before with Nurse Smith. I could figure out how I've been discovered. I didn't wait for Carson to come up the stairs, and I won't wait for whoever this is to stay ahead of me.

I consider the three who definitely know. Lily is self-explanatory. Lily would never tell. She's my sister, and she's too afraid.

The second person is Lauren. My best friend. Now I know that might not mean anything. Hell, I *know* it doesn't mean anything. I've seen enough to know better—best friends can betray you. But Lauren thinks I quit. She thinks I hacked because my dad made me, and now that he's gone, I don't have to anymore.

Then there's Joe. Joe could be dangerous. He's a black hat, a hacker who preys on everyday people. He's a digital pickpocket, and he taught me almost everything I know, but he doesn't know how I've been working to keep women safe. He thinks I work only for him . . . and my dad.

With the exception of Lily, no one really knows how far it goes. They only know pieces, and that's what keeps me safe.

Well, I *thought* it was what kept me safe. . . . So what do I do now?

Fix this.

Or fix someone else.

Now there's a lovely thought. I roll it around in my brain, liking the way it feels. I spin my chair and stick my hand behind my headboard, searching for the pushpin I use as a hook for my special jump drive. The one I use for storing my personal information and programs. Superheroes have Fortresses of Solitude. Hackers have external hard drives. Whoever's doing this has been spying on me. I could return the favor. It'd be easy enough.

I yank the jump drive from behind the bed and plug it into my computer. What I need is a Trojan horse virus.

Trojans are kind of my specialty. I make variations of them out of my Pandora Code, a hack I created to invade hard drives. I've embedded Trojans in Flickr accounts, YouTube links, and now, a simple email. The plan would basically go down like this: I reply to the email and embed the virus within a link or an attachment. I could write something about how I'm willing to take the job and instruct them to follow the link. It's that simple.

Because who can resist a single little click? Not many people. It's bait, and once they click, I have a trapdoor into their digital lives.

I could go through their computer files, check their internet history. If I'm really lucky, they'll have a webcam, and I can turn it on and watch them. I'll be in and they won't know the difference.

I scrub one hand along my mouth and realize I'm still shaking. I'm exhausted, and the trembling just makes it worse. It makes me feel weak. Vulnerable.

If I'm going to fix things, I've got to be at my best.

My jump drive's file listings pop up on the screen. It takes me a minute, but I scroll through the file folders until I find what I want and do the upload. There are few things prettier than perfectly written computer code. It's another language. Hell, it's another world—one that I create. In the digital world, I'm powerful.

In reality . . . not so much at the moment. My head is throbbing, and the edges of my vision are going blurry. I stick one hand into my desk drawer, feeling for a fat orange pill bottle pushed all the way to the rear.

I paste the virus-embedded link into the email, dry-swallow two pills, and hit send, immediately feeling better. It's not the meds. It's the chase. I shouldn't enjoy hunting, but I do. Whoever made me their target just became my prey.

It's amazing how you can measure loss. I wanted him so badly, but after I had him . . . it was the silence that told me all about how I was still alone.

—Page 23 of Tessa Waye's diary

"Wick?"

I am lying facedown in bed, drooling on myself. My bones are complete mush, but my head doesn't hurt anymore.

"Wick!"

Shit! I bolt upright. Bren is hovering in my doorway like there's some invisible line keeping her from stepping inside the room. One hand plays with her pearl necklace, twisting the beads between her fingers. "Lauren is here to see you. She brought you today's math assignments."

I squint. *What? Math?* I rub my tongue against the roof of my mouth, grinding away the gritty feeling. *I don't have math with Lauren.*

"Are you up to having guests?" Bren asks. "I could just, you know, keep the notes for you until you're feeling better."

I fork my fingers through my hair, trying to wrench my brain around. "No, no! Don't do that!" I push away the covers with both feet and realize I went to bed with my shoes on. There are pale, dusty tracks across the blue bedsheets. "Sorry, I'm just feeling a little spacey."

Bren drops her pearls and both hands round into fists. For a moment, I think she's going to launch herself at me, feel my forehead, check my pulse.

Blast me with a Care Bear Stare.

"Why are you feeling spacey? Are you getting sick again?"

"No, I just took these pills—"

Bren sucks in a noisy breath. *"Drugs?"*

Oh God. These are the side effects of watching too much Dr. Phil. Bren is convinced that after growing up with my dad, I'm one step away from becoming Lindsay Lohan. "Sort of. I took two of those pills Dr. Norcut prescribed for me. You know the ones she wanted me to take when I get headaches?"

A wide smile slings across Bren's face. She looks . . . proud? "Did they help?"

"Uh, well, I went to sleep, so . . . I guess?"

"That's good. That's good." Bren's nodding hard enough to knock something loose. "You need to sleep. Dr. Norcut says your insomnia and migraines are linked to your stress levels."

"Uh-huh."

"I'll just have Lauren come back another time. You need your rest."

"Oh, no! Don't do that." I give Bren a big smile like my head isn't swimming and *Find me* isn't resurfacing in a chorus line. "I'm feeling lots better, Bren. I should take a look at the assignments. Don't want to fall behind."

Bren's lips go all thin like she doesn't agree. "Okay, then, if you're sure."

"Definitely."

She turns toward the hallway and calls, "You can come up, dear."

Someone stomps up the stairs, and Lauren appears in the doorway with a black eye that's as bad as any my dad ever gave my mom. And yet she's grinning like this is some sort of toothpaste ad.

"Thanks, Mrs. Callaway!"

"You're welcome, hon." Bren smiles at Lauren, but her gaze hitches on the girl's face like she's worrying. "Let me know if you two need anything."

"Sure will!" Lauren waits until Bren's footsteps hit the bottom stair and then bumps the door shut. "You know, when you hang your mouth open like that, you look just like Bren. It's kind of freaky."

"What happened to you?"

Her grin widens. "You should be asking what happened to the other chick."

"You were *fighting*?"

"Holly Davis said you were acting like a freak, and I got a little pissed." Lauren wanders to my computer desk and drops into the roller chair like a careless puppy. "What can I say? Apparently, my abandonment issues have manifested into anger management issues."

I know I shouldn't, but I laugh. I can't help it. Most people meet their best friends at church or school. Lauren and I met in Dr. Norcut's waiting room. She's adopted, and her adopted mom worries that Lauren will grow up with Issues because her biological parents gave her up.

Lauren was four when it happened. She loves her new life with her mom, dad, and brother and says she doesn't remember anything that came before. But that hasn't stopped Mrs. Cross from sending Lauren to Dr. Norcut every Tuesday and Thursday.

"Is that what Norcut told you?" I lean against the headboard. "You have anger management issues?"

"Among other things." Lauren notices the meds bottle I left next to my keyboard. She picks it up, reads the label, and shakes it at me. "Imitrex? I guess she's been telling you stuff too."

"She thought it would help."

"Did it?"

I shrug. "I went to sleep."

Lauren nods like this is normal. "Anyway, I just wanted to see if you were okay."

"I'm fine." I summon a smile and find it's kind of easy when all your insides are in pieces.

"Really? You're fine? Because you look kind of rough."

"Thanks."

"I didn't mean it like that. I meant it like—" Lauren looks up at my ceiling like it will somehow shower her with answers. She scowls when it doesn't. "I saw you in the hallway at school, and you looked really bad. . . . I thought maybe the whole Tessa thing made you think about your mom."

Nurse Smith thought so too. It's understandable. Our town is pretty small, and for a time, my mom's suicide, and later, my father's escape from the police, were all anyone could talk about. I'm sure it wasn't a big leap of deduction for everyone to assume I was having flashbacks.

"I'm better. It was just . . . shocking. Are you okay? You and Tessa cheered together."

Lauren's eyes go empty like she's examining her hidden corners. "I feel shaken . . . upset . . . not betrayed like Jenna does. She's devastated over Tessa."

Lauren gives me a sad smile. "You know you've been to a lot of therapy when you can turn your feelings into a list. I know I should feel guilty about Tessa. But even though we cheered together, we weren't really *friends*—not like you and me."

I look away, fiddle with the edge of my comforter.

Lauren and I have only known each other since she moved here five months ago, but she's definitely my best—my only—friend. Most of the town knows about my dad and, by extension, about me, but Lauren's the only one who knows a little about my online activities.

Only a few weeks after she arrived, some lacrosse players thought it would be funny to send her dirty anonymous emails. Any other girl would've flipped, but Lauren got pissed. I took a risk and offered to find out who was sending them. And once we did, instead of going to her parents, Lauren confronted the guys herself and threatened to go public. I think that's when we realized we were so similar. We deal with problems on our own.

That's a long way of saying I should trust her enough to explain what really happened today, but I don't. I tell myself it's because I'm playing it smart, but really, I wonder if I'm just chicken.

"Anyway, that Griff kid from your computer class asked me about you." Lauren gives me an expectant look, ready for an explanation.

I don't have one, but my face gets hot. "Can't you get kicked off the cheerleading squad for fighting?"

"Probably, but who's going to tell? They're all afraid of me."

She says it like it's a joke, even though we both know it's true. Lauren looks like someone's porcelain doll. She's all smooth dark hair and moon-pale skin, but, sometimes, when she smiles, it's nothing but teeth.

"Hey, let me check my email real quick." I slide off the bed and nudge Lauren out of my chair. She ambles over to my closet and starts going through my clothes. For a long moment there's nothing, but when I hear her voice, my stomach drops three inches.

"What's this?"

I turn around and see the diary in Lauren's outstretched hand. The cover is folded over, and *Find me* stares up from the page.

"It's nothing. Put it back."

"It's not *nothing*." Lauren swallows hard, staring at me like I'm a stranger. "What are you doing with Tessa Waye's diary?"

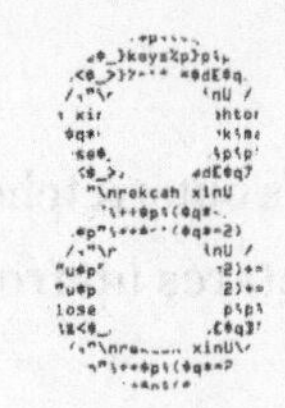

I thought, maybe, keeping a diary would break my fall.

—Page 2 of Tessa Waye's diary

I can tell Lauren about the diary, about everything. The best part of being best friends is that I can tell her anything, or at least I *should* be able to tell her anything.

Back when Tessa and I were best friends, she said I could always confide in her, but look how that turned out. I scoot my chair closer to the desk so there's more room between Lauren and me. "I'm not doing anything with it."

"But why do you even have it?"

She sounds so genuinely bewildered, I waver. I try to think how this might work.

Yeah, so I've acquired another stalker. Oh, I didn't tell you about my first? Well, it's a long story.

Or, *So someone thinks I can find Tessa. Why? Well, I have this little side business. I hack people for money. Oh, I didn't tell you about that, either?*

Stop it. I can trust Lauren. I can. I'm not the girl my dad says I am.

I take a deep breath, but it feels like the air entering my lungs is wearing soccer cleats. "Someone left it for me."

"Someone left it for you?" Lauren's eyes drop to the diary, swing up to me. "That's crazy! Who would do that?"

I stiffen, but . . . she's not challenging me. Lauren's outraged. I don't know what to say. Because for all the times I've told myself she's my best friend, for all the times I've told myself she likes me for me, until now, I never believed it. The realization is horrible and wonderful. I don't deserve this.

So maybe that's why everything vomits to the surface, splashing up chunks of information. It's messy, sticky, nothing like my tidy lines of code. Suddenly, I'm spilling everything: about how I'm watching Detective Carson. How Detective Carson is watching me. How the diary just showed up with the note pasted inside.

"Then I got this email." I double-click my in-box. Lauren and I both read the WILL YOU DO IT? in silence.

After a long time, maybe ten seconds, maybe ten years, Lauren straightens. "What are you going to do?"

"I don't know."

"You don't know?" Lauren cocks her head. Strands of

dark hair slant across her cheek, and she tucks them back with jerky fingers. "How could you *not* know? You have to find her, like the note says."

"Because two words mean so much."

"Wick, you can't ignore this!"

"You're damn straight I can't. Whoever this is knows about my . . ." It's hard to fit my mouth around the actual word. Not because I'm embarrassed. Well, not really. But aside from Lily, I don't discuss this with anyone, and the words stagger on newborn legs. "No one is supposed to know about my hacking."

"Whoever sent this . . ." Lauren studies the email on my computer screen. I watch her eyes trace the words twice more. "Whoever sent this thinks you can help."

And why the hell is that? It's not like Tessa and I were close. I mean, we were friends once, but my dad ruined it. It was one of the few times he actually remembered to pick me up. I was at Tessa's house, and he showed up drunk. I remember being so embarrassed and then just grateful he wasn't angry or trying to hit me. It should have been a good day.

But the Wayes were horrified, especially Mr. Waye, who said he didn't want his daughter hanging around such "trash." Tessa never spoke to me again. She wouldn't want my help. After that afternoon, she never wanted anything more to do with me.

It makes me the worst person for the job.

Or am I better suited because I knew what really went

on behind the Wayes' closed doors?

"Wick?" I jerk to attention. Lauren is still staring at me. "How did someone get the idea you could help? What kind of hacking are you doing?"

Her question smothers me. "I dig up personal information on people."

"What kind of personal information?"

"The kind that wives and girlfriends want to know: finances, other women, jobs."

"Why?"

I start to say something, but Lauren nods. She looks around my borrowed bedroom and she knows.

"I thought you quit, but you never stopped, did you? How long have you been doing this?"

"Three, maybe, four years?" Lauren studies me. I can't tell what she's thinking until her attention swings down to the diary. "What are you doing?" I demand.

"Looking through the diary." She flips past the opening pages, lingers over the torn-out section. "Everyone wants to know why Tessa killed herself. This could have the answers."

"You can't do that!"

"You mean you *haven't*?"

"Yes—no!" I sound ridiculous. "I did glance through it, but it was wrong. Privacy is important. Just because Tessa's dead doesn't mean we can forget that her diary was never intended for anyone else's eyes. It's wrong."

"Fine." Lauren snaps the book shut, thrusts it at me.

"But someone wanted you to read it. Why else would it get left?"

"Who cares?"

"You do. I know you, Wick. You'll never forgive yourself if you don't do something."

"Bullshit, I don't care about Tessa Waye."

But I know I'm lying.

I don't think about my life as having to live up to my parents' expectations. I want to. I'm just doing an epically shitty job of it.

—Page 14 of Tessa Waye's diary

Lauren's right, of course. I wouldn't be able to forgive myself, but that doesn't mean something's not badly wrong here. You don't ask someone to find you if you're planning on committing suicide, and if this is a cry for help or whatever, you sure as hell don't ask someone you haven't spoken to in years.

But of course, none of these objections surface until Lauren's left. After she's gone, I sit in my room for a long time, the sheer weirdness spiraling around in my head in kaleidoscope colors. At first, I stare at my computer, refreshing my in-box every few minutes, waiting for my stalker to take the bait. Then I stare at the diary.

After a few minutes, I pick it up again, turn to the beginning, and read. I'm barely onto the second page before she starts talking about how much she likes this guy. He's funny, hot, and . . . I flip a few pages ahead . . . and he has no name.

What the hell is this? First pages are ripped out and now names are missing.

"Wick?" Bren's voice floats down the hallway. "Do you want dinner?"

Not really, but if I don't, Bren will think I'm developing an eating disorder, and that's the last thing I need. "Down in a minute!" I call.

I tuck the diary away, send my computer into sleep mode, and dig through the gym bag sitting at the foot of my bed for a clean T-shirt and shorts. I find some, but they're wrinkled. Bren hates that, so I try to smooth the fabric.

We've been here for five months now. Lily's been unpacked for weeks, but I'm still living out of my Adidas bag. There's no point in hanging up my stuff. It just makes everything take longer when we have to leave.

I head downstairs, barely making it to the landing before I hear Lily squeal loud enough to make my back teeth click together. Paper bags crinkle, and another round of squealing ignites.

Bren's been shopping again. I round the corner into the living room just as Lily pulls a bright pink dress on top of her school clothes. It has a fitted bodice and full skirt. There's some sort of lace on the sleeves. It's very girly and would take a round of rhino tranqs to make me wear it, but Lily's grin is wrapped around her head.

Bren kneels between the shopping bags, watching my sister spin in circles. She's still playing with her pearls, but you can see the cartoon hearts blooming in Bren's eyes. She's totally taken with Lily, and honestly, I get it. I do. Lily's adorable. It's easy to fall in love with her. She's small-boned and blond with atmosphere-blue eyes and the world's sweetest demeanor.

I am heart-attack serious here. My sister looks like tiny woodland creatures should be brushing her hair or helping her dress. I have never understood how we share the same gene pool.

Bren probably doesn't either, because as soon as she notices me standing in the doorway, the edges of her mouth pull low. Her pale eyes trail down my shirt, snagging on the wrinkles. I start to tug the fabric straight and stop.

I tell myself I don't care what she thinks, and I'm so good at lying, I almost believe it.

"Are you really feeling better, Wick? I could always bring you dinner in bed."

"No, I'm fine. You don't have to do that."

"Wick!" Lily twists to the right and then to the left so I can see her dress from all angles. "Isn't it great? I'm going to wear it to the lake house this summer."

"Wow, Lil. It'll be perfect." I guess. The dress looks a

little fancy for going to the Callaways' lake house, but I've never lived with people who had second homes, so what do I know?

"I got you some things today." Bren nudges a dark blue Abercrombie bag toward me. "I saw them and thought of you."

I peek inside. *She saw baby-duck yellow and thought of me?*

There are two pairs of jeans, a few tank tops, some sort of long leather thing that's either a belt or something to hang yourself with. They're all very preppy, which kinda makes me think of Griff. Somehow I don't think he'd be into baby-duck yellow either, but I'm not really sure.

I put the clothes back in the bag. I don't understand why Bren's doing this. I don't think anyone ever told her you don't have to treat your foster kids that great. I mean, it's not like the last three places liked us that much.

Lily says Bren does extra stuff because she's always wanted kids, and I guess I should be happy about that, because Lily's always wanted a mom. She was seven when our mom died, and even though it's been a long time, there's still a forever hole inside Lily.

So even though I don't get Bren and I'm a little scared to even like her, I think of my sister and summon a smile. "Wow, they're super nice. You shouldn't have."

"I really hope you like them. They had the cutest dresses too. You would look so adorable in—"

"Wicket?"

I look up. Todd's standing in the doorway, both hands braced on either side of the jamb.

"Yeah?"

"There's someone here to see you."

Bren and Lily swivel to get a better look at me; then, simultaneously, their attention switches to Todd.

"Someone from school?" Bren asks.

Todd shakes his head. "No, it's Detective Carson from the police."

Carson stands at the end of the hallway, near the front door. It's not overly bright, but he's still wearing his sunglasses. The aviators are so dark it looks like part of his face has been scraped away, leaving only blackened hollows. I'm about halfway to him when Carson spreads his feet and slumps his shoulders like he's all relaxed.

But when Todd and I get closer, the veins on his neck bulge.

"Hello, Wicket. Do you remember me?" Carson thrusts out his right hand.

I ignore it. "You'd be a little hard to forget."

The offered hand retracts. He shrugs, takes off the sunglasses. "Fair enough."

Except it isn't fair, I want to say. It isn't fair at all. Seeing him makes me start shaking. It also makes me want to rage. The irony is, we're kind of alike. We're both interested in my dad. Carson wants to know where he is so he can arrest him. I want to know where my dad is so Lily and

I can run the other way. Odds are, neither of us is going to get what we want.

I push away from Todd. "Did you find my dad? Is that why you're here?"

Carson hesitates, his attention ping-ponging between Todd and me. "No, it's not. I'm not here about your father. I'm here because of Tessa Waye."

I hear liquid churning in my ears. My blood is humming like bees trying to escape a hive. "What about her?"

"I heard that you girls were friends."

I fight off a scowl. Damn Nurse Smith.

"Did you notice any differences in Tessa's behavior before she died? Did Tessa tell you anything?" Carson asks.

Of course not. Tessa wasn't big on good-byes, or she wasn't five years ago. I remember finding her in the hallway after that awful afternoon, and she just walked right by me like I didn't even exist. Sometimes, I would catch her eye across the lunchroom, but after a while, even that stopped.

It should've pissed me off, but instead I was just . . . hurt. Sad thing is, she could've walked up to me yesterday and asked to be friends again and I would've said yes. Pathetic, isn't it? Thing is, Tessa was the only person who liked me the way I was. Bren didn't. She overhauled me as soon as she could, and Lauren only met me afterward. For both of them, my past is past. They don't understand how it still lives under my skin. But, if Tessa came back, and she was okay with it, maybe I could be okay with it too.

I miss her. Probably always will.

I shrug. "No, nothing was different."

"But you were classmates at school. Surely you must have been around her a lot."

"No, not really."

Carson raises one eyebrow. "But I heard you were awfully upset about what happened."

I open my mouth, half-ready to say I don't even know what, when Todd puts his arm around me. There's no pressure, but my words retreat like they were yanked from the tip of my tongue.

"Everyone was upset to hear what happened, Detective," Todd says, his fingertips brushing my collarbone. "Tessa was a wonderful person."

Carson's attention flicks to me. "And that's why you were so upset? Because she was 'wonderful'?"

"Wicket can feel however she wants." Todd sounds all adult and authoritative. Actually, that's not quite right. He sounds defensive. "The last time I checked, feelings weren't a crime."

Why would he be defensive? I blink. Blink again. He's standing up for me. Part of me wants to say, *What the hell?* But another part of me starts to glow. I'm not alone.

"We've already discussed this, Detective," Todd continues, and I have to hide my surprise. He's already spoken to Detective Carson? "You should be looking closer to Tessa's home for answers. You need to speak with her father."

"Todd?" Bren's in the doorway, holding the cordless

phone to her chest like it might leap away. She doesn't even bother acknowledging Carson. "It's the school's principal again. He needs to speak with you about getting an additional counselor."

"I can call him back."

Why? So he can sit here with me instead? I'm confused until I realize that's exactly what Todd wants to do. In fact, that's exactly what he will do if I let him.

All I'd have to do is ask.

"It's fine," I say, but my voice wavers a little like it isn't.

Todd tenses, turning toward Bren. A charged silent something snakes between them. They heard the waver too. "Tell him I'll call him back as soon as I can."

"It's *fine.*" I sound better now, more like myself. With the Callaways behind me, I feel a surge of courage. The detective can't run me off. He can't keep me scared anymore. I won't let him. I look at Carson and smile. "After all, it's just a few more minutes, right?"

He smiles back. "Right."

Reluctantly, Todd stands, giving me one last, hard look before heading down the hallway. Carson and I watch each other in silence until we hear Todd pick up the phone.

Then Carson's smile drains like a wound. "You're holding back on me. You know something."

"I know lots of things," I retort. "Want to know something about the cop who sits outside my house every night?"

Carson's lips go thin as scars.

I nudge my chin in Todd's direction. "Think he might

want to know about it too?"

"If you were going to tell someone, you would have already done it."

True, but I'm not going to admit it.

Carson's eyes flick to the door and return to me. The skin around his eyes has softened. and his voice tips low. I'm sure he thinks it sounds all comforting, but my dad used the same tone with wound-up addicts. "You can talk to me, Wicket. I'm one of the good guys."

"Who sits outside our house every night."

"There's more to this than you know."

No, dude, there's more to this than you *know.*

Carson's hand lifts like he's going to pat my shoulder. "You have to trust me."

Great. He's going all touchy-feely on me. "I don't think so." I study him for a beat. "I thought Tessa's death had been ruled a suicide."

"It has."

"Then why are you still investigating?"

Carson stares down at me. The good cop routine switches, snaps off like a light, and the detective I remember from my dad's bust emerges. "You know how I can tell you're trouble?"

I don't answer. This is self-evident, I think. But I don't say the word. He probably wouldn't know what it meant. I raise my eyebrows instead, waiting for the explanation I know he's just dying to make.

"Because you have an answer for everything." Carson

pulls a little closer, and I have to stab my feet into the hardwood floor to stand my ground. "You see, nice girls don't. They don't know how to work law enforcement or social services because they've never been in them. But you have. Trash like you always has an answer."

His eyes sweep over me like he can see through the pretty new clothes, the pretty new haircut. That makes two of us.

I glare up at him. "Ohhhh, so that's it! Man, I've really been wondering. Thank *God* you could explain it to me."

Carson's laugh is silent. "You're brave now, aren't you? That's you, Trash. You always know how to play the game." He looks incredibly amused, and motions to the polished foyer around us. "But what happens when all this goes away?"

Yeah, what happens? The question feels so natural. Like it was living under my heart all this time.

"I'll leave my card." Carson flicks out a business card, lays it on the side table. "It has my work and cell numbers. You'll need them, kid."

He flashes me that smile again, the same as this morning's. "After all, if you can't trust the cops, Trash, who can you trust?"

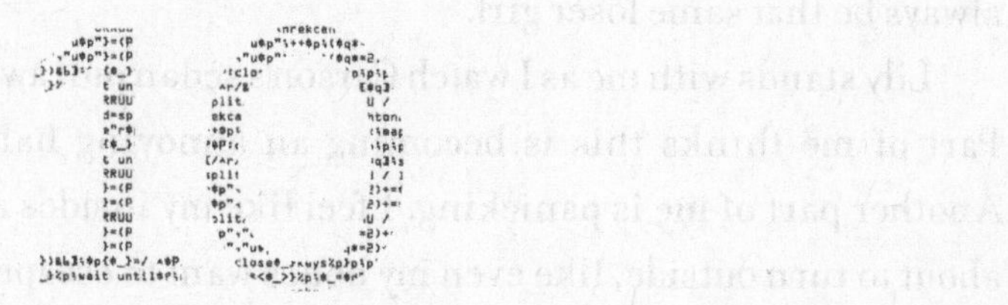

My mom loves him, but he only wants me.

—Page 22 of Tessa Waye's diary

Yeah, who can you trust? Definitely not Carson. Maybe not even me. I know better than to fall for Todd and Bren, and yet here I am. Looking like a Gap ad. In some Peachtree City mansion.

In denial.

Or at least, I was. The soap bubble's burst now. This is who I am: a foster kid living a borrowed life. How could I have been so stupid?

There's a small noise to my left, and when I look up, I see Lily trailing down the hallway. She's been eavesdropping. "That went well."

"What can I say? I'm freaking sweetness and light." I

sound like it's no big deal, and briefly, I'm proud. Then I remember Carson's explanation for my smart mouth: *Trash always has an answer.*

I guess he's right. I might have a new address, but I'll always be that same loser girl.

Lily stands with me as I watch Carson's sedan pull away. Part of me thinks this is becoming an annoying habit. Another part of me is panicking. I feel like my insides are about to turn outside, like even my bones want to escape.

Escape where? It's almost hilarious. I've nowhere to go.

I rub my temples with both palms and realize I haven't heard Todd's voice in several minutes. I look past Lily, down the hallway, but it's still deserted. "Is Todd still on the phone?"

She nods, eyes still pinned to the window and the now empty street.

I sag. *Good.* When Todd returns, there will be questions, and at the moment, I'm too tired to answer.

Lily retreats a single, deliberate step and points her finger at my chest. "What have you done to make him hate us so much?"

I hesitate. Carson's interrogation was hard, but Lily's will be far worse. "He doesn't hate us."

"Is he one of those people you hacked? Maybe his wife, his girlfriend. Maybe someone used you and told him."

"No."

"How do you know?"

"Because I know everyone I hack, Lil. He's just sniffing around for Dad."

"He said he was here for Tessa."

Her name makes me pause. It sounds foul in Lily's mouth, or maybe it's just the way I hear it. I can't really gauge my sister's reaction. Is she upset because of Tessa? Because it reminds her of our mom? Or is she just scared?

"Yeah, well, he said he was, but he's really just looking for Dad. He's just trying to find weaknesses. Why do you think he said that stuff about how I'd need his numbers? He thinks Dad will contact us and I'll get scared."

I can't tell if I sound convincing enough. My tone wiggles between aggrieved and outraged. It would probably fool a teacher, would definitely fool Bren.

But this is Lily. My sister. The only person who knows me. Really knows me. What works on everyone else doesn't work on her, so I launch into another conversational assault tactic: misdirection.

"I'm not the criminal in the family," I say.

Except I am.

I am more my father's daughter than I like to admit. I just have different dirty little secrets. I cross my arms again, trying to look properly pissed off, but it's really to help me hold down the shaking. Now that Carson's gone, my skin is trying to shiver loose from my bones.

"You have to stop, Wick."

And then what? Trust that Bren and Todd will take care

of us? Trust that we're going to be okay? I can't do it. I don't think I have it in me, and for a second, I want to cry. When did I stop believing in happy endings? Maybe I never did.

"We need the money."

"We have Bren and Todd right now."

"Exactly. We have them *right now*. What happens after that?" Irritated, I shove one hand through my hair, resisting the urge to pull it out.

I'm proud of my sister. I really am. She's lovely, and I often wish I were more like her: sweeter, softer, lighter, brighter. Even though I know I'm not and probably never will be. Maybe if I were more like Lily, Bren would like me more. Maybe I'd be happier. Maybe we'd get to stay.

But I'm not like her, and sooner or later, everyone realizes what we are: trash. And then it's finished. I shouldn't have to explain this stuff again. Lily might be younger, but she's seen the same crap I have. She should know.

No, she does know, I decide, looking at the way Lily's mouth is twisted like she's chewing on carpet tacks. *No, she definitely knows. She's just in freaking denial.*

Anger fills me faster than floodwater. "Don't you remember where we came from?"

"Yes! And I don't want to go back! I want to be normal!"

"What the hell is that?"

"Don't swear." She sounds so small I feel like I'm picking on her. "Bren will make you put a quarter in the swear jar."

"All the more reason to keep working then."

She pushes out a short, dry laugh. "You're going to ruin everything."

The words hit with a slap. Actually, I wish she had slapped me. It would have hurt less. But I'm not the only one like our dad. Lily also knows how to wound.

"Everything's already ruined, Lily."

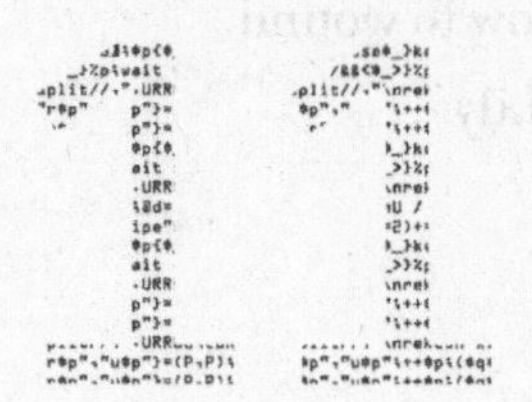

I went after him. It's true. I started it.

I'm just as bad as he is. Worse.

—Page 31 of Tessa Waye's diary

It's almost eleven o'clock, and I'm too wired to sleep. Todd's working late. Lily and Bren have gone to bed. And my stalker still hasn't taken my bait.

How is that possible? I push away from my computer and rub my aching neck. It still doesn't help. The muscles feel like knotted ropes. Am I dealing with someone who knows about Trojan horses? Maybe the email account hasn't been checked? Maybe—

Something scrapes outside my window, and I stiffen. In the dark, the tree branches twitch like spider legs.

It's nothing. Has to be.

Another scrape.

What if it's whoever left the diary?

In my head, I tie up the words, but they still escape. There's no way anyone would dare. I mean, Bren is right down the hallway. Todd could come home any minute. It's too risky.

So why have my palms gone damp?

I roll my chair a little farther back and stare at the open window. The lamplight catches just the edges of the trees, but nothing else. I opened the window earlier because it felt so stuffy after Carson left. I felt like I couldn't breathe.

Something below the window rustles. It's even closer than before.

It's moving *up*.

I drop both feet to the floor, digging in with my toes like a runner ready to sprint. It's maybe three strides to the window. Two if I really stretch. So I'll run over and slam down the window. Easy, right?

Unless I get grabbed.

I make the distance in two strides and seize the window's edge. Outside, the tree shakes hard, and a hand slaps flat on the sill. A scream climbs up my throat . . . and lodges.

It's Griff.

"Sorry." His face bobs into the light, the surrounding darkness making his smile look even whiter. "Didn't mean to scare you."

He's dangling half in, half out of the tree next to my

window. His legs are tangled in a branch, and both forearms are braced on the windowsill. He looks seconds away from laughing.

Like this is some joke.

Like I'm some normal girl who doesn't have to worry about being stalked.

It kind of makes me want to punch him.

"If you weren't trying to scare me, then why the hell are you climbing a tree outside my window?"

Griff's smile freezes. "I wanted to see you."

My heart rate spikes. "What the frick for?"

"You never answered me."

Never answered him? It takes me a full five seconds before I realize what Griff's talking about. The text. I never responded. I bite down on my lower lip, trying to think of something to say. I ought to ask him why he thought I *would* answer. I ought to tell him to piss off.

But I don't. Or maybe I can't. I mean, the guy is dangling from my bedroom window. He scaled a tree for me. And all for what? So he could make sure I'm okay? I don't get it. I chew my lower lip a little harder. "Why do you care? It's not like we talk that much."

"Yeah, I know. I think we should fix that." Griff leans a little farther in and looks around. Heat surges across my face when I realize I have dirty laundry to his left and discarded paperbacks to his right. "So can I come in?"

"Uh." *No! My room is a mess and Bren would have a heart attack and you shouldn't even be here.* "Okay."

Griff's grin slings wide. "Great!"

He heaves himself up a little and pauses, gaze speared to mine. Suddenly, we're close again, and the air between us curls.

His left eyebrow rises. I wish I could do that. "Um, a little space?"

"Oh!" I shuffle backward and my lab partner slides, hands first, onto my floor. He's still wearing the faded polo and khakis from earlier. I'm not usually a fan of anything preppy, but this . . . really works.

Griff looks up at me, his grin crooked, amused. "Didn't think you'd actually agree."

Yeah, well, that makes two of us. I scoot to the side and drop into my desk chair, sitting on my shaking hands. "What do you want?"

Griff shrugs, still looking around the room like he's studying some museum exhibit. I mentally will him to look at me.

What does he find so freaking interesting anyway? I tell myself I don't care what he sees, but inside I'm praying I haven't left any underwear lying around.

"I always wanted to see where you lived now."

"Why?" He's staring at my bed, and the heat in my cheeks, already scalding, turns nuclear. "Were you expecting a coffin or something?"

"Of course not. You sleep hanging upside down, right?"

I give Griff a stony look, but it doesn't hold. He's funny. I've always had a soft spot for funny. A smile starts to worm across my lips, and Griff catches it. The earlier crooked, evil grin stretches even wider, and I have to remind myself not to gawk. But this is Griff. In my bedroom.

Wanting to *talk*. "Why are you being so . . . so . . ." I refuse to say the word *flirty*.

Griff smiles. "Because I wanted to the moment I first saw you, but mostly because Matthew Bradford threw your lunch into the school fountain last week, so you let the air out of his car tires."

"*Tire.* I did only one."

"Yeah, I know. I did the other."

"How did you . . ."

"Know you were there?" Griff stands up, and for the first time, I notice his polo isn't fashionably faded so much as frayed and worn. He doesn't look thin. He looks hungry. "I was one car over, hiding out instead of going to lunch. You're the first girl I've ever met who's smart and never plays stupid. You're small, but you don't back down."

Griff switches his attention to my bookshelf, tracing his fingers over ten different Stephen King novels and pausing when he hits Jodi Picoult's entire oeuvre. If he asks, I'm going to swear they're Bren's.

"So is that a good enough answer?" he asks.

I start to speak, but my computer chirps and my heart leapfrogs into my throat. Someone just clicked on my virus link. Someone took my bait. I spin my chair around and hear Griff move a little closer.

"What is it?" Griff's on the other side of my desk with

Bren's battered copy of *Eat, Pray, Love* in one hand. He eyes my computer with interest. "Something going on?"

"No, nothing."

Except it isn't. It's everything. I press into my chair until the plastic pinches the knobs of my spine.

My Trojan horse virus worked. The email receiver must have clicked my link, which means I'm in. I can see what they see, get into their files, go through their lives.

And take back my own.

"What are you doing?"

I jump, twist in my chair and realize, too late, that Griff is next to me now. He's close. Close enough for me to smell his mint gum. Close enough to make me panic.

This won't work. I need to get rid of him. I stand up, keeping my body between Griff and the computer screen. "You have to go now."

He cocks his head, smiling like I've just said some joke he's desperate to understand. "But I just got here."

"You have to go."

Griff's eyes flick beyond my shoulder to my computer, and then return to me. He thinks I'm being weird. Hell, I *am* being weird, but I don't care. I need some privacy right now.

"Okay, fine, but close the window after me." Griff's devious grin has returned. He straddles my windowsill with more grace than you would think such a thin, tall guy would have. "You never know who might climb up that tree again, Wicked."

Wicked. It makes my heart do a silly, flippy thing. I open my mouth to retort, but Griff's already gone. The tree shakes twice as he scales down the trunk, and then there's nothing. I shut the window, check the locks, and close the blinds. When I turn around, the air is straitjacket tight. It feels like those moments before a movie begins, like the whole world is waiting.

But I'm not waiting anymore. I kick my chair out of the way and, still standing, hunch over the keyboard, pulling up another program. I punch in a few lines of code, accessing the remote computer's webcam.

"Come on, you little bastard," I mutter as the computer processes, turning my code into a rope bridge into someone else's world. Another few seconds and the black camera window at the top of my screen flickers.

I'm in.

Now I can see them.

Or rather, I can see her, and when I do, my stomach hits bottom. Suddenly, I'm hollow.

I know that girl. I knew her when she was in third grade and I was in middle school. I knew her when we passed in the grocery store and no longer said hello. I knew her.

I *know* her.

The girl who clicked on my virus is Tally Waye. Tessa's sister.

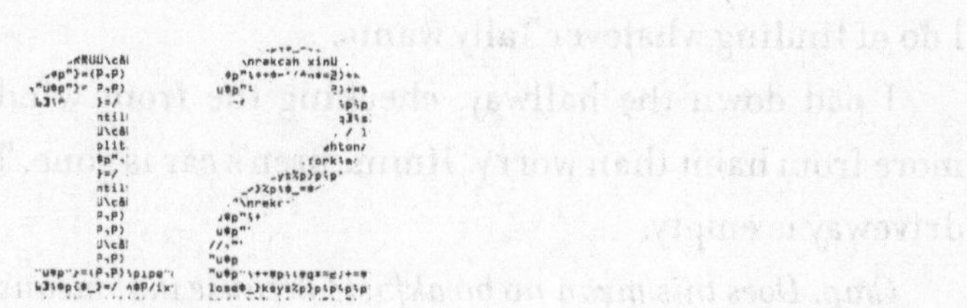

I think my mom knows something's wrong.

No matter how many times I say I'm fine,

she just keeps asking.

—Page 24 of Tessa Waye's diary

When I wake up, it's after ten. The house is quiet. My bed feels great. I want to go back to sleep.

But I'm wide awake.

All I can see is Tally Waye's hollowed-out face framed in my computer's screen. Even if I close my eyes, she's still there.

Find me.

Not freaking likely. I roll onto my side, eyes drifting to the window Griff came through. I'm not sure I want to think about that, either, but it's too late because I already want to smile.

Dammit. I'll find coffee instead. It's Saturday morning, which should mean one of Bren's big breakfasts is waiting downstairs, and if she's distracted by making pancakes or whatever, I have a way better chance of finding coffee than I do of finding whatever Tally wants.

I pad down the hallway, checking the front window more from habit than worry. Hmm. Bren's car is gone. The driveway is empty.

Crap. Does this mean no breakfast? Because that means no coffee.

At first, I think it's odd she's gone, because Bren lives for using her Williams-Sonoma waffle maker, but then I remember she was taking Lily for ballet sign-ups this morning. It's just me.

"Morning, Wicket."

I jump. "Holy shit!"

"Sorry! Sorry!" Todd's standing at the foot of the stairs with two cups of coffee. It's Saturday, but he's in a suit and tie. Headed for the office? If he is, he shouldn't. He looks like hell. His eyes are bloodshot, like he didn't sleep at all.

Shit. I've been so wrapped up in myself, I didn't think how much Tessa's death must hurt Todd. He wants to save the world, and he couldn't even save this one girl. It's got to be devastating. Todd was so quick to stand up for me; what would he have done to save someone like Tessa?

"Really didn't mean to scare you," Todd says.

I wave away his objection. At the rate I'm going, I'll have a heart attack and none of this will matter anyway.

"Don't worry about it." I rub my right temple, where I can still feel an echo of yesterday's headache coming back. "I don't suppose one of those is for me?"

Todd gives me a little smile. "Only if you don't tell Bren." He passes one mug to me, and I take a deep gulp. He's put too much sugar in it and the coffee's hot enough to burn off a layer of my tongue, but it's still wonderful. Two more swallows and I can feel my skin start to perk up. By the fourth my eyelids don't feel so saggy.

"Mum's the word," I promise, and finish off the last of the coffee in a long pull.

Todd laughs. "You're funny, you know that?" He sips at his, watching me. "Bren thinks the caffeine will stunt your growth."

I grimace. "Too late for that."

"I was wondering if you could look at Bren's computer for me. I think I hit a wrong button again."

"Yeah, sure." Todd is always hitting wrong buttons. He knows the Blue Screen of Death better than anyone I've ever met. It would be annoying if I weren't kind of grateful for the distraction. In the five months we've been here, I've reformatted Bren's computer twice because of "wrong buttons." Luckily, their office manager keeps up with the work computers; otherwise, dealing with the Callaway computers would be a full-time job. "No problem."

"Thanks. . . . So what are you going to do today?"

"Don't know." I have an English paper due on Tuesday, the last of the financials to finish for my customer, and then there's Tally Waye. I inspect the bottom of my coffee cup and think I should just go ahead and have my nervous breakdown. It would save time. "What about you?"

"The Wayes are having a prayer vigil at their house this afternoon. I thought I'd go."

"I didn't know you were close to them."

Todd shrugs. "We know them through church. . . . Would you like to come?"

Oh, hell no—then again, Tally would be there and I could return the diary. Staring at Todd, the opportunity seems kind of perfect.

Perfectly dreadful.

"I can't. I'm sorry."

"You know, you could do a lot with what happened to you, Wicket. You could turn it into an opportunity to help others."

Like he did? I don't think I have it in me. I damn sure know I don't have the words anyone would need to hear. "The Wayes are not . . . big fans of mine."

Todd nods like he was expecting this. "I understand. Mrs. Waye told me all about it one day before Sunday school. But you're not that girl anymore, Wicket. You don't have to be afraid, but it's okay if you don't want to come."

Todd takes my coffee mug and turns toward the kitchen. "Bren wanted you to stay quiet, rest. I think she was planning to take you to get your nails done later—"

"Todd?" His name sounds all strangled, and we both pretend not to notice. "I'll come."

If only because it's my best inroad to Tally, and I'll take what I can get.

"Great! And you're sure you'll be okay? I mean . . . after your mom and what happened yesterday . . ."

I'm kind of glad he's fumbling. It makes him seem less assured, less heroic, less . . . dad-like. I hate thinking about Todd in those terms, but it's true. Todd is practically a sitcom dad come to life. He's someone you could confide in, someone who would cheer you on, someone who would never hit you. He's pretty much the exact opposite of my real dad.

Which is a ridiculous thought. I'm almost seventeen—way too old for this shit. I don't need a father figure. I don't need someone to confide in or anyone to cheer me on. I don't need whoever Todd is or could be, but sometimes, in moments like these, I realize how much I want someone like him anyway.

Stupid. Really stupid. Dangerous even, because he will only let me down. So I push the idea under, hold it until it stops thrashing.

After my mom and all. Concentrate on that. There should be a good way to explain this. God knows I've had enough opportunities. Our community is pretty small, and after the newspaper ran a front-page article on my mom's suicide, everyone talked about it. They wanted to know why she did it and how she could leave "her responsibilities."

I don't think they ever understood that was the point. She couldn't *handle* her responsibilities—that's why she jumped. They never understood that they weren't supposed to understand. It was something she felt she had to do, and it made sense to her. It's been four years, and even though I've worked some stuff out in my head, I can't express any of it.

Except maybe this: Everything comes after "my mom and all." That's what comes from loss. There's Before When You Had a Mom and then . . . Now When You Don't Have a Mom. You don't get over it; you just learn how to endure. It isn't just the loss of your mom. It's the birthdays she'll miss. Your graduation. Your first date. All those little losses light up her absence with torches.

You deal. I did.

Tally will.

I swallow. "Maybe you're right. Maybe I could do something good with everything that's happened to me."

Not the worst lie I've ever told. Might even be a little true.

But Todd's still watching like he's looking for cracks. I keep my face blank and shrug. "After all, I know how they feel."

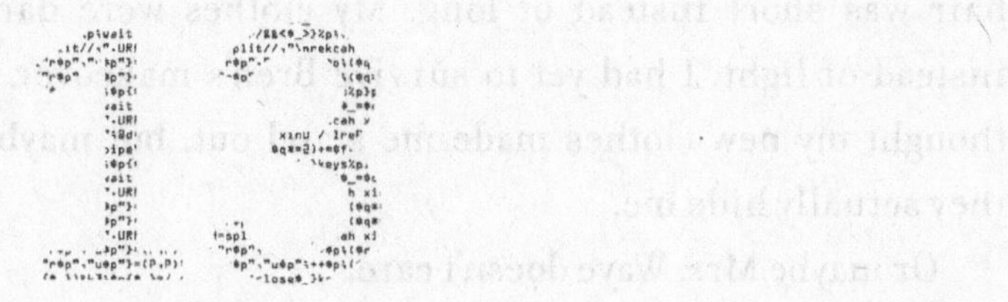

I would do anything for my sister.

—Page 23 of Tessa Waye's diary

Usually Brandy, the Wayes' housekeeper, opens the door for visitors, but this time it's Mrs. Waye herself. She pushes the door wide, and for a second, I feel like I'm an eleven-year-old again, getting dropped off for a playdate with Tessa.

I had forgotten how pretty her mom is, how Mrs. Waye can cry and still keep her makeup perfect.

But it cracks around her strung-up smile.

"Hi, Becky." Todd runs one arm across her shoulders, pulling her into a brief hug. "How are you holding up?"

Mrs. Waye doesn't let him go. "I'm so glad you came."

"I'm glad we could be here." Todd motions toward me and I catch Mrs. Waye's attention, but I lose it even faster.

Her eyes slide so smoothly over me it's as if they were always on their way back to Todd.

Did she recognize me? Maybe not. Five years ago, when Tessa and I made forts out of couch cushions, my hair was short instead of long. My clothes were dark instead of light. I had yet to survive Bren's makeover. I thought my new clothes made me stand out, but maybe they actually hide me.

Or maybe Mrs. Waye doesn't care.

We're barely away from her before Todd is pulled to the side by another mother, leaving me to stand around and look at kids from my school I don't know well enough to talk to. This is weird. On the way here, I was nervous as hell, but now I feel curiously . . . lost.

And horribly sad when I see the pictures of Tessa scattered around the house. Most of them look like they were taken at the church Todd teaches at. There's Tessa's first communion . . . Tessa doing an art project with some younger children . . . Tessa smiling for the camera.

I try to keep moving, but the whole house is super crowded, and between the sheer number of people and their palpable grief, every room is suffocating. I don't see Tally anywhere, and it seems weird to ask strangers where she might be. I give up, ready to return to Todd, when a lone girl catches my attention. The diary tucked under my shirt trembles.

Tessa's younger sister, Tally, is looking right at me. Her eyes are a little glazy and her face is pinched. Everyone else is talking and crying, but Tally's motionless, staring at me like I'm the only person who has ever mattered.

Like I'm a hero.

Tessa's sister is sitting on an overstuffed couch between two overstuffed women. If I had to hazard a guess, I'd bet they were her aunts. And the way they're crying over her head, I'd bet they're self-involved aunts.

One of them keeps plucking at Tally's arm as she wails. The other keeps reaching across her. Yeah, I'd definitely say self-involved. Tally could be a stuffed animal for all the consideration they're showing her.

Tally looks like she'd probably agree with me. When our eyes meet, the girl's mouth goes crooked, and I can't tell if she's holding back a smile or a scream.

She slides off the couch, heads for a set of stairs to my left. I follow, half expecting someone to tell me to stop, but no one does.

On the second floor, the master bedroom is off to my left. The door hangs partially open, revealing a collection of dark furniture and light-colored walls. Like the rest of the house, it's immaculate and, for some strange reason, makes me think about how much Tessa loved to doodle and draw.

She wouldn't have fit in with parents like these. She would have always been reining herself in. And suddenly, I'm sad for Tessa all over again.

I trail farther down the hallway, and it's just closed

door after closed door until I hit the end. Edging around the corner, I see Tally sitting on a flower-print bedspread, staring at the floor. She doesn't move, and looking at her, you wouldn't think she knows I'm here.

But I know she does, because her hands roll into fists.

"Tally?" I slide into the bedroom, nudging the door shut behind me. You can still hear the wailing from downstairs. It crawls up through the floorboards.

"You came," Tally breathes. The girl sounds . . . grateful, and it funnels my throat shut. How am I going to turn her down?

"Yeah . . . I'm sorry, Tally. I know everyone probably keeps saying that to you—"

"Doesn't matter. You came. You're going to fix this."

"I . . . I think there must be some sort of mistake."

Tally twists her head to one side like she's sure she didn't hear me right.

I hold up the diary, give it a shake. "Take it back."

There's a moment of silence before Tally's eyes spear mine. "No, I won't." She has Tessa's mouth: thin and pale. It stretches across her face like a scar. "I shouldn't have to. This is what you do, isn't it?"

"I don't know what you're talking about."

The girl makes a strangled noise, like she's choking, like my denial is some bone lodged halfway down her throat. "Liar. This is what you do. You find people. You uncover the truth for money."

My insides free-fall. "How do you know?"

"Lily."

My sister? I didn't even know Lily and Tally were friends, and even if they were, how could Lily have betrayed me?

"Tessa was crying one day when she came to pick me up. I was afraid to ask what was wrong, but Lily wasn't. Tessa told us it was 'a boyfriend problem,' and Lily said you could fix it. She said you fixed a lot of women's problems."

I stare at Tally, trying to break the situation down so it fits in neater lines. Fix her sister's problems? *Find* her sister? Tessa is already gone. She's already destroyed. You can't fix this.

I start to turn away and realize I, of all people, know the math doesn't have to work—that you can still hope, even if everything's ruined.

"There's nothing I can do, Tally."

"Yes, there is." Her eyes turn huge and glazy again. She's only a hairsbreadth from tears and now, suddenly, I feel like crying too. "We can't save Tessa anymore, but we can punish the man who raped her."

Raped her. The words sound awkward and practiced at the same time. "What are you talking about?"

Tally swallows hard. "The man who made her jump. She wanted him because he made her feel beautiful, made her feel perfect. She wanted him, and my dad says girls like that deserve what happens to them, but Tessa didn't deserve any of it—" Tally breaks off, shakes her head as she considers me. "You're missing the most important part."

"No, I'm not."

"Oh yes, you are." Tally jams one hand under her pillow, pulls out a fistful of torn papers.

It's the rest of the diary. She holds them out, and before I even realize what I'm doing, I've grabbed them.

"You haven't read this. It's all about Lily. He wants her. She's next."

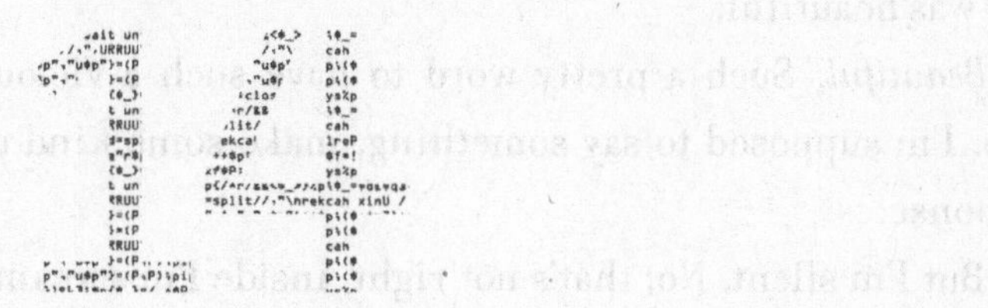

He's done with me. I should be horrified,

but I'm really just relieved.

—Page 84 of Tessa Waye's diary

"You're lying."

"I'm not." Tally's gaze crawls over me, snags on my hands. She watches how they tighten. "Her name is right here."

Lily. I don't say anything. I *can't* say anything. I'm drowning.

Tally nods like she somehow understands. "Page sixty-three. That's the first time Tess mentioned Lily. Do you want to know why she's in there?"

Her eyes meet mine again, and I'm suddenly struck by how flat they look, how empty . . . how familiar. Tally looks like one of my dad's junkies, the one who went on a four-day bender, coming down so hard she doused herself with gasoline and struck a match.

"Tessa wrote about Lily in her diary because *he* thought Lily was beautiful."

Beautiful. Such a pretty word to have such a vicious slap. I'm supposed to say something, make some kind of response.

But I'm silent. No, that's not right, inside I'm screaming. But outside?

Outside, all I can manage is the softest, "What?"

Tally leans forward, scooting a little closer to the edge of the mattress. Her feet reach for the floor, and I retreat a step. She looks like she's going to stand up, but her hands plunge fist-deep into the comforter.

She isn't going anywhere, I realize. She's holding herself back.

"The second time Tessa mentioned Lily it was because he had decided Lily was the One. I guess what he really meant was that Lily was the *Next* One, because you want to know what he said the third time?"

No! Another step away. "Yes!"

"She wrote about Lily because he had decided Tessa was going to help him." For the first time, Tally's voice cracks. She sucks in a breath, holds it, and then smiles. "Weird, isn't it? That Tessa should spend so much time writing down Lily's name, and never once did she write down *his*, even after he wanted to make her . . . make her a part of what he did. I wrote 'Find me' because I thought you might be more likely to do it if you thought it came from her. You might think you were rescuing Tessa, but now . . . now you better do it to rescue Lily."

My shoulders are flat against the wall, and it's still not far enough away. "What guy are you talking about—the one from the beginning? You don't have any idea who he is?"

"I didn't know this was even going on before she died, and I still don't have a clue who it might have been." Tally's twisting the comforter with both hands now. Her forearms tremble with the strain, but her face stays serene. She's still smiling. Anyone glancing in would think we were having a grand old time. "But I bet you can figure it out."

Tally's smile freezes. The corners of her mouth draw in until her lips are only a knot. "Face it, you'll *have* to figure it out if you want to save Lily."

"You should take this to the police."

"And let them see how perfect she thought he was?" Tally sucks in a rough-edged gasp and still sounds like she's choking. "Let them see how she wanted him before it happened? How he told her all kinds of pretty things so she would trust him? They'll look at Tessa differently. They'll think she *deserved* it, just like my dad would.

"And what good would it do anyway? Tessa told me all about your mom. How your dad used to beat her, how the police couldn't help her, and now . . . now they can't even find your *dad*."

Tessa still talked about me? My hand tightens around the

torn pages. I would never have guessed. Maybe she wasn't the only one who let our friendship slip away. Maybe I should've tried harder.

"If you helped," Tally continues, "maybe it would be different."

"Is that what you really think?"

"Even if they have the diary, it won't change anything. It'll only hurt my mom and piss off my dad." Tally gives me a knowing, bitter smile. "You know what he's like. You remember. He finds out about all this and my life is over. I'll never get away. Tessa's dead, but I'm not. . . . If he knows what Tessa did, I'll wish I were dead."

"Wicket?"

We both jump. It's Todd, calling me from downstairs. I'm thrilled. Grateful beyond measure, and I bolt for the door, Tally on my heels. It's like being followed by Lily. Maybe all little sisters are like this. Maybe it's because they're used to their older sisters leading the way.

But Tally doesn't have a big sister anymore.

Downstairs is exactly the same. The aunts are still wailing. Mrs. Waye still looks strung up. Todd still looks like a Ken doll.

I'm being ugly. He looks like a hero. He looks like someone who could save you. Briefly, I think about telling him everything, launching myself across the room so I can press my face into his chest like the other women do.

I'm scared.

But because I'm scared, I can't trust anyone else to do it but me.

"You mind waiting by the car?" When Todd turns to me, his face is tight. My feet stall as I try to study him. Something isn't right here. There's a hush that's fallen over the room, like everyone's holding their breath.

"I didn't tell Jenna what happened to upset you, Jim." Behind Todd, Mrs. Waye is crying again. She presses a tissue to her eyes, and it comes away black with mascara. "I didn't think she would tell everyone like she did."

"Exactly, you didn't *think*." The voice is low and hateful . . . and familiar. I slowly pivot until I'm facing Jim Waye, but this is not the man I remember. There are smudges and sweat stains on his dress shirt, and his hair is standing on end. Everyone else looks close to coming apart, but Jim *is* coming apart.

"She had a right to know," Mrs. Waye continues, her voice climbing. "I told Jenna because she loved Tessa—we all did. The least I could do was be honest with my daughter's *friend*."

Mr. Waye jerks, and for a second, I think he's going to hit his wife, but then I realize he's not going anywhere. Todd has Mr. Waye by his shirt.

"That's enough, Jim."

"'That's enough'?" Mr. Waye swings around, fists cocked. "I'll tell you what's enough. *You.* What the hell are you doing here after telling the police I was to blame?"

Todd glances toward me. "Outside, please. I'll only be another minute."

Like I want to be around Mr. Waye for a nanosecond longer. I spin around, and Tally follows me through the front door. We've barely reached the steps before I see a low-slung sedan parked on the other side of the street. My chest tightens before my brain even realizes it's Carson. It's too far away to see properly, but I think he nods at me.

"Why's he here?"

"He comes by sometimes." Tally's hands are pinned behind her back, but she looks ready to run. "He came by a lot before Tessa . . . died. But every time I told my mom, he was gone by the time she came outside."

My insides leap. "Oh yeah?"

"Yeah." The girl's mouth goes tight. "You think he cares about us? I don't. No cops, Wick."

I fold up the diary pages, pocket them. "You know I might not find anything, right?"

"I know." Tally's staring hard at the sedan sitting over my shoulder. She's watching Carson watch us. "But for Lily's sake, you better."

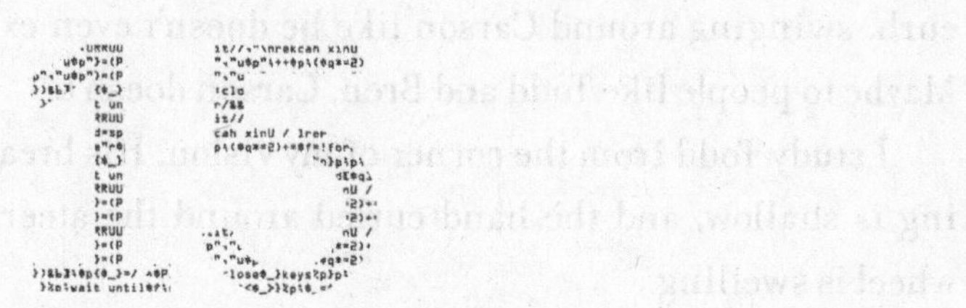

Sometimes he cries. He says he never meant for this to happen, and he's worried about what he'll lose if anyone finds out.

—Page 21 of Tessa Waye's diary

First comes the shouting. It's loud, indignant, and definitively male. Mr. Waye says Todd should get the hell out of his house, and Mrs. Waye is begging them to stop. Something crashes.

Then comes the smack of flesh on flesh.

Next to me, Tally jumps. Okay, if I'm being honest, we both jump. Someone just got punched, and inside, I'm totally set to run.

Except it's Todd who flings open the front door.

"Remember," Tally says.

Like this shit is something I'm going to forget. I follow Todd to his Range Rover, and when I look behind me, Tally's gone.

Todd shifts us into drive and we pull away from the curb, swinging around Carson like he doesn't even exist. Maybe to people like Todd and Bren, Carson doesn't.

I study Todd from the corner of my vision. His breathing is shallow, and the hand curled around the steering wheel is swelling.

"They teach you how to punch in therapy?"

Todd looks down at his right knuckles, tucks his hand under his leg. "Not exactly."

"But you did it anyway."

Todd shoots me a quick look, something wordless clouding up his eyes. He's trying to make a decision, and after another beat, he decides. "I did it because he was going after Becky again. Jim's absolutely unhinged. He's upset because she told Jenna without asking him first. He's more upset about how Tessa's death reflects on him than he is about the loss of his daughter. I punched him because . . . it needed to be done."

I nod. Now there's something I can understand, though I wouldn't have thought Todd would understand it too. He did what needed to be done, and so will I. Tessa's stalker will never touch my sister.

"Jim Waye has bullied his family—his *daughters*—for years," Todd continues. "Tessa was afraid of him."

Afraid enough to jump off a building to get away?

We come to a red light, and Todd spends a moment examining his hand. "I knew Tessa was afraid. . . . Maybe I should have done something. Maybe I could have saved her."

I look out the window. It's understandable. Everybody thinks that after a suicide. Believe me, I know all about the doubts and blame. I feel terrible that Tally and Mrs. Waye are going through it, though. I also feel bad for Todd. The guilt looks like it's eating him from the inside. He looks like he might cry.

I really hope he doesn't. Oh my God, I so hope he doesn't. I would have no idea what to say. I would have no idea what to *do*. People aren't like computers. You can't fix them. They're too messy.

"Hey, Wicket, let's keep this between us, okay?"

The question shoots out of Todd like it's greased. He's so earnest, it surprises—no, shocks the hell out of—me and then . . . I feel kind of good about it. Bren would have an epic shit fit if she knew about this, and he's trusting me not to tell. He's trusting *me*. The juvenile delinquent. The girl no one trusts with anything.

"Sure thing," I say, sounding awfully calm for some-one whose heart is doing a funny leap. If he can trust me, maybe I could trust him. Maybe I could tell him about the diary.

But I don't.

I roll down the window and thread my fingers through the fast-moving air. This is enough. I won't tell him, but maybe I don't really have to. Maybe it's enough to know I'm not the only one with secrets.

By the time Todd gets us home, Bren has dinner ready. The moment we open the door, I can smell warm tomatoes and chopped-up garlic.

"Bren's making spaghetti." Lily meets us in the hallway, and she sounds almost reverent. I can't really blame her—it does smell pretty amazing. The last time we had spaghetti it was microwaved noodles with ketchup on them. Dad said it was basically the same thing, but it's not.

It's *so* not.

"She's already thrown away two batches," Lily continues. "They weren't perfect."

No idea how that would be possible. Bren is the most exact cook I know. Directions exist so we can follow them. Todd says she approaches their business contracts the same way.

"Hi, honey." Bren's fiddling with the garlic bread, carefully pulling it away from the pan's hot edges. "How are you holding up?"

"How do you think?" Todd blows through the kitchen and slams his office door behind him. Briefly we're all quiet; then Bren turns around with an incandescent smile.

Too bad it isn't quick enough to hide the hurt.

Or maybe it's just that I recognize it. In that moment, she looks crushed that he won't confide in her. The disappointment reminds me of my mom.

I feel terrible for her.

"It smells really great, Bren," I offer, and she rewards me with another too-bright smile. It doesn't make me feel better so much as . . . relieved, like a crisis has been averted, even though Bren isn't like that.

And I don't want to say it, but here's the thing: Bren isn't like my mom.

Having a parent with depression kind of forces you to play psychic. You don't know what's going to make her angry. You don't know what's going to make her cry. You don't know. Period. But you better try to anticipate, because you'll feel the fallout. My dad made it worse. He got off on it.

"It smells great because it's going to be great." Lily is already sitting at the kitchen table with a fork in one hand. "Wash up, Wick."

I should say no, but I'm hungry—starved, actually. After scrubbing my hands with the vanilla soap that makes Bren always smell like cookies, I flop into the closest chair and watch Bren add tiny sausages to the meat sauce.

"I ran into your friend's mom today," she says after a moment.

As in a friend other than Lauren? Bren hands me my plate, and I check the size of her pupils. They're normal-looking, but she's talking like she's high on Windex. Interesting—mostly because I don't have friends. I have Lauren, and Bren knows Lauren's mom.

Could she mean Griff's mom? I hope not. I don't think

Griff qualifies as a friend . . . although I'm not sure what that makes him.

"She was really nice," Bren continues, passing Lily a plate full enough to feed a football team. She looks at me. "Wick, sweetheart, please sit up. Posture conveys how you feel about yourself."

Dutifully, I scoot up in my chair, and Bren smiles like I've just done the cutest trick. "Anyway, she said you had physics with her Ronald."

My breath dries up. On the other side of the table, Lily stiffens.

"Ronald?" I put down my fork and focus on not shaking. "You're sure she said *Ronald*?"

Bren's studying the progress of her garlic bread, but hearing my questions, her head whips around. "Of course I'm sure. Why? What's going on?"

What's going on is I am dangerously close to blowing my cool. *Get a grip, Wicket.*

I pull my mouth to one side, try to look like I'm thinking. "Oh yeah, Ronald. He sits a couple rows away from me."

"So you do know him." The muscles in Bren's neck relax.

"Yeah, I just forgot about his real name." I push my food around. So much for my appetite. At this rate, I doubt I'll ever eat again. "We call him Ron."

We also call him Joe, my dad's best friend. The message is one Lily and I were told to expect. It goes down like this: Joe sends his girlfriend—although girlfriend is kind of stretching it. Flavor of the week is more accurate. Anyway, Joe's girlfriend is supposed to contact us by posing as Ronald White's mother. She would ask Bren to say hello to us for her. Bren, thinking she was speaking to a nice Peachtree City mom and not a meth-head, would pass on the story.

And I would know my dad's back and I need to make my way to Joe's place.

I focus on my plate, but inside my ears, my blood is rushing. My dad's home. He's *back*. And he wants us back too.

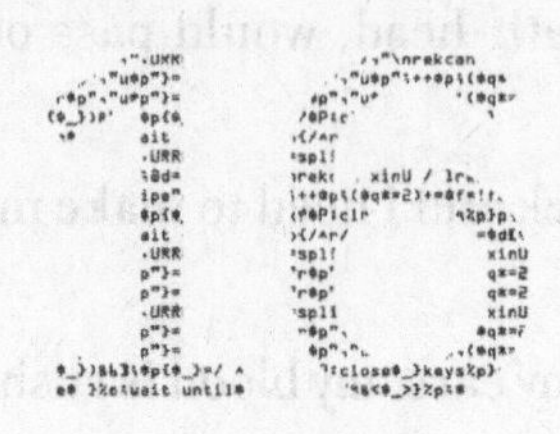

Even when he's not there, I feel like he is.

—Page 19 of Tessa Waye's diary

"So we chatted for about a half hour," Bren continues, pausing only to examine her spaghetti sauce. "Strange really that I've never seen her at the PTA meetings."

Jesus, they were close enough to touch her. Bren could have been hurt. Easily. The thought makes me even queasier.

"Lily?" Bren notices my sister has pushed her plate away. "Aren't you hungry? Don't you like it?"

"No, I'm just not as hungry as I thought." Lily's tone is suitably blank, but her face is tight, like she's seconds away from tears. Her lying could use serious work.

"Do you mind if I take this upstairs, Bren?" I motion to my spaghetti, knowing I'm pushing boundaries here, but

I'm pretty sure I'll get away with it. As much as Bren wants us to not eat like gypsies, Dr. Norcut also told her Lily and I could end up with "food issues" after everything that's happened, so she's supposed to cut us slack if we get weird about eating at the table.

Sure enough, the skin around Bren's eyes creases in disappointment, but she nods. "Okay. Just put your plates away afterward."

We go straight to my room, where I leave the two dishes on my computer desk and Lily shuts the door. For a while, we don't say anything.

"Are you going to go?" Lily asks at last.

"Of course not."

"But what if he gets mad?"

Yeah, what if he does? I shake my head, act like it's no big deal, like I'm not jumping at every shadow that might be him. "So what? He can't touch us, Lil. Don't worry about it."

Lily scrunches up her face. She looks like I just said the sky is green. "But . . . we have to go. Dad said."

I try to nudge Lily's plate into her slack hands. She needs to eat. "We don't have to do what he says anymore."

"Does he know that?"

I concentrate on starting up my computer, but I can still hear all the questions Lily won't ask, like: Who are you kidding? Or don't you remember what Dad was like? But mostly: What if he comes for us?

Scary thought, that one.

We have a lot to lose these days. Maybe I do need to go.

If Joe knows who Bren is, he definitely knows where we're living. If he came here to look for us . . . I grip my chair's armrests.

No, it can't happen. I can't have him here. We can't risk Bren freaking. Getting kicked back into the foster care system would be a disaster. We're safer with Bren and Todd. *Lily's* safer with Bren and Todd.

Which means I'll have to go.

I can't think about this right now. If I do, my head will explode, so I'll concentrate on Tally and Lily and how I'm going to protect my sister, because deep down, I'm pretty sure I'm the best chance she has.

You see, adults mess things up even when they're trying to fix them. No. Check that. They mess things up *especially* when they're trying to fix them. I mean, think about how they tried to save us from our dad, how they tried to help my mom. Failure all the way around.

In a way, I guess, it's not their fault. They're bound by rules.

But I'm not.

I can make my own rules. Online, I'm in charge. I rule the world. I can find this guy.

I slide a quick look at Lily, who's reading on my bedroom floor. She betrayed me, but she did it to save someone else. My sister might not approve of me, but she believed I could help. I'm not sure how I feel about such faith.

"You told Tally Waye about me."

Lily's eyes lift. "Yeah."

"It's supposed to be a secret, Lil. What part of 'do *not* tell people' didn't you understand?"

"I wanted you to have the opportunity to do something good for once."

For once? For once! "I do help people."

"Yeah, but how many of them really need it? Tessa had some boyfriend who made her cry."

"Boyfriend? Did she ever tell you his name?"

"No, but you should find him so he knows what he's done." Lily tucks a strand of curly blond hair behind her ear. It's such a small gesture, but she looks so . . . fragile.

Because she always has been?

Or because of what I know now?

Either way, it doesn't change what I have to do. I pull out the diary pages, force myself through them and . . . it's useless. Nothing more than emotions gutted onto the page. I don't want to read Tessa's perceptions of him. I want to know about their interactions. I want evidence.

Good thing there's another way. I pull my chair closer to the desk, turn the computer on, and start hacking Tessa Waye's email account.

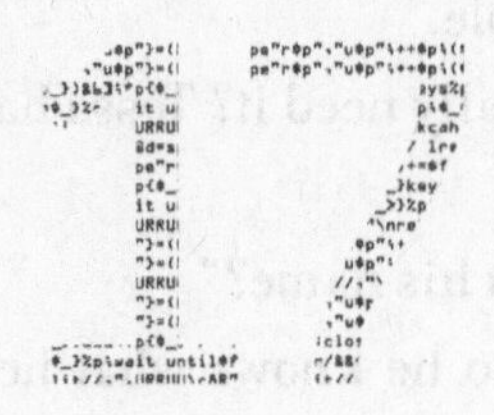

I have all the stuff anyone could want.

I look normal. I look happy. Makes me wonder

how many other girls are faking.

—Page 51 of Tessa Waye's diary

Thirty minutes later, I'm in.

Usually this elicits a happy dance. I learned the Dirty Bird from watching football with Joe. I learned the Funky Chicken from Lauren. But this time?

This time I don't feel anything like dancing. This time I just feel sad.

And super paranoid.

I can't afford to make mistakes in here. It's not just about the police aspect. I'm pretty sure I can duck them even if they are checking all the accounts. It's about Tessa's family. Lauren's not the only one who's had too much therapy. I know what I'm playing with here, can probably spell it out in Norcut-speak.

It's been four years since my mom committed suicide, but I can still feel all those moments and hours and days afterward. When I thought I was getting over it and I wasn't. When I realized I should've known and stopped it.

Except, as Norcut always reminds me, you can't stop it. Wish I could believe her.

But no matter how many times people say they understand . . . they don't. No one gets what it's like to waver between what you had and what you have now. Your new reality perches on top of your old life, but you cannot, cannot, cannot get your head around the fact that you no longer have a mom . . . or a daughter.

And how are you supposed to live without them anyway?

If Tessa's parents knew someone logged on to her account, they'd immediately think maybe, somehow their daughter was alive and had checked her email. Irrational, yes, but that's what I would've thought—what I would've *hoped*—until reason squished it flat.

Then they'd wonder what kind of disgusting person would do that, maybe the press or some hateful classmate. They would worry, period. I want to spare them that.

So I'm extra careful, but I go through everything. All of Tessa's deleted emails, all of her sent emails, everything she saved, and there's nothing—absolutely *nothing* useful. How is that possible?

She had to have contact with this guy. I just have to find how they did it. Cell phone records are usually a great starting point, and once I have access to the target's email account, they're pretty easy to get into. It's all just clicking the carrier's "Forgot Password" link, sending the new temporary password to the hacked email address, and wham, bam, thank you ma'am, I'm in.

But in this case, it won't work. Tessa would've been on her family's plan, and I'd waste too much time tracking down the email address associated with her carrier.

I rub the skin between my eyes, feeling the beginnings of another headache, probably from caffeine withdrawal. I'm at least two cups of coffee low, and it's making me feel fuzzy and dull.

I'm not sure how long I've been staring at my computer, but Lily's been asleep in my bed for hours. A while ago, I heard Bren and Todd put in a movie, but even that's gone quiet now.

I crack my knuckles and decide to switch things up. If the email is a dead end, I'll try something else. Opening a new window, I log into Tessa's Facebook account—easy enough, since it's the same password as her email—and I read through all the comments posted to her wall. Too many go on and on about how she shouldn't have given up and how much her friends miss her. I shouldn't read any further, but I can't seem to stop myself.

Poor Tessa. Is this how they remember you? Matthew Bradford posted he was "sorry she couldn't take it." Jenna's remembering her as a girl who was "afraid." It makes me stiffen. There was more courage in Tessa's leap than they will ever realize.

I click on the Friends link and scroll down through the list of names, recognizing almost everyone from our school.

Football player . . . football player . . . Griff. I wonder if Tessa asked him to be her Friend on Facebook or if he asked her.

That really shouldn't matter to me, but it does.

I keep scrolling. Cheerleader . . . oh wow, Layla Howard. With practically no social skills and even less fashion sense, poor Layla makes me look normal. I like that Tessa was friends with her, even if it was just on Facebook. I bet that made Layla's day.

Then I spot the name under Layla. Marcus Starling. That's not familiar. I click on the name, and it takes me to an almost empty profile page. There's some information near the top—birthdate and stuff—but no wall postings . . . and no other friends besides Tessa, even though he says he attends our high school.

Interesting. I click on the only picture at the top. It enlarges to show a good-looking blond-haired guy, maybe eighteen or nineteen years old. I still don't recognize the name, but the guy looks oddly familiar . . . and not quite right.

He looks staged . . . and that's when it hits me. I don't know the guy. I know the *picture*—specifically the shirt from the picture. Lauren showed it to me when she was ordering a birthday present for her brother and wanted my opinion. I open Google Images and search for Ralph Lauren polo shirts . . . there it is. Third from the bottom. Marcus Starling is using a Ralph Lauren model as his profile picture.

That's weird. All of Tessa's other Facebook friends seem to be from school. Unless Marcus is some friend-of-a-friend-of-a-friend exception, she would have known it was a fake picture. So is it fake because Marcus's a three-hundred-pound shut-in hiding behind a generic-looking model, or is it fake because he was trying to blend in with her other friends?

Some parents check their kids' Facebook accounts, and it's not much of a stretch to think Tessa's would do the same. By putting up some cursory information and how he's "attending" our high school, Marcus looks legit. Tessa's dad or mom probably would have glossed right over him. Could this be the unnamed "he"?

Could be . . . but it's not enough. I click on Tessa's wall again and scroll farther down, looking for past postings. There isn't a lot. Considering Tessa's popularity, that seems strange. Did she find Facebook stupid? Or was it something else? She was selective about what she wrote in her diary. Maybe this is the same kind of thing.

I keep scrolling down, clicking the Older Posts link until I'm looking at entries from almost a year ago. Interestingly, this far back, Tessa's online activity was more frequent. There are the usual shout-outs to friends and comments about weekend plans, but there's also a link to a newspaper article on National Night Out, and Tessa labeled it as "Another Weekend with the 'Rents." The article itself is pretty fluffy—lots of talk about community involvement, which is not a lot of help to me.

But then I see the picture near the end. The caption labels it as "Local Community Leaders Fight Crime," and it's your standard group shot with everyone lined up and grinning. I'm a little surprised to see Todd and Bren at the far right, all happy and smiley and at ease with each other, but this is the kind of community stuff Todd loves, so I guess it makes sense they would be there. Farther to the left is some guy I don't recognize, but on the other side of him is Jim Waye.

He's in the dead center of the picture, with a game-show-host smile and one arm wrapped tightly around Tessa, who looks stiff and uneasy, her eyes slanting sideways like she's looking for someone.

I double-click the picture to enlarge it. Tessa's looking at Carson. The detective—hands stuffed deep in his pockets and scowling—is standing on the far left. He seems oblivious to the photographer and is looking in Tessa's direction as well. Coincidence?

Maybe, until you think about how Tally said Carson kept coming by their house. I push closer to my computer and try to evaluate the detective's expression.

He looks pissed. Why? Maybe he doesn't like Jim's attention whoring, or maybe he's just tired, or maybe he's jealous someone else is touching Tessa.

It's this last thought that sticks.

But just like Marcus Starling, it's not a good lead. I need something more. I close the picture and hit the back button until I'm on Tessa's Facebook page again. There are no new posts to her wall, and for a long moment, I just reread Jenna's comment.

Maybe that's why I open up the diary again—because there are no more options and I'm stuck. I push through, telling myself this is just another job—even though every word makes me wonder if this was the way my mom felt or, even worse, how Lily will react if he gets close to her.

It takes me just under an hour to finish, and when I get to the end, I'm back to where I started. There's nothing helpful. I think the guy is older. She wrote he was "worried about what he'll lose" if anyone discovered them—that doesn't sound like a guy from school. Then again, they started as friends and then it became more . . . and that makes him sound like a classmate.

Tessa wanted him, but after they slept together, she slowly, very slowly, became afraid of him. He was not the man he pretended to be; being held by him was wonderful until it became too tight; being desired by him was perfect until it meant no way out. She tried to end it, and *that's* when the abuse turned violent. If he was older, that means it was rape. Even if they were the same age, it would still be abuse. Once she told him no, he began to hit her where no one would see the bruises.

I lean back in my computer chair, stretching until my spine pops. I don't really know what to do. I have no definite leads. I don't know anything except that I'm dealing with a very specific kind of monster, one who hides his victims in plain sight.

I need more information, but he's so hidden—how will I get it? How do I drive him out of the shadows?

With bait.

I pull closer to my computer, wiggling my mouse until the computer emerges from sleep mode. I've never hacked without a plan, and what I'm about to type is no plan. It's not even a good idea. What I'm about to type is a bullet shot into the dark to see if someone else will shoot back.

In other words, it's a Hail Mary shot, and I hate those.

I click on the Facebook comment box at the top of Tessa's wall—say a quick apology to Mrs. Waye—and press my feet into the floorboards, because part of me is kind of scared I'm about to float away as I type:

`I know who killed me.`

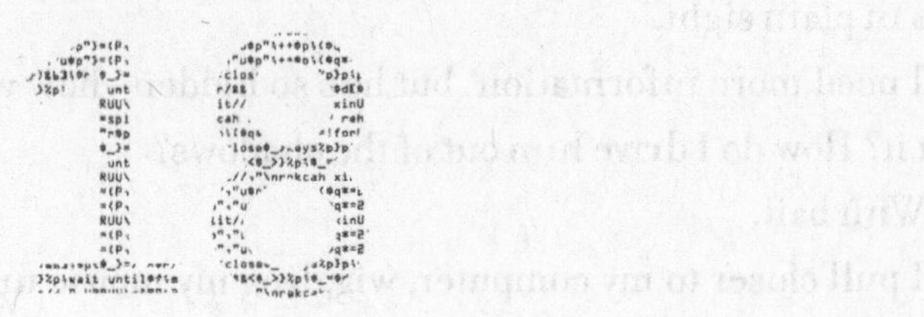

After we did it, I ran. I ran and I ran and I ran. Must have put two miles in between us, but it didn't matter. All that space and I still sobbed under a sky the same color as his eyes.

—Page 33 of Tessa Waye's diary

Joe lives in the west end of Peachtree City in a subdivision called Twin Creeks, and until that dawn raid when the cops came for my dad and found Lily and me instead, we lived there too. It's a funny place. Drive five minutes farther into the city and you'll find multimillion-dollar homes. Here you can find Hispanic families living nine and ten to a house. You can buy meth from one of my dad's dealers. While other kids went to camp, I learned to code. While other dads taught their daughters to play soccer, mine taught me to scam. I think the newspaper once called the neighborhood a "blight," but Lily and I always thought of it as home.

I'm almost at the front porch when the door opens. Joe Thompson, my dad's best friend and my "mentor," ambles onto the warped deck. The wooden planks creak under his feet. Big to begin with, Joe must have put on another fifty pounds since I last saw him. It's like looking at a Baby Shamu crammed into human clothes.

"Well, well, if it isn't Wicket Tate herself."

"Drop the act, Joe." I stand at the bottom of the stairs and glare up at him, all attitude, even though I'm pretty sure I look like I was dragged through a bush. A five-mile hike down the bike paths in ninety-degree weather doesn't do much for your appearance, but it beats the hell out of having to explain why you need your foster dad to give you a lift. "What do you want?"

"To see if you would come when you're called."

I don't say anything, mostly because there isn't anything to say. I hate the idea that he can yank me around like this, and he knows it.

Joe rubs one hand over his mouth, but it does nothing to hide his grin. There's something dark and satisfied sitting behind his eyes. He looks like he's been fed with secrets. "I mean, you're living in that big house, wearing all those fancy clothes. I just thought you might get the idea you're too good for your own family."

Family. Great. If that doesn't make me want to scrub

myself with bleach, nothing will.

"You been watching me, Joe?" I don't know what disturbs me more—that he's been spying on me or that I've been too distracted by Carson to notice.

"Yeah, I have." Joe's daring me to smart off. I look at his catcher-mitt-sized hands, however, and decide to decline. The last time he smacked me, my ear hurt for a week.

Joe looks me up and down again. You can see his thoughts ticker-tape through his eyes: different clothes, same girl. He thinks I'm a coward, and he's probably right.

"Come on in." Joe palms the screen door wide and motions for me to pass beneath his arm. This is the part where I should march right on in like a good little hacker, but I don't move. Not sure I can, actually. If I step across that threshold, I'll step into my old life.

Joe gives me a knowing smile. "Saw you out with that lady you're staying with," he says. "You two looked awfully comfortable together. Then there was that dark-haired girl you've been running around with. Has a smile so pretty I want to ruin it."

Bren and Lauren. Briefly, I'm ashamed of myself. I know better than to make friends. I know better than to let myself get close. I made myself vulnerable.

I made Bren and Lauren vulnerable.

I look up at Joe and realize I'm not stepping into my old life. I never left it. Whatever Joe wants, I will deliver.

And we both know it.

"Go wait in the living room," he says as I pass. "Your timing couldn't be better. We're having a meeting. Heather's already here, but the other guy's late."

I duck under Joe's arm and head for the living room. Inside, dead beer bottles and pizza boxes are scattered across the floor and a thin, blond girl—*Heather, I'm guessing*—is draped across the sole armchair. She looks up as I come in, and her eyes narrow.

Guess we're not going to be besties. I ignore her, turn for the couch, and have to shove a mix of nudie magazines and computer catalogs onto the floor so I have a place to sit. The fabric under my legs is alternately stiff and sticky. I pray to God that it's just spilled soda or juice, because I do *not* want to contemplate the alternatives.

"What do you want, Joe?" I lean against the armrest, trying to get comfortable, and watch Joe hover near the front window. He looks nervous, and I don't like that. It makes me start checking for the nearest exit.

What's he looking for? Is he worried about the cops? Carson? It would not go well for me to get busted while I'm here with Joe. The very idea makes my skin pop up in fresh sweat.

"I can't be gone for long, Joe, or else they get suspicious. What do you want?"

"Don't get your panties in a wad. The little shit will be here soon."

Charming. I wonder what my nickname is. Except I don't

really want to know. I'm sure it's worse. I do, however, want to know what's up with Joe's new chick. Heather doesn't look too good. She's drawn herself into a tight ball. With her knees tucked up like that, I can see bones ghosting through her skin. Another junkie.

I offer her my hand. "I'm Wicket Tate."

"I know," she says, staring at my open palm like she might bite it. Behind us, I think I hear Joe snigger. I guess it is pretty funny. Me trying to make friends with a cracked-out junkie. I should know better, and I do.

Just like I know better than to feel sorry for her.

But I do anyway.

Fine. Whatever. I lean my head against the faded couch cushions, force myself to take a long, deep breath. It actually works a little. My heart rate ratchets down a few notches. Norcut would be so proud. "So I'm guessing this has something to do with a job?"

Joe snorts. "Aren't you the genius?"

Well, if we're judging by the people in this room. "So when did we start discussing jobs in front of junkies?"

Heather leaps to life, fingers arched into claws. "I ain't no junkie!"

"Is that what you tell yourself?" I stare at her. "Seriously?"

"Shut your damn mouth, Wick." Joe takes a step toward us, and I tense. With this much distance between us, I could easily outrun the fat bastard. I've been in Joe's house enough to know that if I jump the couch and head for the kitchen, I can duck through the back door.

But he'll still know where to find me.

Joe glares at me. "Heather's straight up. She's part of the job. A real necessary part of the job." He jabs one finger in her direction. "Show her the voice, baby."

Heather sinks down into her armchair and clears her throat a couple of times. When she finally speaks up, her voice has lost all its raspiness, all its broken-off edges. Instead, it surfaces smooth as sun-warmed honey.

"That was Bonnie Tyler's 'Total Eclipse of the Heart,' and I'm Larissa Miller signing off for the night. Be southern and be sweet." Heather picks at a stain on her tank top with a shaking hand. "I'm gonna be a radio host, and then I'm going to get my own talk show. I'm gonna be just like Nancy Grace."

Well, dare to dream, Heather. I look at Joe. Is he thinking about doing a phone scam with this chick? He's got to be high, but Joe interprets my shock as being impressed.

"That's right," he says. "Heather's got the voice of an angel. Ain't nobody going to suspect her. So shut the fuck up, Wick." Outside, there's the low growl of a motorcycle pulling into the driveway. Joe stiffens and hurries to the window, pushing the dirty curtain farther aside. "Oh, good, the little shit's here. This kid can hack almost as good as you, Wick."

Joe opens the door and I look up, ready to greet Little

Shit. Maybe I'll call him LS for short. Maybe I'll call him *Pequeño* Shit to be multicultural.

Except as soon as the kid walks in the door, I know I won't. I've only ever called this guy by one name.

Griff.

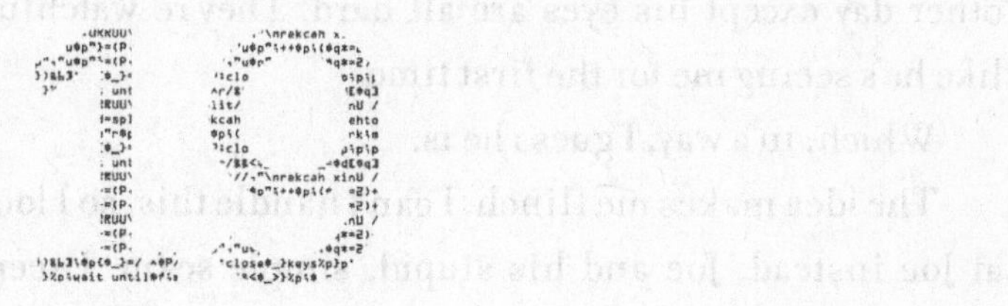

Are there more like me? Has he had other girls?

Or am I supposed to be special?

—Page 23 of Tessa Waye's diary

I have to struggle not to gape. It's just not possible. Griff can't be a hacker. He's too quiet. His grades are too good. He's too . . .

He's too much like me. The realization stings. We're hiding behind the same habits, the same mask. I make my living by looking underneath people's surfaces, and yet I never suspected his.

"Do you have the new firewall program?" Joe asks.

Griff nods and pulls a jump drive out of his jeans pocket. He hands it to Joe, who plugs it into one of the laptops left on the coffee table, leaving the rest of us to stare at one another while he goes through the files.

I guess this is the part where Griff and I are supposed to say hello. I can't tell if he's surprised to see me too. His face is blank, and he doesn't say a word. This could be any other day except his eyes are all hard. They're watchful, like he's seeing me for the first time.

Which, in a way, I guess he is.

The idea makes me flinch. I can't handle this, so I look at Joe instead. Joe and his stupid, simple scam. Except it's not stupid or simple when you unravel how it works. The plan goes like this: Joe has set up a legitimate charity organization. It even has a legitimate website. He's telling everyone he's collecting money for tornado victims. Georgia's been hit hard this spring. Scam-wise, this is smart on a couple of levels.

One, he looks legit to the cops. They might suspect, but they'll need more evidence to get a warrant, and evidence takes time. Speed is essential in a good credit card scam. By the time the police get what they need, we'll be gone.

Two, the scam taps into the marks' pity. Almost everyone has seen the horrible pictures. Whole towns have been decimated. People have been left with nothing. Marks are always more likely to hand over credit card information if they think it's for their neighbors.

And with Joe's official-looking website and charity paperwork, they'll feel comfortable revealing their credit card information. That's the beauty of the plan—he won't have to steal their financial information. They'll just give it to him.

"I want to make sure we have distance on this. Heather will call them up and get their email information." Joe shoves Heather aside and flops down in her chair, sweating. "It'll reassure them that we're not asking for money up front. We'll direct them to the website and tell them to input their donations there."

And those are the donations that will be reported to the IRS, continuing Joe's front as a legit charity. I rub the tight skin across my forehead. There's a faint thumping behind my eyes, another headache begging to get in. *Bravo, Joe. You've definitely stepped up from dealing meth and stealing ATM passwords.*

"And when we send them their email confirmations, when those rich bastards click to print off their donation receipt, you'll have them, Wick," Joe says, looking at me, his face all flushed.

I don't want to see it. I close my eyes, but it doesn't help. His expression is tattooed on the backs of my lids. I know the look because I've had it myself. Joe's thrilled to be hunting, and I hate, hate, hate that it's something we share.

"Griff here's a whiz with firewalls," Joe continues.

Really? As good as he is with graphics? I open my eyes, take a shaky breath. *I liked him better as an artist.*

"I can't do this, Joe," I say. "I'm already under surveillance."

"That thin cop?" Joe spits the question like Carson doesn't matter and isn't a danger. Joe has no idea, and that scares me even more.

I focus on the skin between his eyes. "Yeah."

"He's not a problem yet. No warrant, right? No security breaches?" Joe leans forward. Sweat is beading along his upper lip. "'Cause you of all people should know."

We stare at each other. I can see where this is headed. If I'm being honest with myself, I saw it before I even opened my mouth to object. I don't know why I bother trying to get away from this crap. Once you become useful to the wrong sort of people, you'll never get free. It doesn't work like that.

"Well?" Joe's getting pissed off now. His hands start to round into fists, and instinctively, I retreat. "Have the cops traced you?"

My nervousness dissolves, and I almost laugh. *As if.* Then again, if I were to say yes and tell him I was compromised, I'd be useless to them. I'd be out.

For a brief, shining second, I see myself away from all this, but reality swings into focus. I know too much to be let go. I'd go from compromised to liability, and looking at Joe's fists, I know what happens to liabilities.

I swallow hard. "No, they haven't traced me."

"Then we're good—at least for a little while longer." Joe rests both hands on his belly. For a second, he looks like Buddha in a wife-beater. "Don't go soft on me, Wick, or I'll have to toughen you up. There are all sorts of ways to hurt you now, and I remember how your old man used to do it."

I nod. I want Joe to shut up, because I know where this is going. I was five when my dad destroyed my only doll, eight when he got rid of my dog, and ten when he broke Lily's arm. It was all to punish me.

And Joe watched all of it. We both know how this works. Love is leverage. Caring is dangerous. Dangerous for me, but also—*mostly*—for anyone I care about.

"You might think because your dad's on the run that you're beyond his reach, but you never will be. He'll always have me, and I'll always have access to his people."

His people. His drug dealers. His junkies. People who are afraid of Joe and my dad and people who want their approval. My life is worth nothing to them. Bren's and Todd's and Lauren's are worth even less.

"I will fix you so you have nothing, understand?" Joe stares me down. "Do you *understand*?"

"Yeah," I manage, and if I didn't know better, I would think Griff just stiffened. But I do know better. It's stupid to think he cares.

So I stare at Joe. I listen as he runs through the scam again, and I know, without a single doubt, that this is who I am and who I will always be.

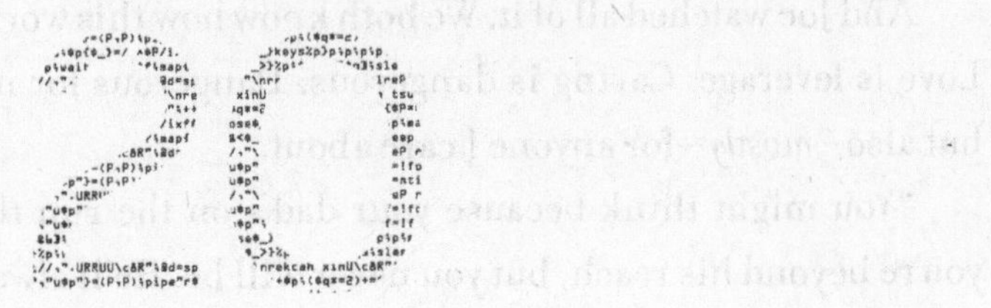

Everyone thinks I'm a good girl. If they only knew.

—Page 11 of Tessa Waye's diary

An hour later and we're on Joe's front porch, blinking up at the sunshine. The way we're both squinting, you'd think daylight was a hacker's natural enemy. I study Griff's pale skin and my equally pale arms and think I might be on to something.

"You okay?" Griff asks.

Am I okay? At first, the question startles me; then it just makes me sad, because I have no idea how to answer him.

"Yeah, sure." You'd think I'd feel more comfortable around him now. He's apparently like me. He steals. He cheats. He takes advantage of people's natural urge to help. It doesn't make me feel any better at all, though. I stare at one of the few people I should be able to say almost anything to, and I can't think of a single word.

"How do you feel about the job?"

I grimace. "Oh, it feels peachy. Nothing like knowing Joe's boinking a junkie he's involved in his scam to make me feel all warm and tingly inside."

I sound bitter, and I am. It's dangerous for Joe to do this. You can't trust a junkie. If something comes loose, it'll be from Heather's end. There are too many lives tied up in this. Lauren, Lily, Bren, Todd. Naming them off makes my chest shrink.

Griff nudges his chin toward the bike parked in the driveway. "You want a ride home?"

Ha! Bren would die if I rode up on the back of a motorcycle. I rub the tight muscles along my neck and realize she would die if she knew about any of this.

I drop my hand. "I don't think it's a very good idea."

"Why's that?" Griff's voice is as even as ever, but his eyes are still hard.

Because I shouldn't trust you as far as I can throw you. Because you're using your powers for evil, but when I look at you, I still see the guy who kept Matthew Bradford from punching his girlfriend. I see the guy teachers adore, and that makes you . . . Dangerous?

I don't want to know. Seeing him involved in this disappoints me more than I care to think about. I want to ask how it happened, but I don't think I could handle the details. I liked him better before. "You don't have to be nice, Griff."

Something flickers inside those bottle-green eyes again, but I head for the sidewalk, walking fast enough that I don't have to think about it.

Until he comes after me.

"Let me give you a ride. It's got to be almost an hour's walk, right?" Griff's hand cups my upper arm, and I yank it away.

Stupid move, though. It only makes his fingers trail down my arm, shooting stars across my skin. "It's forty minutes."

"So let's ride." Griff pushes his hair away from his eyes. I've known the guy for almost three years, and he's always needed a haircut. Except I haven't noticed—really noticed—until now. "Forty minutes turns into ten."

"No."

"Then I'll walk with you."

I back up another step, but it's no good. Griff still follows me. What's the deal here? He's a criminal with a conscience? Doesn't want me walking home alone? "No."

"Why not?"

"Because your bike's here."

"So?" He's too close again. "I'll get it later."

"If it's even still here." I stare at him like he's an idiot, and it might not be that far from the truth. "You should know how easy it is to steal those things. I mean, all someone would need is a van and two guys to just pick it up and . . ."

And I just backed right into his argument.

Griff's smile is lit-fuse bright. "Exactly. So you should just say yes and save me from getting my bike stolen. Come on."

Reluctantly, I follow him. It's a ride home, for God's sake—we're not getting married. It doesn't mean anything. Except it feels like it does. Before now, we barely spoke, and now I know what Griff really is . . . but I still keep seeing him as a good guy.

Griff's Honda is lowered, black, and stripped down. Minimal chrome. No accessories. Even the stripe is just a glossy black strip against the tank's flat black paint job. It's not what I ever would have pictured for Griff.

But it's perfect for him.

"You like it?" He hands me an extra helmet. I hesitate, almost ask if all the bimbos he picks up wear it, but then decide not to bother. It's none of my business, and I don't want to know anyway.

"Yeah, it's a cool bike." I pull the helmet on and buckle the chin strap. It's a little snug, which is good for head injuries, but seriously bad for my hair.

"It's a different-looking bike, though," I say. "You don't see many Hondas like this around."

Griff's face lights up like I just said something wonderful. It kind of makes me cringe and glow.

"No," he explains. "It's vintage. Everyone around here goes for Harleys, but this is a 1978 Honda CB400. My dad and I stripped it down to be a café racer."

I have no idea what that means, but I smile anyway. It's

getting easier and easier to do that with him, but it's not something I'm going to think about. Griff smiles too, but once I slide behind him, his shoulders stiffen.

Wonderful, my touch repulses him. I try to shift away, put a little more space between us, but Griff's right arm snakes around to pull me closer. Suddenly, I'm smashed up against his back, my heart knocking around in my chest like sneakers on a spin cycle.

"You okay?"

"Um, yeah." I ease my right hand around, groping for the usual handholds. The bike doesn't have any. If I want to stay on, I'm going to have to hold on to Griff. "So how did you know where I live, anyway? How did you know which window was mine the other night?"

"I know a lot about you."

Especially now. Griff fires the engine to life, and the bike shifts forward like it's eager to take off. He cuts a quick look over his shoulder, grinning again.

It's probably the helmet making my face hot. There's no way he just got me to blush. "You 'know a lot' about me? Stalk much, Griffin?"

His grin stretches even wider. "I like it when you're mean. Don't be a chicken, Wick. Hold on to me."

"Right. Like you scare me," I say, and force myself to slide one hand round his waist. Griff isn't what I'd call super built. He's not like some of the football players or wrestlers who go around with biceps shaped like softballs and no neck. He's . . . spare. Wiry. And when my arms circle his waist, I realize he's also incredibly hard.

I tug back a bit. That is something I *so* do not need to know. Except I'm grabbing hold again, way harder than before, because Griff guns the bike onto the street, leaving a smear of tire and smoke behind us.

Fine. Excellent, actually. We whip around the corner, heading for the highway, and my heart leaps. This is faster than I was expecting. A lot faster. Griff seems to be enjoying the speed and, if I'm being honest, so am I. The faster I can get away from Joe and my dad and their plan, the better.

Except it shadows me. I press my cheek between Griff's shoulder blades and hear my fear grow pulse and breath. The faster we go, the faster it follows.

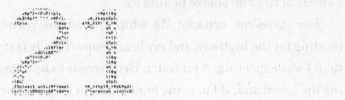

He says I'm beautiful, and it only makes me feel ugly.

—Page 40 of Tessa Waye's diary

Okay, so this might be all kinds of awesome. Griff's bike is fast, but he's also a pretty amazing driver. The way we whip through the turns like we're weightless, the way he slides us through traffic like we're greased . . . Yeah, it's all kinds of awesome.

It still takes me to the first red light before my shoulders begin to unknot. I straighten, belatedly realizing two guys in a minivan are admiring Griff's bike. To our left, there's a cop eyeing us. I go back to looking at the Minivan Men until one of them waves.

"Friends of yours?" Griff coasts the bike forward as

the light changes, and I hope we're going too fast for him to hear me laugh.

Shame how the elation all goes away as soon as we pull into my driveway. I slide off the bike and face Griff, feeling heavy enough to sink through the concrete. "So how'd you get caught up with Joe?"

"He stopped by the school."

"Seriously?" I pull off the helmet and hand it to him. "Was he trying to steal something?"

"No, I think he was looking for you."

Me? Shit. I hug my arms close around myself, try to look like I'm not thinking about how much that scares me, how much it makes me wonder if Joe ever came looking for Lily.

Griff watches me. He keeps turning the helmet around and around in his hands, his eyes all wrinkled up. "My mom's brother was picking me up. He knows Joe, and they started talking. Paul—that's my uncle—told him I was good with computers. One thing kind of led to another."

"No, one thing does not lead to another." I stare at him, lost between sad and pissed. "We're *scamming* people. How the hell does a nice kid like you get caught up in credit card fraud?"

"First of all, I'm not a kid." Griff twists off the bike, scowling. He shoves my helmet onto the seat and, fast as a blink, grabs my hand. "Secondly, I'm not so nice."

Oh, right. Because giving me a ride home instead of making me hoof it was a real dick move. I give him my best Whatever look. It usually makes guys back off. Actually, it usually makes them run for the hills, but this one just gets closer.

"I'm not nice," Griff repeats. "If I were, I wouldn't have been there and you'd still be avoiding me." He pauses, waiting for me to agree or deny, and when I don't do either, he shrugs. "Look, I *really* need the cash."

The admission makes me relax, more than it probably should. I've known Griff for three years, and until this moment, I've never been comfortable talking with him, but now that I know he's like me . . . Jesus, Norcut would be all over this.

I nudge my chin toward the bike. "Looks like you're doing okay."

"This was my dad's. Only thing he left behind when he took off for California . . . aside from me, aside from my mom, who still thinks he's going to rescue us. She's not even getting out of bed anymore she's so fucking depressed. She lost her job because she stopped showing up, and the food stamps go only so far."

"Sorry, I didn't mean—"

"I know. Sorry. I shouldn't snap at you. I'm just tired." He sags a little, and for the first time, I notice the shadows smudged under his eyes, how the skin around his mouth is pale and tight.

And yet he's rubbing my palm like he wants me to feel better.

"Even after everything Joe said, I never expected to see you sitting there," he says.

I shrug like it's no big thing. "Life's just full of surprises."

"No shit."

We stare at each other and neither of us says a thing . . . and yet . . . and yet. "You should quit while you still can, Griff. It's not good for you. *I'm* not good for you. I appreciate the ride home and all, but it doesn't change anything. You really should stay away from me."

I tug my hand, but he doesn't let go. With anyone else, this would totally freak me out, and okay, maybe I am a little freaked. There's the familiar lump of panic rolling up my throat, but there's something else there too. Something inside me that flips when his fingers skim farther up, hitting the inside of my wrist.

Everywhere he's touching and everywhere he's touched is lighting up. I feel like I've swallowed the sun. His fingertips streak light across my skin.

"You sure you're not good for me?" Griff's voice is deeper now, rougher, but he's holding me like I'm the one who's about to break.

He might be right. Griff makes me feel funny . . . happy and worse. Is this because I know what he really is? Or is it because he knows what I am?

"I'm very sure I'm not good for you," I say again, pushing hard against his chest even though I didn't really have to. He lets me go. For a second, I regret it. My legs are shaking. "And I don't think you're very good for me either."

I hustle up the sidewalk, expecting to hear his engine start any second now. It doesn't. Griff's watching me. Part of me wants to run, but the other part wants to go down there and tell him to knock it off.

I have the front door almost closed behind me before he responds. His voice sounds a lot more normal. There's the familiar laugh, but underneath, he sounds like he's flaking into pieces. "I think you're wrong, Wicked. I think you'd be great for me."

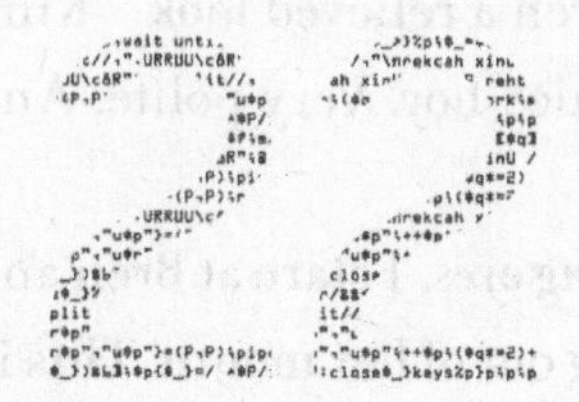

It's getting harder and harder to play normal.

—Page 62 of Tessa Waye's diary

"Who was that?" I don't even have my shoes off, and Bren has already materialized on my right. "Was that the Griffin boy?"

The Griffin boy? I was going to squeeze past, but her question brings me up short. "How do you know Griff?"

"I met his mother at a PTA meeting. She was late and looked really lost. We talked a little and she said she'd be back, but I haven't seen her since." Bren nudges the curtains to one side, studying Griff with the same wrinkled-eye look she saves for reviewing work contracts. "The woman's name is . . . Karen? Kelly?"

"Kim."

I didn't realize Lauren was even there until she spoke. I twist and our eyes meet. Great. There's no way I'm getting out of explaining. Lauren looks seconds away from choking on a belly laugh.

"That's it!" Bren throws Lauren a relieved look. "Kim. Kim Griffin. Her son is a very nice boy. Very polite. And those eyes—they're so striking."

Nice boy. Very polite. With striking eyes. I stare at Bren and try to reconcile the words coming out of her mouth. This is so not what I was expecting. She should be busting me six ways from Sunday. I mean, it's a boy, for God's sake. We've never talked about boys, but I'm sure she has rules about them. Plus, I rode up on a motorcycle. We've never talked about that, either, but I *know* she'd have to have rules for motorcycles. This doesn't make any sense. Bren's not mad and I'm not in trouble.

"So we'll just go upstairs." Lauren slings her arm through mine, drags me up the first few steps. Up this close, I can see how her bruised eye has gone eggplant purple. She isn't even bothering to hide it with concealer. Knowing her mom's commitment to perfection, it must be driving the poor woman nuts. "I have a history project I want to show Wick."

"Okay. Have fun." Bren continues to stare at me. Her mouth is a little open and her eyes are wide, and now I really don't know what to do. My foster mom looks astonished and also . . . a little happy.

"What's going on?" I mutter. "Why's Bren watching me

like she's waiting for an alien to crawl out of my chest?"

"You brought home a boy." Lauren is almost vibrating with excitement. She tightens her arm so I'm caught against her side. "A very *cute* boy. Bren's probably tearing up with joy. You're finally doing normal teenage stuff."

"That's what it takes to make her happy?"

Lauren shuts my bedroom door behind us and grins, the bruised skin around her eye wrinkling into purple folds. "If you really want to make Bren happy, ask her to braid your hair."

"Oh, nice, and everyone thinks I'm the smart-ass."

"I get away with it because I'm adorable. I can't help it. It's my burden. So. Since when did you and Griff start talking?"

Since I discovered he's as awful as I am. And is that really the reason? Can I talk to him now because we're alike? I can't really reconcile the new Griff with the guy I liked. He's horrible now. He's like me. He cheats his way into people's lives.

And yet he's also the nicest guy I know.

My fingers drift to where Griff held my hand. It's still warm, and touching where he touched, I get warmer. "We've always talked. We're computer lab partners."

Lauren nods but doesn't look like she believes me. "Well, whatever. We need to talk, but . . . are you okay? You kind of look like you're going to be sick."

"I'm fine." We stare at each other and I cave, slumping into my desk chair and rubbing my temples. "Actually, no,

I'm not. My dad's back."

Lauren gasps like I've just confirmed the bogeyman's for real.

Which I guess, in my case, is about right.

"Is that where you were?"

"Sort of. I was meeting with his partner. He has this new scam."

"So how does Griff figure into this? I mean, I'm guessing you two didn't just run into each other."

"He was there too." For a second, I don't want to say anything further. I'm cramming down my feelings pretty well—even though they're threatening to erupt. It isn't my secret to tell. Then again, Lauren's already made the connection. "Joe recruited him for some of the security work."

"Who's Joe, and why does he want either of you?"

"Joe is my dad's best friend." If you could call it that. Joe doesn't really have friends. Joe has contacts, sources. . . . My dad is protection. Even though Joe is afraid of him.

"He needs my help. He needs *our* help," I correct, suddenly remembering Griff's role in all this. "There's this credit card scam. Joe's spearheading it for my dad."

I offer Lauren a wobbly smile. "I think this is the part where you run screaming from the house."

"Don't push it, Wick. I'm actually thinking about doing just that."

"Then why haven't you?"

"Because . . . I don't think you'd do this without a really good reason." Lauren turns away, retreats to my bed, and starts unpacking more new clothes Bren bought me. "So what do you have to do?"

"Some hacking. They have a way to scam people into making donations by appearing to be a charity for tornado victims." I plug in my computer, and while I'm stuck waiting for it, I swivel my chair side to side. Power-ups take longer with my computer than they would with most. I have a mess of firewall hardware, an entire platform of anti-spyware protection, and I *still* unplug the computer to prevent anyone from powering it up remotely. It's the only way to fully sever my line to the outside. I can't get out, but no one else can get in either. "Joe and my dad need me for the credit cards."

"I just . . . I just don't like you doing this. I mean, when are you going to quit?"

"Do you have any idea what will happen if I do?" She doesn't have an answer, and because I don't either, I look away. I turn to my computer and pull up my email. Wire transfer. Wire confirmation. A follow-up email from a past customer. This is what my life used to be.

"Your dad can't touch you, Wick. You're not part of that world anymore."

"I'm not?" The argument is so familiar it pisses me off. These are the same lies I told Lily. I might not be part of my old world anymore, but I'm sure as hell not part of this new one. "Joe knows where we are. He knows how to reach us. I can't risk pissing him off. Think about what he could do to us."

"You mean what he'd do to Lily."

"I mean *us*. Bren and Todd and you," I add. "If Joe knows about you, my dad knows."

Lauren nods like she gets it, but I can see in her clouded eyes and pressed-thinned mouth that she doesn't. She's worried about the hacking, not what the hacking protects. I could try to explain it, but the words won't come. They're lodged in my gut.

I click my link to Facebook and plug in Tessa's log-in. The page takes only a heartbeat to load, and when it does, there must be twenty messages under mine, but only one makes me cringe:

`When I find you, you'll bleed for that.`

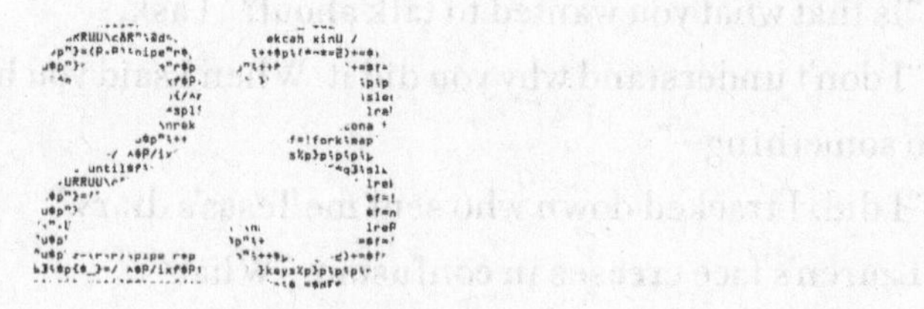

His promises scare me.

He always gets what he wants.

—Page 34 of Tessa Waye's diary

When I find you, you'll bleed for that.

Well, hello, Marcus Starling. I stare at the screen, wavering between excited and spooked. There are no other comments from Marcus, but there are *plenty* from Tessa's other friends. Matthew Bradford called us both "freaks." Holly Davis says, "Whoever hacked Tessa's page will go to hell for this stuff." There's more, of course. Everyone knows Tessa's account has been compromised, but they're assuming it's been hacked by a nasty classmate. This could work to my advantage . . . as long as the Wayes or the police don't report the page as being compromised.

"Are you the one who posted on Tessa's wall? That comment about knowing who killed me?"

I look up, catch Lauren staring at me from across the room.

"Is that what you wanted to talk about?" I ask.

"I don't understand why you did it. When I said you had to do something—"

"I did. I tracked down who sent me Tessa's diary."

Lauren's face creases in confusion. "What?"

"It was Tessa's little sister, Tally. She found the diary, read it, and contacted me. Tessa was involved with some guy—I don't know who, but I think he was older—and when she tried to break it off . . . it turned violent."

Lauren puts one hand on my bed to steady herself, but her knees keep pressing toward the floor.

"It gets worse," I continue. "Tessa wrote about the guy in her diary, and even though she never used *his* name, she did name someone else he wanted, his next target—"

I know this part so well it should be easy. Lily's name is living under my tongue, but I end up having to rip it out of myself.

"It's . . . Lily, Lauren. He named Lily. She's next." I tilt my computer screen in Lauren's direction. She hesitates, then comes to join me. "I've been trying to run down Tessa's inner circle—figure out who he might be—and when I looked through her Facebook friends, everyone seemed legit.

"Except for this guy." I point at Marcus Starling's avatar.

"He has no other friends but Tessa. It's a fake profile picture, a fake name. I think he could be our guy."

"He sounds way pissed, Wick. Could he really find you?"

"No, I logged in as Tessa. There's no way he could know who I am."

Then why are goose bumps still climbing up my arms?

"But what if someone tells the police? Could it get tracked back to you?"

"No, I used a secure IP address. Worst case, they're going to think it's cyberbullying and delete the account."

We both spend another minute rereading the message, and for the first time, I notice the time stamp. It's barely twenty minutes after I posted my message. Good. I can use that. Hacking is all about knowing your code and programs, but it's also about knowing your prey. Marks with high emotions are often the easiest to hack. They can make themselves vulnerable. The right email, the right phone call, the right touch can push them in the direction you want.

But how do I keep pushing him?

"I guess I just . . . I just don't get why you threw it up there like that." Lauren pulls her thumbnail from her mouth and gestures at the screen with a half-chewed finger. "'I know who killed me.' It's kind of, I don't know, inflammatory. It isn't just Tessa's attacker who's going to get upset. What about her mom?"

I think of Mrs. Waye's cracked smile and wince . . . then I think of Mr. Waye's fists, and I cringe. "It'll be horrible, but she'll think it's some cruel kid showing off. Lauren, if I make him angry, he'll be easier to find."

"Or you could go to the police. What if you took all this to them?"

"One of the detectives—his name's Carson—might be involved. He kept waiting outside their house. Tally's suspicious."

"Are you?"

"Yeah . . . Carson's shown up here too. I think he's dirty. He might even have something to do with it."

Lauren sits down hard on my floor, watches me with a kind of horrified wonder.

"Even if I did give them the diary, it wouldn't help. It doesn't name the rapist. It will focus them in the wrong direction, and they'll be chasing their tails. Trust me, I know this stuff. I'm usually the one they're chasing." I run both hands through my hair, rubbing my scalp until I'm sure I look like I stuck my tongue in a toaster.

I look at Lauren. "Do you know how many times my mom called the cops about my dad? A bunch. Ten times? Twelve? Even after she slapped him with a restraining order, he still didn't stop. He'd beat the hell out of us, steal her paycheck, and disappear again. There's some evil that can't be caught by playing by the rules."

I expect to see denial in Lauren's expression, but her chin lifts. "Yeah, the police play by the rules, and this guy won't."

"Exactly. If Lily's going to be saved, it's up to me."

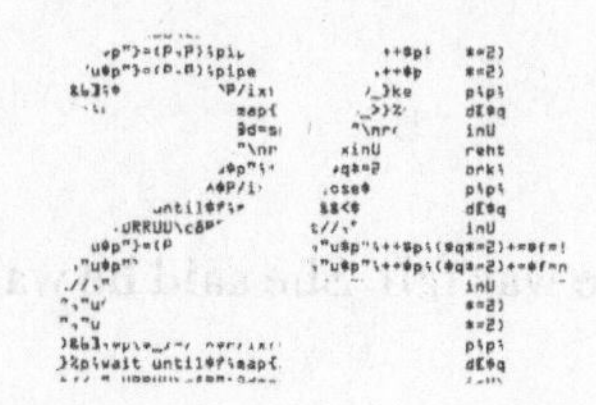

I love the way he looks at me.

It's like he's starving, and I'm food.

—Page 10 of Tessa Waye's diary

I'm awake long after Lauren leaves. *When I find you* is branding everything I see. I have to catch up, but how? The IP address he used is hidden. I followed the proxy server connection from New York to London to a tiny town in the Virgin Islands and gave up. He's using a software program to bounce his connection, routing it through different servers around the world. So annoying when noobs do this. Makes them think they're better than they are. Eventually, he will screw up, and I'll have him.

But how long until that happens? I roll over, bury my head under the pillow. Marcus Starling is my guy—only someone who's guilty would use that much protection to keep from being found—but it brings me no closer to the man behind the name.

I toss the pillow aside and reach for a pen. I'll start with what I know.

He likes young girls.

He has access.

Tessa mentioned once that he was tall. She said he was hot probably twenty times.

Attractive.

I look down at my list. Great. Tessa's rapist could be in a boy band. I'm not doing this right. I flip the paper and start again. Possible suspects.

A friend.

Technically, it works. It could explain *some* of what I know: access, liking young girls, attractive, but it doesn't explain *everything* I know: He seems older, they were both hiding the relationship, he had a great deal to lose.

A teacher.

That could work too, and it seems more likely than some random guy from our school . . . but if it's a teacher, then *which* teacher? If I assume Tessa's relationship started about a year ago when her Facebook postings started to decrease, then that leaves the field pretty open.

A relative.

Same problem as the teacher angle. Could be a possibility, but how do I narrow down the relatives?

4 . . .

Hmmm. I don't have a Number 4.

Unless I do. What if I consider Tessa's life outside of school? What if my Number 4 is someone her family knew?

If I think about that . . . What if it's Todd?

The thought makes me go very, very still. I mean . . . it's logical. He had the opportunity. He had the contact, the trust.

But it's also Todd. The guy who is everybody's hero. The one who almost cried the other night. He's a *counselor* for Christ's sake. And, while I know—I *know*—that doesn't excuse him, I can't stop thinking of all the ways it won't work. He's too kind. He's too squeaky clean. He's too . . . computer dumb. I tap my pen against the page. I need more clues. I grab the diary off my nightstand; flip it open, and go slowly through the first twenty pages.

There it is. Page twenty-two. Tessa wrote how her mom loves him, but he only wants Tessa. It's definitely worth asking Tally about.

And as long as I'm trying this from a different angle, what if I looked at people Tessa was afraid of?

Her dad.

She was definitely afraid of him—even Todd knew. And of course, Mr. Waye would have access. Now that I think about it, Tessa never names her father in the diary either . . . even though she complains that her mom won't—or can't—stand up for them.

Maybe Tessa was afraid to name her abuser . . . because he's her dad.

Or maybe I'm thinking horrible thoughts about Mr. Waye because he forbade Tessa from being friends with me.

I sit back. It's a stretch to think her dad would be involved, but he definitely belongs on the People Tessa Was Afraid Of list.

I chew on the end of my pen and read through my notes again. Whoever this guy is, he can cover his tracks. He knows how to hide his location. IP blocking software doesn't make him a genius, but it does make him smarter than the average user. He would also have to have access to Tessa and be able to get her to trust him. If not a relative or a teacher . . .

What about a cop?

Unease squeezes my chest. What if she was afraid of Carson?

Think about the picture where he was staring at her and how Tally said he sat in front of their house. Cops always seem so trustworthy, but Carson's already proven he's bold enough for a break-in. He tried our locks. He laughed as if our attempts at protection amused him. Because he figured he would eventually catch Lily? That was the night Tessa died. What if he decided it was also the night he would attack my sister?

What if I've been watching too much *Criminal Minds*?

I crumple up my list; toss it in my book bag so I can throw it away at school and not worry about Bren accidentally discovering it in the trash. I'm getting paranoid.

But what if I should be?

I flip off the lights and rub my eyes until colors starburst behind the lids. It's two in the morning now. I'm going to be a zombie at school tomorrow and I should just go to bed, but it's so not going to happen. My body is exhausted, but my brain is on overdrive.

Headlights slide past my window, and even though they've become as familiar as my own code, my nerves still shiver.

Two in the morning. Carson's right on time.

I pull my desk chair closer to the window, expecting to see Carson wheel into his usual spot, but the car doesn't stop. It drives past our house and rounds the corner. The street is empty . . . or is it?

Something moves in the shadows, and as I watch, a man emerges from the neighbor's tree line, steps across the deserted street, and looks up at our house.

It isn't Carson.

It's Jim Waye.

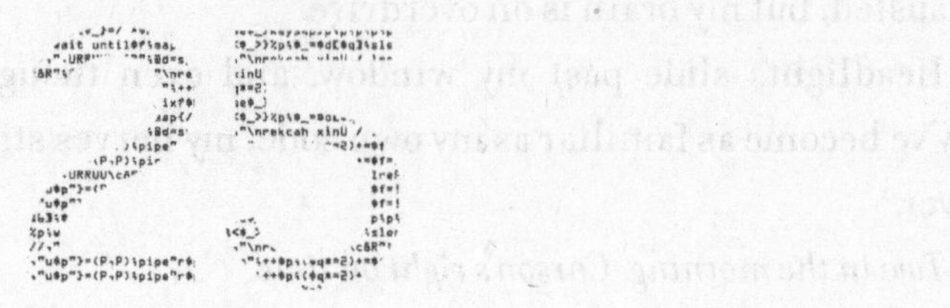

My friends would say they know who I am, but really they just know who I wish I could be.

—Page 41 of Tessa Waye's diary

All hell breaks loose at school. The next morning, Jenna Maxwell is crying. Again. Counselors are circulating. Again. And all the students have to attend a mandatory cyberbullying workshop in the auditorium tomorrow.

"You might have had a point about the whole 'inflammatory' Facebook comment."

"You think?" Lauren is waiting for me after fourth period, arms tight across her chest. "If you wanted to draw attention to all this, you got it, Wick."

"That wasn't the point."

"I know." Briefly, Lauren closes her eyes, and when they

reopen, they're hooded. "I know that wasn't what you were doing, but it doesn't make me feel any better. If someone traces it to you, you're screwed. I'm worried you're walking around with a target on your back."

That makes two of us. Right now, I feel like my life has gone totally surreal. Everywhere you turn, people are talking about Tessa, her Facebook page, and the posts. Even though they don't know who's behind it, it still scares me.

In some ways, I'm used to being gossiped about. Everyone knows how my dad beat my mom and how my mom jumped because she couldn't take it, but this is the closest anyone has ever gotten to me—the *real* me—and I don't like it.

"You look exhausted," Lauren says.

"Yeah. I was up most of the night. We had another visitor, and even after he left, I still couldn't sleep."

"That cop again?"

"Nope. Jim Waye."

Lauren blinks. "What? *Why?*"

"Hell if I know." I open my English notebook and check to make sure my homework is tucked inside. "He just stood across the street and stared up at our house."

"Okay, that's creepy."

"No doubt. The thing is . . . I don't understand why he would do it. I mean, he hates Todd, since Todd sicced the police on him. He's not a big fan of mine—"

"Doesn't matter. No one *normal* hangs around outside someone's house in the middle of the night. The guy is seriously strange. You know he's still showing up to cheerleading practice?"

I stare at Lauren.

"Yeah. Exactly. I mean, he used to watch our practices almost every day after school, and that was weird enough, but now that Tessa's, you know, *gone*, he's still showing up." Lauren fidgets with the strap of her book bag, attention trained on the counselors circulating at the other end of the hallway.

"Look, I gotta go," she says. "If I'm late for history one more time, Mrs. Gavin's going to give me detention, and my mom will flip. Try to be good, okay?"

"Gee, Bren, you look awfully young today."

Lauren stalks down the hallway, middle finger raised, and a group of freshman girls scatter in four different directions to get away from her.

Norcut might have a point about the anger management issues. I turn to my locker, ready to get going, but I don't move fast enough, and Jenna Maxwell, her boyfriend, and her flying monkeys cruise past, heading for their own lockers.

Usually, Jenna's mere presence makes me remember I need to do something, anything really, that's far away from her. In fact, it's so instinctual my feet are already moving, but I can't seem to stop . . . staring.

This was Tessa's best friend—and yeah, that's obvious—but knowing what I know now, it feels different. This is the girl who should've known what happened, who should be tracking down her best friend's attacker, and instead, Tessa's stuck with me.

I pretend to trade books again and watch the girls from the corner of my eye. I tell myself it's reconnaissance. After all, this was Tessa's world, and that's something I'm trying to piece back together to discover where it all went wrong.

Except it kind of just shows me where *I've* gone wrong. It's funny the way they all touch one another, the natural way they hug. Makes them seem like a different species entirely—or maybe it's just that I am. Jenna's friends have none of my hesitancy or awkwardness. They're stroking her arms and trying to soothe her tears in a way that makes me pause. I might be even a little . . . envious? Tessa felt so alone, but how could you ever be alone in the middle of all these friends? How could you feel alone when you're so damn perfect? When your friends look after you so well?

"I just don't understand why she did it." Jenna smacks her locker shut with a flattened palm, and her friends draw away in surprise. Anger. It's even more familiar to me than Jenna's sneer.

She doesn't understand, and she's furious. I get that. Sometimes I hate my mom for doing it too. Sometimes I understand. Jenna will feel the same way about Tessa, and I want to tell her it will get better. I want to—

"My mom says she'll go to hell for it," Jenna announces. "Says Tessa's going to burn for eternity."

It hurts more than any blow. I don't want to believe in a God who would turn his back on someone who needed him so much. Suicides, more than anyone, deserve God's love. They're the lost ones, the forgotten ones, the ones he's supposed to notice.

And did he? Did *anyone*?

Sudden nausea threatens to curl my knees into the floor. Jenna prattles on and on and I shouldn't be listening to *any* of it, but I can't shut down her words. Is this part of the reason Tessa didn't tell anyone? Part of the reason she jumped?

"She deserves hell," Jenna continues, brushing pale blond hair behind her ears. "Committing suicide makes you a coward."

"You're a bitch, Jenna."

She rounds on me in one smooth pivot. "What did you say?" she demands.

For a second, I really don't know. The words just snaked out of me, and now I want to call them back, because in four little words I just reminded them I still exist, and even worse, I revealed how much I still hurt.

And Jenna sees it too.

Her mouth tilts into a sideways smile. "What's the matter, Wicket? Hit a little close to home?"

"You shouldn't talk about Tessa like that."

"Why's that?" Jenna gets a little closer, and without thinking, I retreat a step, but my shoulders hit the lockers and she's closer than ever now, so close I can smell her citrus gum and see her eyes aren't even bloodshot. All of Jenna's crying has been *fake*. It's been for attention.

It makes my hands curve into fists. I ought to punch her—for Tessa's sake, for my mom's, but suddenly I feel like crying. How can Jenna live with herself? She's making her best friend's death into an accessory, wearing the grief like it's a Kate Spade purse.

"You think Tessa cares?" Jenna sneers.

"No, but I do." I swallow and take a small step forward. Maybe it surprises her, maybe no one's ever been so stupid, but it forces her back. "She was your friend."

Jenna makes a strangled little noise like a gasp caught halfway up her throat. Her palm shoots out, catching me in the shoulder, slamming me into the lockers. It doesn't hurt. Not really. But people are staring now. I glance around for help, but even Jenna's friends won't meet my eyes.

"You're nothing more than trash, Wicket."

For some reason it stings worse coming from Jenna than it ever did coming from Carson. Jenna pulls away, smiles at her boyfriend. "And do you know what you do with trash?"

What do you do with trash? I have no idea until her no-neck boyfriend laughs. *Oh shit. You throw it out.*

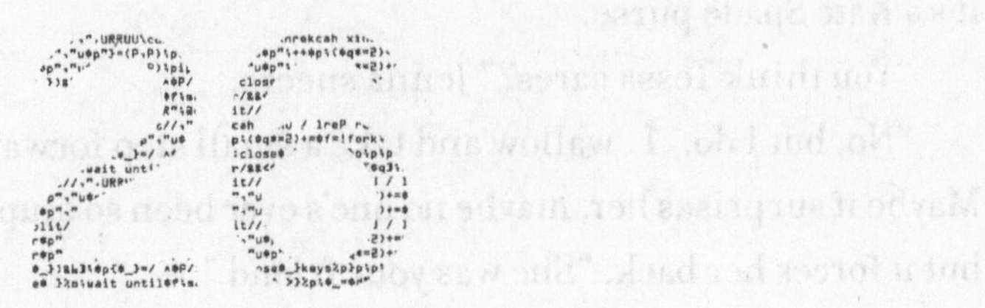

In the beginning, I loved his attention. I would do my hair and makeup so he'd find me pretty. Afterward, I never bothered, and he wanted me even more. He said it was better for him when I was broken.

—Page 53 of Tessa Waye's diary

I hate being thrown in my school's Dumpsters for a lot of reasons. The first is because it's all *kinds* of nasty. The second is because it's humiliating. The third is because Griff ends up finding me.

"You've got to be kidding." He's looking over the Dumpster's edge, shaking his head. It kind of makes me want to punch him, but I can't really deny the guy his moment. Or rather, I *won't* deny him his moment. I'm just hoping he'll haul my sticky self out of here.

Sometimes, this is the closest a geek can come to being a superhero.

"Yeah, yeah, spare me the astonishment." I glare up at him, realize damsels in distress probably never glare at their heroes, and try to soften my expression, but I'm pretty sure it looks like I have a hemorrhoid grimace. Words cannot describe how embarrassing this is. Of all the places for him to find me. *Ugh.* "Like this never happened to you."

"No. In all honesty, I can say that it hasn't." Griff reaches down, offering me a hand stained with blue and green ink. He's been drawing again. "What the hell did you say, and who'd you say it to?"

"Why does it always have to be my fault?"

Griff grins. "Because it's you and your mouth."

This is the part where I should growl at him, but he makes me laugh instead. I take an unsteady step toward him, my feet squishing deep into overstuffed Hefty bags. I'm not usually prone to praying, but I immediately start making promises to stop lying, be a better person, and improve my potty mouth to any god willing to listen.

Please, dear God, just let the bags hold. If I get lunchroom pizza on my feet, I may hurl.

No, I'm lying already. I *will* hurl.

"It's nothing, really. Jenna Maxwell was just bitching about Tessa—" I grab his hand, dig my right Converse into the metal wall, and scramble. I briefly end up straddling the Dumpster edge before tipping, face-first, toward the concrete. I brace for the impact.

Griff catches me before I hit.

"Graceful," he teases, easing my weight against his chest. One arm tucks me close. The other sweeps my legs around, steadying me. Oh. Wow.

Um, I should be able to stand up now. I really should.

So why the hell am I leaning against him like I'm about to fall?

"She was saying shit about Tessa, about how she was going to go to hell." Crap. I *so* wasn't planning on saying that. Leaning into Griff is dangerous stuff. I should know better.

"What was she saying?" Griff brushes a strand of hair out of my eyes. It's all very sweet . . . until I realize he's just picked a piece of garbage off my cheek too.

Yeah, okay, I can totally stand up now. Moment is officially over.

Griff lets me go and takes a step back, watching me dust off my jeans as I try to explain. "She just said shit about how suicides will burn in hell and . . ." And I don't want to explain any further. I look at Griff, ready to tell him *Never mind*, and realize I don't have to explain. His eyes have already gone flat and dark, like he knows. The realization licks something inside of me.

"So Jenna was being Jenna and that got you into the Dumpster how?"

"It just got out of hand." I brush my jeans a little harder, and something warm and slimy connects with my skin.

Oh. God. I swallow really, really hard, holding my contaminated hand as far away as possible. I might have to cut it off. Seriously.

"Here." Griff rifles through his backpack and hands me his Windbreaker. It's very tempting, but I feel bad. What if I give him the plague? Isn't that how the Black Death got started? I didn't really pay much attention in history class, but—

"Oh, for God's sake." Griff grabs my wrist and, before I can get away, uses the fleece side of his jacket to wipe off the slime. He turns the jacket twice, making sure to get all of it. The crap does come off, but I still want to break out Brillo pads and bleach. "You must have cared a little, or you wouldn't have started anything."

"Oh, please." I pull my hand back just as his thumb skims across my palm, but it's too late. When Griff touches me, I feel like something inside me pitches sideways and breaks. "As if I ever needed an excuse to run my mouth."

Which is mostly true and yet kind of a lie. Sure, I don't need an excuse to smart off. In fact, I like to think of it as one of my better qualities. But in this case, I had a reason to smart off to Jenna, which is what Griff's hinting at and I'm pretending I don't understand.

"So what'd you do?"

"I called Jenna Maxwell a bitch."

Griff's brows shoot up. "Seriously?"

I give him a *What can you do?* smile but don't elaborate any further, and it makes Griff's features harden. He knows this is a dare. Boys always do, and it's what makes them back off from me.

All of them except for Griff. "I want to know, Wick. Why would you even bother?"

"Because someone had to say it." Suddenly, the weight of his eyes is too much and I look away. I end up studying the tops of my Converses, and the smiley faces I drew on the toes smile up at me. They're entirely too happy. "She's telling everyone Tessa's going to go to hell because she committed suicide."

It sounds super lame when you put it like that. I'd even say it lessens my anger to throw it into the open . . . but it doesn't.

"Then she's an idiot." Griff leans toward me. "I'm sorry about what she said, though. People are stupid, thoughtless. I'm sorry you had to hear it."

I open my mouth. Close it. He's *sorry*. The word has been thrown around in my life so much it should be meaningless by now. Sorry isn't like a computer game's magic sword or medic kit. It won't fix anything, but, right now, it kind of does. He sounds so genuine, and I've known so much fake.

Maybe that's why everything bubbles up.

"I want to know if Tessa saw the same things my mom saw." I can't really look at Griff while I say this. It's too close and personal, and yet it's coming so fast and hard I don't think I can stop it. "I want to know if she came to the same conclusion—if they both did. I mean, she must have, right?"

Just saying it makes my chest swell with guilt. I'm

choking on a sob now because I can't, I *can't* cry in front of this guy. "How can we all just keep swimming along when some of us are drowning? How can we not *know*?"

"Because you can't save them all, but sometimes, if you're lucky, you can save one." Griff hangs one arm around my shoulders. I've never understood before why some girls like that. His arm is heavy, and it makes me feel unpleasantly small.

And yet . . . and yet . . . it does make me feel like I might not fly apart, like I might not explode into a million pieces, because his weight will keep me pressed together.

Griff leans down, just enough so his cheek brushes my temple. "Sometimes you have to save yourself by asking for help."

Help. I could ask. He's good with computers—he's like me. He sees the other side of things. At least, he saw the other side of me and he didn't turn away.

But can I trust him?

Can I *not*?

"Griff." I clear my throat, but it doesn't matter. The words are still ragged. "I need your help."

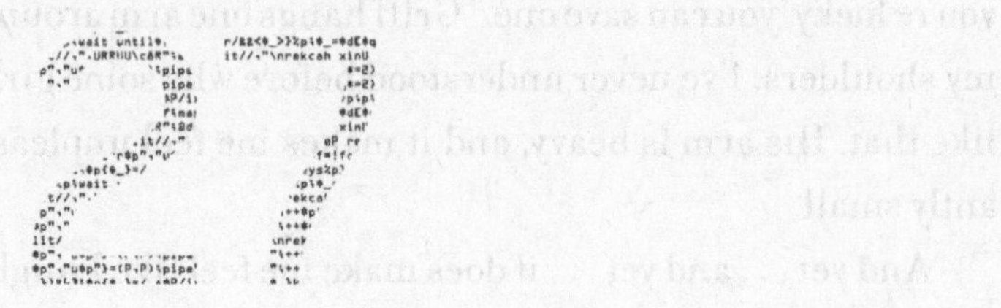

I don't want anyone to ever know.

—Page 17 of Tessa Waye's diary

Griff doesn't say a word while I explain. He doesn't say anything about Tessa. He doesn't say anything about Tally. He just listens.

And, wrapped in his silence, I start to hear how I sound.

Like I'm crazy.

Like I'm *scared*.

I push my chin up higher. "Aren't you going to say anything?"

Griff's looking at me with horror—no, worse, with *pity*. I squeeze my eyes shut so I don't have to see, but in my head, one word lights up with glitter: stupid, stupid, stupid.

"Why do you care? Tessa Waye didn't know you existed."

My eyes fly open, meet his. I'm not sure what I was expecting. I just laid a mess of shit at his feet. How was he supposed to react? With reassurance? With confidence?

That's exactly what I wanted. I just didn't realize until this minute. But I'm not looking for a hero. There's no such thing. I'm just looking for some help.

"We were friends . . . once."

"There's more to this. What aren't you telling me?"

I don't—suddenly *can't*—answer.

Griff shakes his head. "Yeah, I don't do the work if I don't know the deal."

"It's Lily." I push my feet hard against the ground so I don't sway. "Lily's his next target. I need help getting to the guy."

"Wait. Are you the one who posted on Tessa's Facebook page? Who said the thing about knowing who killed her?"

I nod, and Griff's mouth unhinges. "Wicked . . . if this is true . . . you're taunting a fucking psychopath."

"I—" The first bell rings, and we both jump.

"We can't do this here." Griff weaves one hand through his hair. "We need to get going."

And I need an answer. "Well?"

"Griff? Wick?" Mrs. Harding has come around the corner with Shane Hallowell in tow. They're both heading for world history, which is where Griff and I should be heading too.

"Hey, Wick. Hey, Griff." Shane gives us a small wave. I've known Shane since kindergarten. He's almost as short as me, with red hair and fluorescent-orange freckles. He enjoys Halo 4, downloading pictures of Olivia Munn, and playing Angry Birds while sitting on the toilet.

And people wonder why nerds get beat up.

"I've been looking for you, Griff." Mrs. Harding comes closer. She's within touching distance of me now, and I can see her blanch. Can't really blame her. By now I probably have cartoon stink waves wafting over my head.

Mrs. Harding blinks at us as her eyes start to water. "You need to come with me, Griff. They've asked to see you in the front office."

The front office? Griff never gets in trouble. Right? But Griff won't meet my eyes.

"Sure, Mrs. Harding."

Mrs. Harding look at me. "You're going to be late, Wicket."

"Right. On my way."

Except I'm not. I want an answer. Griff seems horrified, but surely he understands what I had to do. What I *have* to do. I just want a glance, a look, *anything*, so I know he's with me.

So I know I haven't just made a horrible mistake.

But I don't get any of those things. Mrs. Harding and Griff turn for the office, leaving me standing there with Shane.

"What the hell, Wicket?" Shane leans in and sniffs me. "You smell like roadkill."

"Go on without me. I forgot my math book."

"But you'll be late. Harding will give you detention."

I'll get way worse than that if the Tessa situation goes public. I rush off after them, taking a separate hallway so Harding doesn't spot me. I have no idea what I'm going to do.

Funny, but it ends up not even mattering.

I hit the entrance just in time to see Griff get escorted into a dark sedan with government plates.

The sight roots me to the tile, and for a second, I don't know how I'm still standing, but I do know this: I recognize the guy slamming the car door behind Griff.

It's Carson.

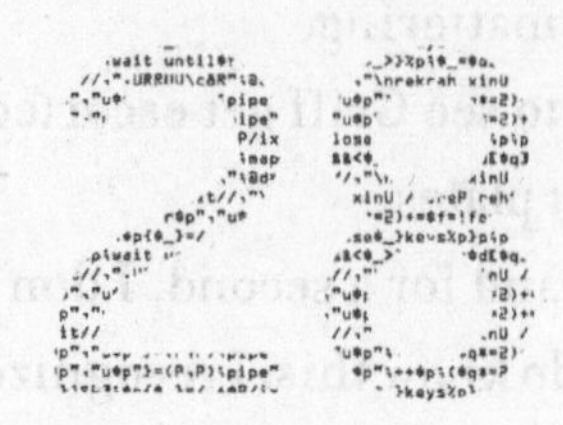

When people ask me how I am, I have to struggle not to scream.

—Page 15 of Tessa Waye's diary

I can't stop worrying about Griff. I leave school fully expecting to see cops waiting for me in the parking lot, but there aren't any. None on my way home. Or at the house.

I have no idea what this means, and it kind of makes my head want to explode.

I unlock our side door quietly, but Bren catches me before my feet even hit the stairs. Swear to God, the woman must have supersonic hearing. It's like her superpower or something.

"Wicket, are you home?" Bren comes down the hallway from the kitchen, wiping her hands on a pale pink dish towel. She makes it about four feet in front of me before her nose wrinkles.

"Why do you smell like meat loaf, Wick?"

Oh God. The cafeteria served meat loaf on Wednesday. Now wearing cafeteria meat loaf is bad enough, but wearing five-day-old cafeteria meat loaf is grounds for vomiting.

I try to nod like it's no big thing. "Yeah, I've been recycling."

Bren's brows rise, and I nod harder, mentally willing her to believe me. I don't know if she does, but thankfully, she doesn't push it. The last thing I need is my foster mom streaking down to the principal's office to complain. If that happens, Jenna will make sure No Neck holds me under the garbage bags until I stop kicking.

"Maybe you should take a shower," Bren suggests.

"Or ten." I offer her a slight smile, and to my surprise, Bren smiles back. Poor Bren. They don't cover this shit in her parenting magazines.

I don't think this really qualifies as a Moment, but it's still kind of nice. She doesn't even remind me to put my clothes in the hamper.

Doesn't even bring me a vat of bleach to douse myself in either, which, honestly, is pretty generous of her. If my kid (or, you know, whatever I am to her) came home smelling like meat loaf, I'd probably hose her off in the yard.

I shampoo my hair for the second time and decide I might be making progress on the Bren front. Until I dry off and realize she's thrown away all my clothes from today.

Including my Converses.

Scowling, I turn my computer on, wait for the internet browser to load. Plenty of time for me to worry about what's happening to Griff, what I may have done by telling him about Tessa, and what Griff may do by telling Carson. I rub my eyes, sudden exhaustion making me want to curl up in a ball.

Then there's Tessa's attacker. Griff's right after all. I am taunting a psychopath. He'll retaliate. I know he will.

But that's how I'll catch him.

Or at least, that's what I tell myself, because the alternative is pretty horrifying to admit. He could come after me. Worse, he could come after Lily.

My Google home page populates, and I use my Gmail account to send Tally a quick message. We need to talk. I want to know more about what Tessa meant when she wrote her mom loved this guy. Maybe Tally will have a few ideas, but I don't want to explain myself over email, so I ask her to meet me tonight at the path by her house instead. I hit send and feel a little better.

Even though I know I'm obsessing, I type in the Facebook web address. My computer's history takes me to Tessa's page, and I'm almost surprised her parents haven't taken it down. Tessa's profile picture still grins at me and I scroll, quickly, to get away from it, heading down the page to find my comment and his reply.

It's still there, but so is something else. Marcus

Starling's written to me again, added a picture, and the image makes a sob claw up my throat.

It's a picture of Lily. And when I scroll down to the comment below, he's written:

`See who's next?`

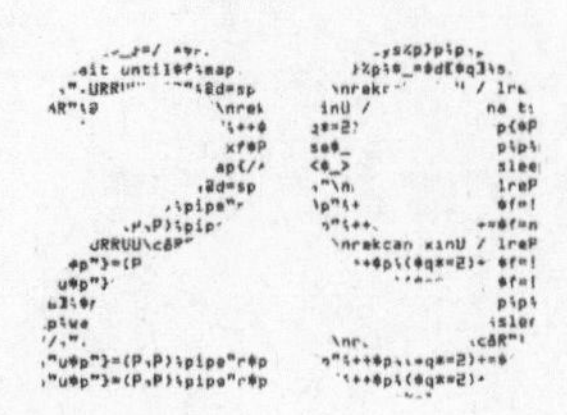

I can't really eat around him anymore, but it doesn't stop him from eating. Sometimes, it's like he's empty, and nothing can fill him up.

—Page 44 of Tessa Waye's diary

In the picture, Lily's coming down the front steps of her school. She's smiling. Whoever took the photo is close to her . . . or maybe it's taken with a zoom lens. Doesn't matter, he could be a hundred feet away and it would still be too close.

"Wicket? Are you okay?"

I jerk, minimizing the website and spinning around to meet Todd's gaze. Freaky, sometimes, the way he can move without a single sound. My foster dad is standing in my doorway, but I can't guess how long he's been there. Long enough to see the Facebook site? Long enough to see Lily's picture?

I sit up straight. "Yeah, I'm fine."

"Really?" Todd's face screws up in disbelief. "You look like you're going to be sick again."

You have no idea.

I smile at Todd and dig my fingernails into my palms until I feel blood well up. "I have everything under control."

Todd nods. "I'm heading to the church for a while, and Bren's on conference calls for the rest of the afternoon." He turns to go. "Will you be okay on your own for a bit?"

"Sure thing," I say, and smile at his retreating back like it's all fine and Marcus Starling isn't a three-hundred-pound weight sitting on my chest.

This is why Tessa jumped.

I'm not a jumper. It's not in me. But I can run. I am my father's daughter after all. I can make it so this man who wants my sister will never find us.

Even though Lily's home by five, I have both of us packed and ready to go. My sister says nothing until I get to the end of my explanation, which isn't really an end, I just run out of steam.

"We have to go. Tonight." I haven't told her the truth, of course. I told her it was Dad. It was Joe. But somewhere, I underestimated my sister . . . or overestimated myself.

Probably both. Because she's not buying it.

"We don't need to go anywhere," Lily says. "We have Bren and Todd now."

Bren and Todd. Like they're our parents. Like they

care. Does she think if she repeats it enough, somehow it'll make it real? I start to ask her and stop. After all, for her, it might be real. Or real enough.

An unwanted thought flickers: Would Bren and Todd adopt Lily if I weren't in the picture?

Yes. No doubt.

She'd be safer without me.

Then again, how safe are any of us? Look at Tessa. Safety depends on everyone playing along, and not everyone does. Tessa's abuser didn't.

I look at Lily. "We need to leave, Lil."

"Why?"

"You have to trust me."

"And go where?"

"Wherever you want. Seattle? Miami?" My eyes skip around the room for inspiration and fall on a National Geographic calendar. "What about Europe?"

"What about *here*?" Lily's voice scrapes up. "I want to stay here, Wick. I want to go to school. I want to go to college. I don't want to run."

"It isn't running. You want to go to school? Fine. Seriously, Lil, where do you want to go? I can make it happen."

"No, you can't. Not for real. You can only do it by hacking."

Well, duh. "I can enroll you in any school you want to attend. And I can put on the rosters that you graduated with straight As."

Lily gives her head a quick, tight shake. "It would be a lie."

"Better than lying to yourself that we'll ever belong." I'm being evil now, but I can't seem to help it. Hacking is really all I have to offer, and it's not good enough. Not like Bren and Todd. Not like this borrowed life we're living. "Look around you, Lily. We don't belong here."

"I do." Her chin hitches up. "I will."

And what about me? I thought I belonged where she was. Lily drags her bag out of my room, slamming the door hard behind her.

How can she want to stay?

How can she not *want to stay?* Our lives are supposed to be perfect now.

Tessa's attacker might think he's above all this. He might think he won't be caught. But he can think again. I can do this. Everything just feels different because it hits so close to home, because it involves Lily.

It feels different because it is different.

Then comes Griff's voice in my head: *He's a fucking psychopath.*

"Yeah, he is," I whisper. "But I can't trust you, either. I have no idea what you're going to tell Carson."

It's another problem. In the meantime, though . . . I scan the other posts below Marcus's. People are spooked, and two of them say they're going to contact the police—and yet I can't seem to stop myself from reaching for the keyboard and typing into the comment box:

`I'm going to make you pay for that.`

And I will.

I hit return, and there's something satisfying about seeing my response . . . but at the same time, my insides feel hollow.

He's close enough to take pictures of my sister. I need to make my threats a reality.

I check the time stamp on Lily's picture. It's almost six now, so it was posted nearly three hours ago. At that point, most of Tessa's friends were still in school, so there's a good chance not all of them have seen it, but, even if one or two people did, this could be a serious problem. Lily and I keep a low profile out of habit, but still . . . people know us. Rumors will spread. Someone will call the Wayes or Bren.

She'll bring in the cops, and with everything I'm doing for Joe, it's too dangerous.

I have enough weak spots in my defenses. And even though I don't want them to, my thoughts cling to Griff again. He still hasn't called, hasn't texted. Something's very wrong. Have I opened myself up for betrayal?

My computer blips again. A new message loads into the comment box below mine:

`Not if I find you first.`

My hand clenches the mouse as my feet hit the floor. He's pissed, but so am I, and briefly, it flattens my fear. Angry people make mistakes, and I cannot afford to screw this up.

He replied to my message in less than a minute. That's not much time to secure your identity. Any mistake, even a small one, would help. I just need a little information, a small tear in his anonymity so I can rip him wide.

I open another window, log on to Tessa's webmail account. There must be forty or fifty new messages, but the notification from Facebook about the latest posting is right at the top.

I copy the long series of numbers at the email's very top. Then I pop onto www.myiptest.com and input the copied numbers into a search.

Holy shit. I stare at my screen and think I can't be seeing what I'm seeing . . . but I am.

The bastard didn't use his hiding software this time. That's an IP address.

Stifling a war whoop, I paste the physical address into Google. IP addresses are like phone numbers for your computer. Track them to their server and you can locate the owner. I have to drill down through the information, but it takes me less than thirty seconds to find it.

Only what I find isn't what I want.

Shit. I squint at the screen, my excitement trickling through my feet. I have my location. It has fifteen computers, running seven days a week. People are moving through pretty much constantly. This doesn't narrow my focus—it throws it wide open.

Lily's picture was uploaded at the Peachtree City Library.

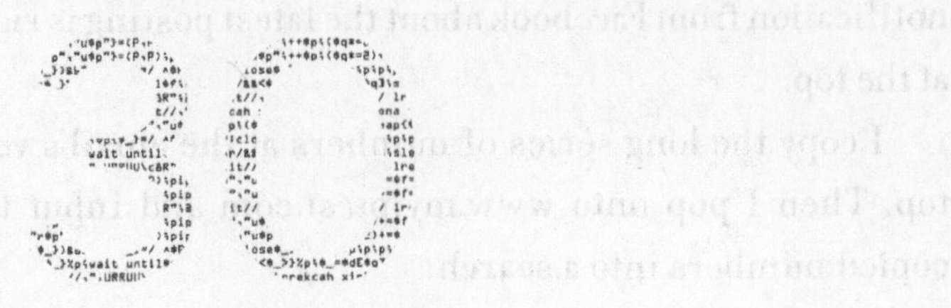

I do not understand how nerds can be happy.

Then again, according to every sitcom on television,

my life should be perfect.

—Page 44 of Tessa Waye's diary

It takes me fifteen minutes to delete Tessa's Facebook page. My comments? Gone. His comments? Gone. And the rest of Tessa? That's gone too.

It kind of feels like she's being killed again.

I erase all the evidence I can, even running a Gutmann-grade scrubber on my computer to delete all the files and histories associated with Tessa's Facebook account. It should buy me some time.

Time enough to track down who was using that computer to upload Lily's picture? God only knows. I have no idea how to get the information from the library. I doubt they keep the names in an electronic format I could hack, so that leaves me . . . ?

Nowhere. I check my email once more, but there's still no response from Tally, so I retreat to the kitchen where Bren is pacing back and forth on a conference call.

"Lauren's here," she mouths before telling the person on the other end of her Bluetooth that his pricing is ridiculous.

"We can go elsewhere," Bren continues, clicking her pen nonstop. "If you want to play ball, then you need to come to the table with a legitimate offer."

"She always like this?" Lauren hops up onto one of the dark wood bar stools lining the kitchen island.

"Pretty much." We watch Bren stalk down the hallway, continuing to pop her clicker pen. "I think it's all part of the plan for world domination."

Lauren nods. "Anyway, I came by to get you. I'm having a party at my house tonight, and I want you to come."

"I'm not big on crowds." Which is a shorthand way of saying I'm not big on hanging out with the same people who dropped me in a Dumpster.

"It's a pool party, Wick. You need the break, and it'll be fun." Lauren puts one hand on my arm, talking to me like I rode in on the short bus. "They won't bother you. I'll make sure of it."

I stare at her. Lauren had to have been dropped on her head at cheerleading practice if she thinks Jenna won't bother me anymore. "Why are you even friends with Jenna?"

Lauren shrugs. "If I weren't, she'd think I'm scared of her."

"Lauren." Bren reappears, pulling off her headset and looking tired. "So nice to see you."

"Hi, Mrs. Callaway. I was just stopping by to pick up Wick. My mom said I could have some people over tonight—kinda like the last fling before we start SAT preps next week."

"SAT preps start next week?" Bren's eyebrows knit. "Wick, did you tell me that?"

Not likely. "I didn't really see the point in taking the SAT."

Lauren cocks her head. "But you have really good grades. Why wouldn't you take it?"

"Yes, exactly. I don't understand," Bren adds. Now both of them are watching me like I'm some sort of performing poodle.

Which I am *so* not. "Well, um, I've had quite a bit going on."

You know? Like surviving? I shoot Lauren a pointed look. You can't have a normal life when your meth-dealer dad is on the run and you're scamming innocent people for money and dead girls' diaries are showing up on your doorstep. "I don't think anyone in my entire family has ever gone to college. I'm lucky I have the grades I do."

"That has nothing to do with luck," Bren says quietly.

She's right, of course. Around here, teachers don't give you a good grade because you're the plucky poor kid. This isn't a freakin' Lifetime movie. I've had to work for everything.

"So can she go, Mrs. Callaway?"

Bren fidgets with her Bluetooth headset, clearly conflicted between fury over my not telling her about the SAT preps and giddiness that I'm being included in a quasi-school function.

"Absolutely. I really think you should go, Wick."

"Bren, do I look like the kind of person who goes to pool parties? Do I look like someone who even *swims*?"

Lauren sighs. "Yeah, you are kind of pasty."

"Pasty doesn't even begin to cover it." I lean one hip against the kitchen counter. "People see me in shorts, they're going to think an angel has landed."

"No one is ever going to see you and think of angels," Lauren says. "You have to come. I could drag you, you know. I am bigger than you are."

"Not by much." But I edge away a little to be safe. Lauren has freaky head cheerleader strength. She weight trains with some of the football players. And I . . . well, I spend my time tapping on my computer.

"Besides," Lauren continues, "Griff's going to be there. I told him you were coming, so he said he'd come too."

I stiffen. "When did you see Griff?"

"Just before I came here. Why?"

"No reason."

Lauren leans in a little closer, and her innocent smile worms its way wide. "Griff says you two have something really important to talk about."

I try to smile back, pretend my insides aren't suddenly twisted. "Oh yeah?"

"Yeah. He said something about having the names of an IT address."

"What—an *IP* address?"

Lauren snaps her fingers. "That's it. An IP address. He says it's really important for your computer science project."

"Anything else?"

She shrugs. "He said something about how he has names associated with it. Honestly, all I really remember is 'Blah, blah, blah, need to see Wick.'"

What the hell? Is he talking about the library IP address? Could he have the real name of the person who used that computer? I check my phone. Six thirty. I have thirty minutes before I'm supposed to meet Tally. If I hurry, I can make both.

"I'll be there."

Once Lauren's gone, I head straight for Tally's house and wait by the path, but seven o'clock comes and goes without any sign of her. I give it another ten minutes and wonder if I'm being blown off.

If this were any other client, I'd be so gone. Actually, if this were any other client, I wouldn't even be here. I don't meet anyone face-to-face, and I sure as hell don't march up to a client's house and knock on the door.

But that's exactly what I decide to do. Tally wouldn't leave me hanging like this. Something's wrong. And the closer I draw to her house, the more I think I'm right. The whole place looks shut down. The curtains are drawn. The garage door is shut.

I should turn around and go home. Instead, I grab a copy of *Wired* magazine from my messenger bag and decide, if Mr. or Mrs. Waye answers the door, I'll tell them I'm selling subscriptions to raise money for school. That'll work, right?

Right. I stab the doorbell with one finger. For a long moment there's nothing, and then someone moves on the other side of the door and a face appears in the stained glass.

"Wicket!"

I wave. "Hi, Brandy!"

The door swings open, and I'm grabbed up in a massive bear hug. Brandy has been the Wayes' housekeeper ever since I used to come here as a child. I never saw her after that horrible afternoon, but she holds on to me like we never stopped being friends.

"I didn't see you at the funeral," I murmur into her shoulder.

"I couldn't face it." Brandy pushes me back with such force I might have stumbled if she hadn't been gripping my upper arms. "What are you doing here?"

"Um, well." It would have been easier to lie to the Wayes. I grimace and decide to try for the truth instead. "Actually, I was looking for Tally. Is she around?"

Brandy shakes her head, dark hair falling in her eyes. "No, she's gone."

"Gone?"

"Yeah, with her mom." Brandy sounds very matter-of-fact, but her mouth stretches like she's pressing down tears. "I'm gone too. The Wayes are divorcing. Mrs. Waye took Tally to Charleston to be with her mother. They're not coming back."

"Why's that?"

Brandy shrugs, glances back inside like she's afraid of being overheard. "Don't know. She said she had to keep Tally safe."

My skin goes cold. Safe. Does Mrs. Waye know what really happened to Tessa?

"I'm leaving too. Now." Brandy steers me toward the street, where a lanky guy in a beat-up Toyota pulls up to meet us. "I'm so glad I got to see you before I left, Wicket."

Suddenly, I'm glad too . . . and sorry. I hadn't really thought about Brandy in years, but now I miss the way she used to smile at me, how she used to tell me I could be anything . . . and I believed her.

Brandy throws open the passenger door and passes her purse to the guy inside. She turns around, hugs me again. "Stay away from here, Wicket. I've never seen him like this. He's furious—completely enraged. Do not come back here. You remember how he is."

Of course I do. I stand at the curb and watch Brandy drive off. I remember a man so controlling he selected Tessa's clothes, criticized her behavior, chose his daughter's friends based on their parents' connections. I thought he was awful. I still do. But now I wonder if it wasn't something else driving him. What if Mr. Waye was grooming Tessa? I thought it was all about making her perfect enough to live in his perfect life. But what if he was grooming Tessa to be perfect for him?

It would explain why she never told Tally. It would also explain why he stood outside our house. He's hungry for Lily.

But if that's true and if Mrs. Waye discovered the truth, why didn't she report him? Why didn't she turn him in to the police?

Because she was afraid of him. Mrs. Waye is afraid of her husband, just like my mom was afraid of my dad. Sometimes it's safer to run.

And who knows, maybe they are safe in Charleston. The thought makes me smile as I walk down the Wayes' driveway.

Until I think: Tally may be safe, but Lily's not.

Twenty minutes later, I turn onto our street and stop. There's a cop car parked farther down from me. Carson.

For once, he's not staking us out. He's standing on our front porch, and Bren's about to let him inside.

Shit. I look at my phone. It's after seven thirty, just over four hours since the picture of Lily was originally posted. Carson must've traced the image to my sister . . . or me.

Anxiety makes the low-level thumping in my right temple jump up another notch. Jesus. Of all the times to get a migraine.

Bren shuts the door firmly behind Carson, and after several moments of waiting, it doesn't look like the detective's returning to his car anytime soon. I walk down the street with one eye on the house and one eye on Carson's sedan. My first instinct is to let the air out of his tires, but then . . . then something else occurs to me: Carson can't be a suspect.

Mrs. Waye would have gone to a man she trusted and loved and told him everything—especially since that man was a cop—but she didn't. She ran.

I think about the picture of the Wayes on Tessa's Facebook page. What if Carson somehow knew something was wrong with Tessa? What if he wasn't looking at her with jealousy, but with suspicion and concern?

What if Carson and I are actually on the same team?

There might be a way to find out.

I walk around the car, and unsurprisingly, all the doors are locked. But in concession to the heat, Carson has cracked the windows. The rear passenger window is open a bit more than the others. Not enough to fit a hand or an arm . . . but it is big enough to slide in a diary.

I watch the house, look for any movement in the windows. Nothing.

Before, I didn't think the diary would help the police. It's just too vague. But maybe—*maybe*—it would lead to a closer examination of Mr. Waye.

I take the diary from my messenger bag, turning to page twenty-two and carefully folding down the corner so he'll see the sentence about how Tessa's mom loved her daughter's abuser. It's not much, but it's the best I have at the moment.

I wipe the book with the front of my tee. Paranoid? Yes, absolutely. Then I flick it onto the backseat floorboard and step away.

I run for Lauren's.

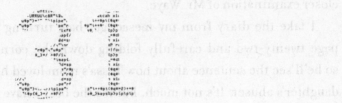

We don't have guns. My mom keeps the knives locked up. . . . There has to be another way.

—Page 51 of Tessa Waye's diary

Lauren's house looks like something you'd see in a grocery store magazine. I guess for them it's normal, but I still find it hard to believe real people live like this. All the surfaces are so clean. All the fabrics are so touchable. The colors Mrs. Cross used are brilliant and soft all at the same time. It kind of invites you to just . . . relax.

But it makes me stiff as hell.

People like Bren and Todd would be comfortable here, but of course, they would be. This is their world, not ours.

I guess I should say it's not *mine*, because Lily is doing just fine. Actually, she's doing better than fine.

So what's my deal?

I probably don't want to know. I let myself in through the side door that leads to the Crosses' kitchen. There must be twenty people crowded around, but I don't make it half a dozen steps before running into Jenna Maxwell. Her pale hair is scraped into a tight ponytail, and she's sporting a candy-colored dress that looks just like one Bren brought home for me last week.

"Why are *you* here?" she snaps.

I try to think of a good answer, but I don't make it very far. Jenna has finely ground glitter smeared across her face and shoulders, and I can't really stop staring. She kind of . . . twinkles. I'm sure Jenna thinks it's fabulous.

But I think she looks like she was molested by a fairy.

"What?" Jenna demands. "Jealous?"

"Uh . . ." There's really no good answer here. If I say no, I'm not jealous because I've seen the same look on strippers, then she'll pound me to a pulp. If I say yes, I'm jealous, she'll probably still pound me to a pulp.

"'Uh,'" Jenna mimics. She looks me up and down, and judging by her sneer, I've been found way lacking. No surprise there.

So why does it still make me feel like shit?

Jenna puts both hands on her hips. "What the hell do you know anyway, Wicket? You think just because you're friends with Lauren that makes you something special?"

"Piss off, Jenna." Griff—wiry, hard, gets-into-unmarked-police-cars *Griff*—slides his arm around my shoulders, and the veins in Jenna's neck pop up like rope. "You're drunk."

"Maybe I am." Jenna looks me over once more. "So what's your excuse, Griff?"

I want to leave, but I can't move. Griff's arm has tightened. He's pinned me, and I don't want to hear any of this, I really don't. Because I know what's coming next. He'll say he's slumming it. He'll blow me off.

And I don't want to hear it.

Jenna's face screws up. "Well?"

Griff's arm loops me closer. His fingers slide up my neck, touching the edge of my hair. Everyone's looking, and he . . . laughs at her.

"You're an idiot, Jenna." Griff pulls me to his side, and we walk straight past her like she doesn't even exist.

And maybe, for a minute, she doesn't. Because all I can feel is Griff, sharp-edged and amused, against me, and all I can think about is how he stood up for me and how I feel about being rescued by someone I'm not sure I trust anymore.

There will be payback for embarrassing Jenna—probably another Dumpster dive in my future—but right now, I don't care. I'm with Griff and I should be suspicious of him, I should be demanding answers, but it feels so . . . good to be under his arm and tucked into his side.

Except as soon as I glance around, I realize how many people are staring.

Whispering.

It could be because Griff made Jenna look like an epic

fool, but the way their eyes inch over me, I know it's something else.

"Lily," one girl mouths to another, and my skin goes cold.

Looking around, I watch my sister's name pass in whispers. Some people back away from us, but others start to come closer, and I realize they know. They saw the Facebook page or they heard about it.

And all at once, my smile—the one I didn't even know I had—evaporates. I'm back in my life. My real life.

"What IP address did you tell Lauren about?" I whisper.

Griff nods at some guys from the baseball team, weaving us through the party like we have all the time in the world. "The only one that matters—the one Marcus Starling used to do the upload."

"Tell me—"

"Not yet, Wicked. Not here." Griff says hey to a few more people, but thankfully, we don't stop. His friends' gazes cling to me.

Because they saw Lily's picture? Or because he's holding my hand?

We push our way toward the backyard, where there's a couple making out in the pool and a game of volleyball going on. Good. No one seems to notice or care about us.

Griff tugs me toward a set of teak chaise lounges. From here, you can overlook the narrow alley separating the Crosses' backyard from the road. And see Detective Carson parked at the curb.

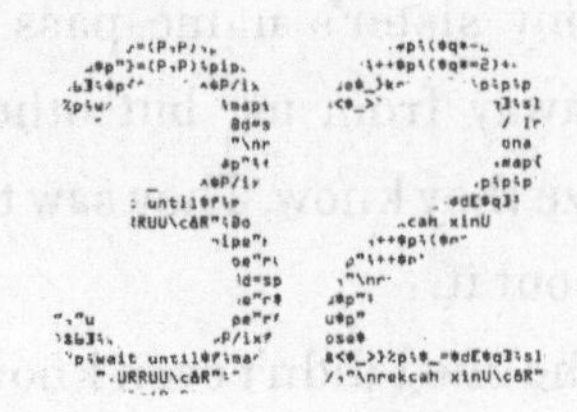

I have the hardest time getting up in the morning. It's not like the blankets weigh that much, but it feels like I've been buried.

—Page 3 of Tessa Waye's diary

"He's here for you."

I blink, force myself to turn around and face Griff, even though it makes the hair on my neck stand up. I hate having Carson behind me. "Oh yeah? How do you know he's not here for you, Griffin? You're the one who jumped into the car with him."

"You saw that, huh?" Griff's lips curl up in a phony smile. It makes me nervous. Faking it is never a good sign. I want to keep my attention trained on Carson, but now . . . now I'm afraid to have Griff at my back.

"And I thought I was supposed to be the stalker, Wicked."

"You're avoiding my question."

"Not really. I guess I'm just surprised you knew about that." His eyes flick over me, and I'm struck again by the color. Traffic-light green really is the best—the *only* way—to describe his eyes. Except, right now, they don't just flash "go." They flash "run."

I push my feet into the ground.

"Considering it's you," Griff continues, passing one ink-stained hand through his hair, "I guess I shouldn't be surprised."

"Yeah, I guess you shouldn't."

Unexpectedly, this makes him grin. Griff drops onto the first chaise lounge and pats the cushion next to him. "You look miserable. Stop drawing attention and just sit with me."

I jerk my head side to side. "I'd rather stand."

"I'd rather you sit with me." Griff's hand snakes up, seizes my wrist. This should be the part where he yanks me down, and I have to fight to get away. But he holds my wrist like I'm fragile as glass and sharper than needles. "He can't touch you here. He can't touch either of us here. Just relax. Please."

No one ever says that to me. And maybe it's the "please," or maybe it's him. Or maybe it's just that, deep down, I really want to be next to him, but I cave. My knees bend, and I fit myself against his side.

And even though I'm panicking, it feels like coming home.

"So what's the deal?" I ask.

"They wanted me to come in for questioning."

"About what?"

"My father. He didn't take off to California just for the weather or whatever. He left to get away from his dealer."

Next to me, Griff fidgets. He's usually so still, like he's always holding his breath.

"It's really no big deal, Wicked." Griff turns his attention to my palm. He's rubbing his thumb in circles across my lifeline now. "I thought it would be better to go with Detective Carson than do the interview in the principal's office."

True, but now he's a liability. It won't matter if the cops were asking Griff about his dad. Joe will think they were questioning Griff about the scam. Oh God, if Joe finds out . . .

I shudder.

As if he can read my mind, Griff slowly shakes his head. "We did the interview in private. No one else knows. I'm seventeen. I'm protected. Carson doesn't know anything about Joe. What happened . . . It doesn't change anything."

"If Joe hears about it," I say, "he'll come after you. It's not safe for you to be involved anymore."

I start to pull away, and this time, Griff grips me.

"He won't know if you don't tell, and I don't think you would do that to me."

My eyes jerk to his. *He trusts me? Why?*

"I'm safe," Griff says. "But you aren't."

He says Carson spent most of the time asking about me. He thinks because we're from the same neighborhood, Griff will know all about me: what I do in my free time, what kind of computer setup I have. Turns out I'm not paranoid; Carson does suspect me of hacking.

It makes my anxiety grow large enough to split my skin. "What did you tell him?"

"I didn't tell him anything." Griff leans back, pulling me with him. He pushes into the cushions until I'm draped across his chest, pressing my breasts and abdomen into him. I usually think of myself as a prickly person, but Griff makes me feel like I'm melting. "You've got to believe me. I didn't tell him anything."

Carson wouldn't have accepted that. There's no way. I start to tell Griff exactly that when I realize he isn't watching me anymore. His eyes are trained beyond my shoulder, watching Carson's car idle.

"Everything I know about you, Wicked, is useless to him."

I snort. Joe and the scam and Tessa are not useless. Jesus. Tessa. I need to ask him about Marcus Starling's real name, but I can't stop thinking about everything Griff knows that could bury me. "Oh yeah? How so?"

"I know your laugh sounds rough, rusted. I know you look hungry even after you've eaten. I know you get pitched into Dumpsters. Everything else is just details."

His eyes slant toward me, darken. "Should I go on?"

"The only thing I'm hungry for is coffee." I sound pissy, but I'm grinning like an idiot, like Lily with a new dress, like my mom when she was still in love with my dad.

My insides twist.

I know better than to look like this. I know better than to *feel* like this.

"That's not what I'm talking about, Griff. You know more than enough about the scam and Joe and me to interest Carson. How do I know you didn't tell him?"

"Because you're still here." Griff curls his hands into my hair. "I would never do anything to hurt you."

I don't know what to say. I try to get my balance, to find the girl I'm supposed to be, the one all of Griff's attention and Bren's nagging and Lily's reassurances are threatening to erase. And I come up with nothing.

"Are you okay?"

"Fine," I say, and push myself up. I'm sitting now, and there's still not enough space between us. I get up and Griff's fingers brush down my hand, disappear from my skin. Good. I think better when we're not touching. "I'm fine."

Griff watches me, and so I don't have to look, I watch Carson.

"Why do you do it?" he asks.

Funny how I don't have to ask for clarification. "Hacking is what I'm good at."

"You're good at math. I don't see you doing people's homework for pay."

"Probably because it doesn't pay enough." Bitchy. I sound bitchy and I don't want to. It's the truth and yet not how I meant for it to sound. "Sorry, it's . . . Why don't you do something else?"

"You have better options than I do."

True, I have Bren and Todd . . . but why does it feel like Griff's leaving something out? He doesn't say anything and neither do I. The silence blooms. I can feel how much he wants me to break it, but I won't. I know better. You can't con a con.

"Are you planning to run?"

I have to smother the laugh. Or maybe it was a sob. Maybe he knows what I'm playing at too. "Yes . . . if I have to."

"But in the meantime, you're catching bad guys."

Another almost laugh. He makes the whole thing sound so heroic, like I'm not freaking terrified. I look at Griff, catch him looking at me like he gets the joke too. His smile is suspended by strings.

I turn to focus on Carson, but the street is empty. He's gone.

"I'm sorry I dragged you into this, Griff. I made it worse."

“I’m not sorry.” Behind me, the cushions whisper as Griff gets up. He comes close, so close his lips hover just over my ear. “You need my help, Wicked. Kiss me and I’ll do it.”

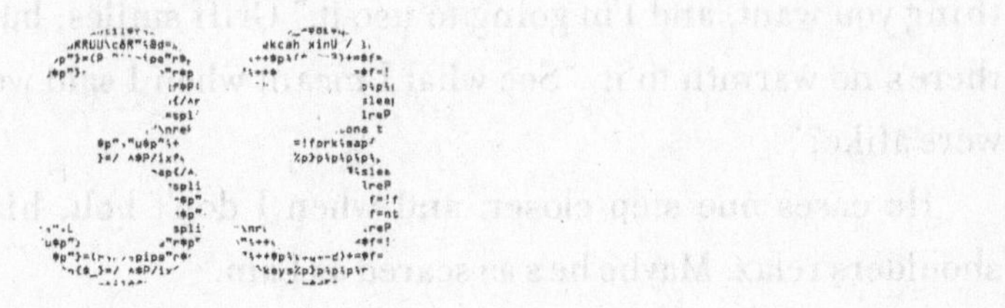

I used to grin like a freaking idiot when I saw him.

—Page 23 of Tessa Waye's diary

"What?" Behind us, the volleyball game has ended, and the winners are trying to drown the losers in the pool. Everything is weirdly normal yet utterly wrong. I couldn't have heard him right.

"Kiss me and I'll help you."

Kiss me. It's a command, but it sounds like a prayer. "Yeah, I so don't do blackmail."

"It's a barter system, Wicked. You should understand that." Griff walks around me. He notices Carson's absence, and his mouth thins. "You want something from me and I want something from you."

"That's not what this is about." That's not what *he's*

supposed to be about. I don't want Griff to be just like Joe or my dad, where it was always about what I could do for them.

I look up at him. "Why are you doing this?"

"Because for the first time in three years I have something you want, and I'm going to use it." Griff smiles, but there's no warmth to it. "See what I meant when I said we were alike?"

He eases one step closer, and when I don't bolt, his shoulders relax. Maybe he's as scared as I am.

It's just a kiss. It's no big deal . . . so why am I afraid? I should just do it.

At the other end of the yard, the volleyball players splash out of the pool and trail inside, leaving us completely alone. I step away from Griff, but it doesn't work. He just gets closer. "Bullshit, you're already in, Griffin. Lauren told me you had names linked to my IP address. So what's that mean? You've already tracked him?"

"I did some research. We both know Marcus Starling is a fake name, and he did the upload from the library. Get the names of whoever checked out the computer with the matching IP address and we have our guy."

"And you're going to do that *how*?"

Griff shrugs. "You have your methods. I have mine. You're taunting a psychopath, Wick. Whoever this guy is, you don't want to mess with him."

No, I don't. I raise my chin. "I have to make this right."

"It's never going to be right and you know it. Some things can't be fixed."

"But we can make them better." I force myself to meet Griff's eyes, and it damn near kills me. I thought he knew what I was. I thought it was evident at Joe's, but Griff's staring at me like I'm something different, and I hate it. Because there's nothing sweet, nothing lovely about me. There is only my anger and determination.

"Fine, I'll do it . . . I'll kiss you."

"I knew you would."

Liar. He swallowed too hard to have known this would work.

"Close your eyes. I'll kiss you, but you have to close your eyes."

The green briefly narrows, but he does it. Griff's hands even go to his sides. He's letting me take my time, giving me control.

I place my hands on his chest and he jerks, mutters, "Fuck" in a way that makes me smile, lets me know how much this costs him. He's holding back for me. Good.

Before I can chicken out, I press my lips to Griff's cheek.

His eyes flash open and I grin. "Deal's a deal, Griffin."

I push past him and get two steps before Griff grabs me from behind, twisting my body around so I'm suddenly over his shoulder.

"Hey!" He picked me up like I was nothing. I freaking *hate* that. I hate being reminded that I'm small.

"Put me the hell down!" I slam both fists into Griff, thrashing as he walks. I expect for him to fight back: shake me, drop me, *something.* Instead, he throws me in the pool.

"Motherfu—" I push toward the surface and wipe sodden hair behind my ears. "You bastard!"

"Yeah, pretty much." I'm not far from the edge, but Griff leans close to give me a hand. Most guys would be laughing their asses off, but Griff's mouth has gone tight. "Not such a nice guy after all, huh?"

I slap his hand away and swim to the pool's edge. "Is that what this is about? Proving you're a dick? How third-grade are you?"

"What can I say? You bring out the worst in me."

And you bring out the worst in me. Griff offers me his hand once more and I grab it.

And haul for all I'm worth.

He falls face-first into the pool, which was the goal. But he also falls on me, which I should have thought about.

Maybe I did.

Griff tilts so he doesn't land on top of me, but my hands are twisted up in his shirt now. His arms drag me close. We're sinking and we're tangled, and when we resurface, he's pulled my legs around his torso and I've tugged my fingers into his hair.

This time, Griff doesn't wait for me. His mouth finds mine, and he pulls me close like he's afraid I'll get away.

As if I'd want to.

Because he's *everywhere*. One hand cradles my lower back, pushing me into him. His other hand plays with my hair, tangling the strands into knots. His tongue traces my lower lip gently, but I still shiver.

Which is all the invitation Griff needs. His tongue meets mine, touching slowly, softly, like he's exploring me, tasting me. At first, it's perfect . . . then it's not. Without even realizing, I wrap my arms around his neck and tug him to me. Griff answers with a low moan, and then the kiss deepens and hardens.

Griff breaks away for breath, and when I open my eyes, he's smiling. "Three years, Wicked. I waited three years, and you were worth every damn second."

Now I'm smiling.

"Again," I whisper, and we kiss and kiss until want rolls through me like honey and lights me up like gasoline.

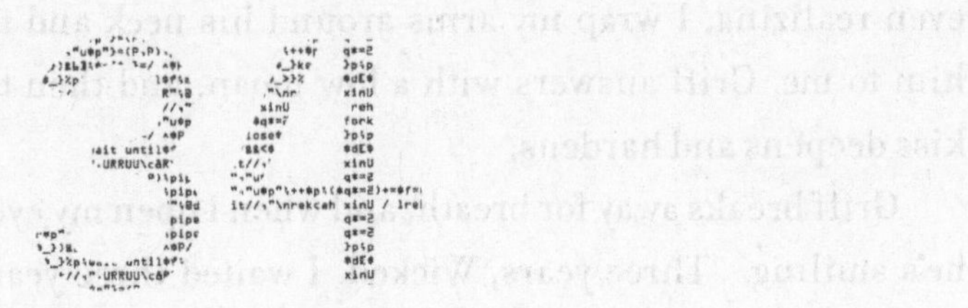

He never stares at me, never does anything improper, when we're around other people. He's too careful. Looking at us, no one would even guess. Funny, how . . . everyone still stares at me. That's why I had to learn to disappear. Right in front of their eyes, I vanished.

—Page 82 of Tessa Waye's diary

When I wake up the next morning, Lauren's guest bedroom is drenched in sunlight. *Oh, shit! What time is it?*

I slap my hand around on the floor, searching for my cell. Find it under my flip-flops. I check the time. Almost ten. Good. I'm not too far behind.

I also have a missed call from Bren. I play the voice mail twice, listening for any telltale voice inflections, but she sounds . . . okay. If Carson had discovered my hacking, Bren would not be okay. She'd be in full-fledged meltdown. Maybe Carson had another reason for coming by?

I'll ask Bren later. I need to get going. We have to be at Joe's before eleven.

Joe's. Shit.

I roll onto my back, stare at the ceiling. Mrs. Cross has painted it a dove gray. I'm sure it's supposed to be soothing and all, but I think it looks like the color of brewing thunderclouds.

"Is it really that bad?"

I jump, making the whole bed shudder. Griff—who's been inches away, who's been watching me this whole time—starts laughing.

"Jesus, no wonder Bren won't give you coffee. Jumpy much?"

"What the hell are you doing?"

"Waiting for you to wake up."

I'm not sure I like that. I don't really remember getting into bed with him. We just kind of . . . ended up here. It was three in the morning, and I needed a place to crash. Usually, I can't sleep anywhere—not really even at home. But exhaustion hit me hard. I could've crashed almost anywhere, but Griff wouldn't let me. The party was still going strong. He found us an empty guest room.

Last I remember, he was sitting with his back against the door.

But now he's here.

I pull the sheets a little closer to me, and Griff's eyebrows rise. His lips start to tip into a wider smile. He thinks I'm being kind of girly, and he would be right. I mean, I'm not exactly doing the whole virginal, cover-yourself bit, but I still feel way more naked than I should. I'm wearing jeans and Lauren's favorite Honey Badger T-shirt, for God's sake. I also shouldn't pull the sheets closer to me, because it pulls them *off* him.

"I like waking you up," Griff says, putting both hands behind his head. Hmm. When he does that, his T-shirt pulls against his chest and . . . and I have trouble concentrating. "You're cute when you're sleeping."

"You were watching me sleep?" *Ohgodohgodohgodohgod.* I narrow my eyes, bump up my chin so he can't see my panic. What if I snored? What if I *drooled*? "You know that's creepy, right?"

Griff's smile spreads into a full-fledged grin. "I couldn't sleep. You kept kicking me."

"I didn't."

He's awfully close again. "You did."

I glare at him. I meant what I said. It's creepy to watch someone sleep. It *is*.

But somehow, it doesn't feel so creepy when Griff's the one doing it.

I rub one hand across my face, try to concentrate on something else. "We should probably get going."

"Sure thing." Griff starts to ease closer to me and I freeze. "But we don't have to rush off. I have my bike. It'll take less than twenty minutes to get to Joe's."

"I—I—" I don't know what to say. We're only inches apart now, and my brain has stalled. Griff's body slides lower along mine, and I have to stifle a gasp. He still smells like grass and chlorine from last night, and his hair has dried in messy spikes.

For a second, I think he's going to kiss me again, but Griff turns his head so his whispers rush past my ear, making my skin leap like it's electrified. "I like waking up to you, Wicked."

I dig my fingers into the covers so I don't dig them into him. "I thought you were awake because I kept kicking you."

"Yeah, true." Griff's hand drifts up, up, up my neck until it's cupping my jaw. "But mostly, I was up because I wanted to do this."

His lips press against the corner of my jaw . . . my cheek . . . my mouth. I roll into him, and he pushes me down, pins me to the bed.

"Again," he breathes.

"What the hell, Griffin?"

It's a really pissed-off male voice coming from the other side of the bedroom door, and it makes me jump so badly I thump my forehead into Griff and my face turns thirty different shades of red.

"We're busy!" Griff shouts, covering my ears with his hands so he doesn't deafen me.

"Like I fucking care," Matthew Bradford bellows, and

starts beating on the door. "Your bike's in my way, man. I'm gonna run it over if you don't come move it."

"Fuck off, Bradford. I'll be out in a bit." Griff smooths the hair back from my face. Where I would be jumping from the nearest window to get away from Bradford, Griff's utterly unfazed. His smile is slow and secret, like I'm the only person left in the world.

"Let's get going," I whisper. "He really will run it over."

Griff laughs. "No, he won't."

But he lets me up anyway, goes to the door while I stumble into the attached bathroom. I shut the door and snap on a light.

Wow. I blink at myself in the mirror. Maybe I should have left that off. I totally need a Ho on the Go bag. I don't have anything that's going to cover up this walk of shame. My hair is a tangled red mess. There's mascara pooled under both eyes. And my clothes . . . yeah, my clothes look totally slept in.

But Griff wanted me anyway.

We pull into Joe's just before eleven. Griff parks in the driveway and shuts off the engine. For a moment, we both sit and stare at the house as Griff's fingers trace circles on my left knee.

"You know," he says at last, "Joe showed me that code you wrote, the one that gets you past the mark's firewall."

"Yeah?"

"Yeah, it was impressive."

"It's not impressive to screw people."

"True." He twists a little so our eyes can meet. "But you're much better at coding than I am."

I search his face for any hints of bullshit.

"You sound surprised," I say, even though Griff doesn't. I'm no good with compliments. It's easier for me to react like he wants to start a fight.

"You know," Griff continues, "most of the time, I back-door my way into a company's system, scam some secretary into giving me system information. I don't code. I lie. It gets me what I need. But you're not like that. You have real talent, Wicked."

I look at him more closely. Now I am suspicious. This has a Hallmark Very Special Moment feel about it. Griff's eyes flick forward, concentrating on Joe's house now. His hands spin his motorcycle helmet in slow circles. "Have you thought about quitting?"

I laugh, swing one leg over the bike so I'm standing.

"Every damn day," I say, and the honesty surprises me. It's one thing to know you're awful. It's another thing to admit it to someone else.

Especially when that someone else is Griff.

He skims his fingers down my arm until they brush across my hand. "Then why haven't you quit?"

"How can I? Everyone has certain skills in life." I turn toward the house, take a deep breath so I can push myself closer. "For better or worse, these are mine."

"What are you talking about?" Griff puts his hand on

my elbow, pulling me to a stop. "If you want out, you just quit. You walk away."

I stare at him, waiting for him to get it. He's already put most of it together. He even said it out loud last night.

The skin between Griff's eyes knots up. "You really are afraid. You really think he'll hurt Lily or the Callaways."

"No, I *know* he'll hurt them. You don't know what my dad and Joe are really like, what it was like to grow up with them. I have to be prepared. Hacking allows me to do it."

Anyone else would start in with the denials. *It doesn't have to be like this. You don't have to run. You have Bren and Todd.* Griff, though . . . He just nods. I pass him my helmet and our fingers graze, making my heart stutter.

He hooks his hand around my wrist. "What would you do if you could do anything?"

"No idea." I refuse to think about it. That's a question that other girls deserve to answer. "What would you do?"

Griff hesitates, then his mouth is on mine again. Both hands cup my neck, my jaw, my face. He kisses me like I'm wonderful.

And I'm grabbing him like I'm drowning.

I press close, curving my fingers around his belt loops, and he responds by bending me into him. All I can do is hold on.

Griff breaks away, breathing hard. We're *both* breathing hard. I can't look at him. I'm too transfixed by how his pulse jerks beneath his skin.

"I would do that," Griff says.

Our eyes meet and we both look away.

"I want to see you again." Griff runs his hand down my spine. "After this. During this."

Our gazes meet again and, even though I know better, something inside me loosens. "Me too." I nudge my chin toward Joe's front door. "Get it over with?"

Griff hesitates. Something's wrong again. His eyes have gone dark.

"Griff?"

"Right." He shrugs and follows me toward the front porch. I make myself grab the door handle and push it open. I've known Joe for years. I've hacked for almost as long. You'd think this would be easier.

We walk into the darkened hallway.

"Well, you two sure took your sweet time." The voice is coming from the step-down living room. Joe doesn't sound particularly pissed, but a chill still climbs up my spine. The lights are low—the computers must be overloading the electrical system again—and I can't really see much apart from Joe's outline. My eyes adjust to the dimness, and my chill turns into a shudder.

Because Joe isn't alone.

"Hey there, Wick." My dad's teeth are a stripe of white in the dark. "Did you miss me?"

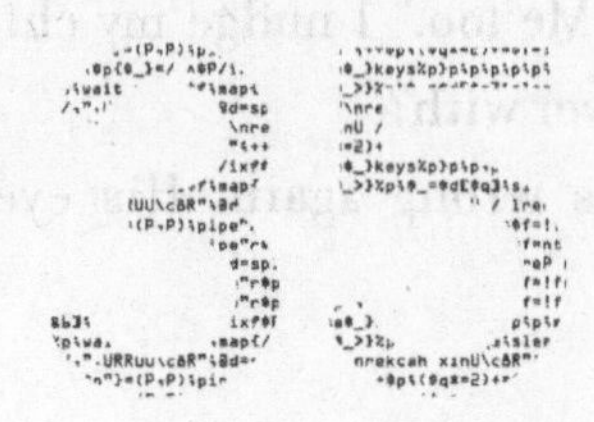

Doesn't matter if it's been fifteen minutes or fifteen days, there's nothing like seeing him again.

—Page 61 of Tessa Waye's diary

He's back. It's been ten months, eleven days, and fourteen hours. There have been cops and reporters and even a special news bulletin. There's been a freaking manhunt. But he's still back. He still slips through.

I want to laugh, but I don't let myself. It might turn into a howl. This is what the cops will never understand and I can never properly explain. You can't catch my dad, and you'll never be safe.

Not as long as he wants you.

"Wow. It's been a while." I try to look him up and down without meeting his eyes. "How did you get here?"

"Magic." My dad's eyes slide over my shoulder. "Since when did you get friendly with Joe's new whiz kid?"

I look around, suddenly remembering Griff. He's closer than I thought. I clear my throat, turn away. This is a loaded question. I'm not supposed to have friends. My dad doesn't allow us to have anything he hasn't given us.

"We're not friendly." I force myself to walk into the living room only by sheer willpower. "So are we going to start this or what?"

But my dad isn't looking at me. He's studying Griff, and the hairs on my neck and arms go rigid. This isn't good. I don't like the expression on my dad's face. He's watching Griff like he's a threat.

I know that look. Too well.

My dad's in that dark place now, that rotten place that lives under his heart until it blooms and he can see nothing but his rage. And I don't want Griff anywhere when that finally happens.

I take another step into the dark. "I don't have time to hang around. I have to be back or my foster mom will get suspicious."

It's an aggressive push and I know better, but I don't stop. I force my eyes to meet his, turn my body so I'm squared up with him. I make myself bigger instead of smaller like he prefers, and the result—sudden tightness in his shoulders, and tensing of his hands—ripples through him. In some ways, this is too easy.

Until he looks at Griff again.

"Don't start with the attitude, Wick. You fuck this up and—"

Griff snorts. Not good. When Dad's like this, you don't want to draw his attention, and that's what Griff keeps doing. He doesn't know the rules—that he should be *avoiding* my dad's gaze. He should be making himself unobtrusive.

Not copying me.

"No one's going to fuck up anything," I spit out, drawing myself up. "In case you haven't noticed, we don't need you here to babysit. We were doing just fine without you."

It works. My dad's gaze meets mine, and immediately I want to look away. My brain is screaming for it. When he's like this, you should never question him, never meet his eyes.

"Is that right?" The question is so soft I think my plan didn't work.

But then he launches.

I make it two steps before his hands lock down on my upper arms, before his weight shoves us backward. We plow into the wall behind us. Dad hits me hard enough to knock the air from my lungs, and even though I know I'm supposed to be the strong daughter, I tear up.

He leans in close and wrenches my right arm back, back, back until the shoulder starts to give in the socket and my vision spots from pain.

"Answer me," he says.

Dimly, I'm aware of a crash, and Joe starts swearing. It makes my father's eyes skate away from mine, assess something I can't see.

"What the hell is that about?" His attention pivots to me. "Did you find yourself a hero, Wick? Did you think your little boy could save you?"

I don't answer, so he digs his fingers into my jaw, twists my head around so I can see Griff.

Griff, whose temple is inches away from the end of Joe's Glock.

Dad wrenches my head around. "You were always my favorite, do you know that?"

He whispers the words like they're some secret, but he's loud enough so everyone can hear. The room is too quiet.

I think of Griff—staring at us, seeing what I hide from the world—and know that's exactly what Dad wants.

He's showing me, showing all of them how I belong to him.

As if I needed reminding.

"I love you, Wick."

Love? How can he even talk about love? He's just using it as a reason to do damage. He doesn't understand it.

Then I think about how much I love Lily, what I would do for her, and I want to sob. I am my father's daughter.

"I love you because you're just like me."

Just like him. Dad sees my wince. I've been away from him too long. I don't remember to mask it, but the backhand reminds me. It brings it all to the surface.

I don't bother putting my hand to my mouth. Not because it doesn't hurt.

Because it does.

And not because I can't taste the blood.

Because I can.

I don't move because now everything really has returned. I suddenly feel stronger. I find my own phantom, the girl who was in danger of disappearing at Bren and Todd's. I find her right under my heart, and she stands up to fit inside my skin. She looks out of my eyes, and we both promise that while he may use me, he will never break me.

Dad leans in again until I can smell the whiskey on his breath and the sour stench of his skin. "So you'll do as you're told?"

It's a question, but we all know it's really an order.

"Yes . . . of course."

It's the answer he wants, but Dad grabs my throat anyway. His long fingers skim up into my hair until they grip hard. "Face it, Wicket. You need me. Our kind needs each other."

His voice is actually lower this time. The words are meant only for me, and I recognize the tone. I can even name it: reasonable.

Rational.

Like all this was inevitable.

Because I'm just like him.

I blink back tears. "Yeah, I am like you, Dad. You're right."

His hand loosens. His eyes search mine, and whatever he sees there makes him smile. He pushes away from me and retreats into the kitchen, where we all listen to the scrape and slide of the bottle. If this is my family reunion, then that noise must be our favorite tradition.

"Make sure you have the coding finished by the end of the week." Joe hands Griff a jump drive, and when Joe turns to give me mine, I study the sweat darkening his T-shirt so I don't have to look in his eyes.

"Fine."

"Text me before you come," Joe adds.

"Fine."

Griff follows me down the porch steps, keeps reaching for me, and I keep stepping away because I don't want to be touched.

"Just give me a minute to start the bike," he mutters.

I nod, but I don't wait. While Griff is turned, I take off and run the whole way home alone.

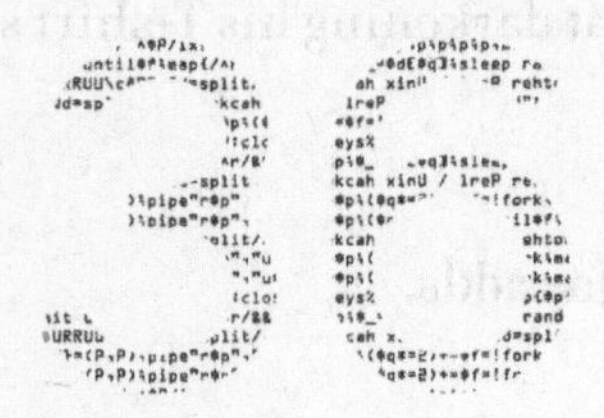

I can't even imagine what life would be like if he hadn't happened.

—Page 23 of Tessa Waye's diary

I'm shouldering open the front door when Griff's fourth text message lights up my phone:

r u ok?

No, I'm not, but thanks for asking, because now I know you are. Griff's okay. He didn't go back in there, didn't try to be a hero for a girl who doesn't deserve him.

I make it upstairs on noodle legs. Bren's heard me come in. She starts calling my name, and I'm scared shitless she'll follow. I don't have an excuse yet. I don't have my lies straight. If she sees my face . . . Someone's footsteps stop right outside my bedroom door.

"Wick?"

"Lily?" *Thank God.* I start crying.

My sister opens the door, and once she sees me, shuts it tight behind her. Turns the lock. She takes one look at my face and knows.

Another text:

Wicked?

I delete it. Lily sneaks up ice from the kitchen. She tells Bren I'm tired from Lauren's party and am going to lie down for a while. This will buy us a few hours. I will come up with an explanation for my bruised mouth. I will fix this.

And another:

Wicked?!

Stop calling me that. Stop acting like you know me. Except now he really does, doesn't he? I fold onto the floor, push off my shoes with one hand.

The only person who knows you any better is Lily, and now they both know you shouldn't be allowed to protect anyone. You can't even protect yourself.

I pull my arms around my sides, even though it makes the muscles in my right shoulder scream.

Five minutes later:

please call me

They just keep coming. I delete them one by one, but it doesn't matter, because he only sends more.

I take two of Norcut's pills and drag myself into bed. My phone vibrates. The screen says I have one new text:

i'm coming over

I flip my cell onto the floor. Bury it under a dirty T-shirt. *Go ahead,* I think. *Doesn't matter. I'm not really here, and I won't be here for you ever again. I can't be. He destroys everything I care about. I can't give him you. I* won't *give him you.*

I roll into a ball, stuff a blanket so far into my mouth, no one can hear me cry.

It's something else my dad taught me.

I wake up after just after four o'clock in the afternoon. My phone is still on the floor, and I ignore it. I pad from my room to the bathroom, keeping the lights off so I don't have to look at myself. But after a few minutes, I know I need to man up.

I flip on the lights, look at my reflection.

Jesus. I get a little closer to my reflection. Between Lauren's black eye and now mine, we're going to look like bookends.

"Wick?"

Bren. I rub the bridge of my nose between my thumb and forefinger. Do I have some sort of invisible bell on me? How does she even know I'm up?

"Wick?"

I crack open the bathroom door. "Coming!"

Yeah, sure. Coming. And what are you going to say when they see you?

I lean my head against the bathroom door as my brain chugs through all my excuses, all my lies . . . and I can't come up with anything they'll believe.

Except for the truth. I could tell them about Joe, about my dad. The police would arrest both of them.

And then they'll arrest me.

Maybe. *Probably.* By confessing, I would hand Carson my ass on a platter. If I'm lucky, I would get a deal, but our dad would be put away for good.

Except he got away last time.

He always gets away. Then I would be locked up and Lily would be alone, and he's taken out his anger on her before. He's punished me by punishing her.

And even if he doesn't get away from them again, there's always the man who got Tessa. He's still there. I can't protect Lily. I can't protect anything I love.

But maybe Bren and Todd could.

Because she'd be safe with them. That's the way it's supposed to work. People like them don't have these problems.

But Tessa came from a wealthy family too, and look what happened to her. There's some evil you just can't catch, because no one recognizes it. I know all about that.

"Wick!"

"Coming!" I wrench open the door before I can find an excuse to keep hiding, but I still have to keep one hand on the banister going down the stairs so my knees don't buckle.

I don't even make it to the landing before I see Lily

coming up. Something's wrong. Badly. She's gone pale. Her eyes meet mine.

"Lil, what is it?"

"Bren," Lily whispers. She's close enough now that I can see she's shaking. "She wants to talk to you about a photo that was on Tessa Waye's Facebook page."

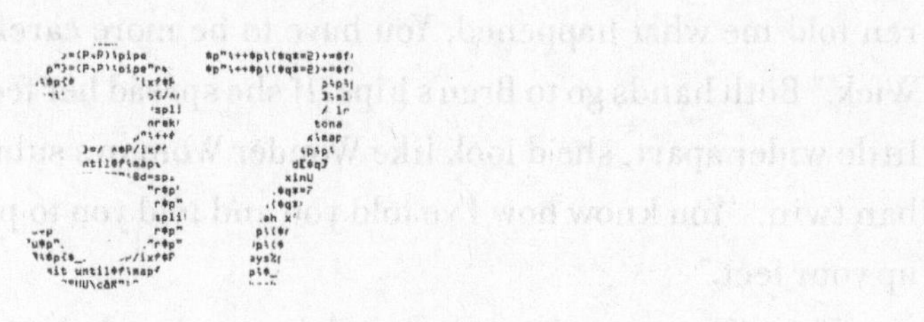

Helped my mom with her scrapbooking today, and it really made her happy. I usually refuse to do that crap, but this time it was kind of soothing. I think I'm really starting to enjoy cutting things into pieces.

—Page 37 of Tessa Waye's diary

In the kitchen, Bren is baking. Both ovens are still going, even though the counters are covered in muffins and cookies. The room smells like brown sugar and vanilla. It's a happy scene, something torn from a Martha Stewart magazine, and yet Bren looks two seconds from an implosion.

"Wick!" She flings down her cookbook and rushes over, pulling me into her arms. Stunned, I let her. "I've wanted to wake you for ages! How are you feeling?"

"Um." This was not the reception I was expecting, and for a very long moment, all I can do is blink.

Bren puts the back of her hand to my forehead like I have a fever. "I'm glad you had a chance to lie down. Lauren told me what happened. You have to be more careful, Wick." Both hands go to Bren's hips. If she spread her feet a little wider apart, she'd look like Wonder Woman's suburban twin. "You know how I've told you and told you to pick up your feet."

What? The tone—accusatory and disappointed—is more familiar, but I have no idea what she's talking about.

"Maybe if you wouldn't shuffle, you wouldn't slip, Wick."

Shuffle? Slip? My sister gives me the world's smallest nod. I get it. She called Lauren. They made something up.

And here I was, thinking my baby sister couldn't lie.

Her eyes meet mine, and for a moment, it's just us. We're a team again, and my heart grows wings. But then, just as quickly, I think about how Lily had to cover for me, how she had to lie.

And I'm ashamed of myself. How can I say I want to save my sister when she has to become a liar like me?

I have to tell them everything. I look at Bren—and Lily interrupts. "Wick says she doesn't know anything about the picture, Bren."

I never said anything. When Lily told me Bren knew, I just kept putting one foot in front of the other.

Lily's eyes are huge and hard. We don't need words

right now. She's willing me to go along with her.

Reluctantly, I turn to Bren. "What picture?"

"Well." Our foster mom fidgets with her Kiss the Cook apron, ties the front knot a little tighter. "I'm not really sure. I didn't see the picture myself. I just heard about it from Detective Carson. He came by last night to talk about Tessa Waye's Facebook page."

"Oh yeah?"

"Apparently, there's a really bad rash of cyberbullying going on at your school. People have been trading threats on Tessa's wall, but as of last night, everything was deleted."

Lily sits up a little. "They deleted the account?"

"*Someone* did." Bren's tone turns ominous, and briefly, her eyes settle on me and I think she knows. But just as quickly, her gaze jerks away. She doesn't suspect me. She has no idea what's living under her roof.

"What really worries me is the picture of Lily," Bren continues. "I don't know who took it. I don't know why it was there, but I want *answers*."

Jesus. Bren sounds like she's about to start one of her contract negotiations. She's kicking into Executive Bren mode, which is ten times more demanding than Regular Bren.

"Does Detective Carson have any suspects?"

"No, and while they're investigating, we're going to take a trip." Bren sounds breezy, but underneath there's a razor edge. "Just the three of us. I think we all need some time to, you know, get closer as a family."

I have no idea what Bren has in mind, but my stomach is already sinking.

"What about Todd?" I ask.

"Todd can't come." Bren unties her apron and folds it into a tight square. "His counseling sessions have doubled since Tessa's suicide. It's important for him to be here, but we're leaving. We'll stay in Atlanta so we're in time to catch an early flight to San Francisco. We'll stay for a week. Let the detective do his job."

Bren's smile is so wide now I know it's fake. I recognize the look. Her smile is just like my mom's when she kept telling us everything was fine, just like my teachers' when they said Lily and I would be okay.

Bren stretches *that* smile until her eyes narrow. "Start packing. I want us to leave this afternoon."

I think I've found a solution. It's three stories up and no one is watching the fire escape.

—Page 54 of Tessa Waye's diary

Go? I can't *go*. Running won't change anything. It might even make it worse. Our dad's returned, Tessa's attacker is closer than ever, and Carson isn't doing anything with the diary. Now is not the time for me to take off.

"I can't go, Bren. I have school."

"Well, yes." Bren won't look at me, but her words march forward in a perfectly rehearsed line. "But they'll understand, Wick. I'll write you a note. You can make up the work later."

Holy shit, she's really serious.

"I can't make the work up later," I lie. "I have a project

that's due for my computer class. I'm on a team. They're counting on me to be there."

The corners of Bren's mouth pull down. "That class is so demanding, Wick. I think we should look around for something else. Maybe you should diversify a bit. Take an art class, or maybe try out for one of the teams. You would be a fantastic cheerleader. You're so small you could be a flyer!"

"I don't like the cheerleaders." *And they really don't like me.*

"You like Lauren." Bren reaches for me, straightens the hem of my shirt. "And, maybe, if you would just—"

"Don't!" I explode, way, way angrier than I expected. "Just don't, Bren. I'm not some pet project. People can't be fixed."

She blinks. "Are you broken?"

Of course. "Of course not."

"Of course not," Bren echoes softly. "That's good. I'm glad, though I don't think anyone can get to adulthood without a few cracks." She gives me a small, shy, totally un-Bren-like smile. Suddenly, she isn't the woman who runs a million-dollar corporation. She's someone I don't recognize. "It makes sense that you're the unbroken one, Wick. I think you might be the strongest person I know. Nothing scares you."

You have no idea, lady. I've been very, very careful to keep it that way. It was supposed to be a good thing. It *is* a good thing. Except that now . . . now I want to explain. But there are too many lies between us.

I stare at Bren and feel ten thousand miles away. "I didn't have a choice."

"I can see that." The oven buzzer goes off, beeping like a perky fire alarm, but Bren barely seems to notice. "I want us to be friends, Wick. I want . . . I want us to be more than friends. I spoke to your social worker about drawing up adoption papers."

And just like that, I feel like I've been dropped from three stories up.

"You spoke to her about *what?*"

"Adoption papers. I want to adopt both of you. I want you. *We* want you."

Not if you really knew who I am and what I've done.

"I always wanted kids," Bren continues shakily. "But I couldn't . . . have them. For years, I just couldn't understand why I was so unlucky, but now I get it. I was supposed to wait for you. It was you all along, you and Lily."

Bren's eyes are shining. "I know Todd wanted to be here when I told you, but he's still helping Principal Matthews, and I wanted you to know, and now that dreadful picture went up and we have to go."

Go. I force myself to breathe. *We're back to that again.*

And maybe that's where we need to stay. If they're in San Francisco, they would be safer than if they were here. I need Bren to take Lily.

"I know you still have a dad, Wick, but Todd would love to be your father too."

My dad. Another reason they need to go and I need to stay. Because there's nowhere I can run that our dad will not follow. Getting close to Bren only gives him someone else to hurt.

"So what do you think?" Bren asks softly. "What do you say?"

"About the adoption? Or about the trip?" Stupid questions, but they buy me time, give me a few more seconds to savor what it feels like to be wanted.

Bren nods. "Both. Either. No, *both*. I want your answer on *both*."

Any way you look at it, it all comes down to the same answer: no. No, I can't leave. No, I can't involve them. No, this won't work. No. No. No.

But if I say yes, I'll have what I want. I'll get away. I'll have Bren and Lily.

I'll . . . I'll be a coward.

"I'll think about it, Bren."

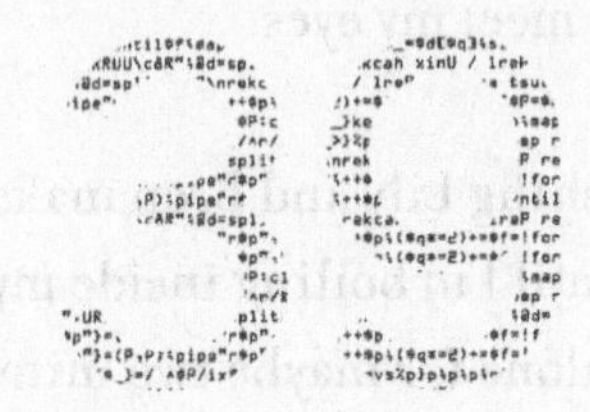

Pretending to be normal makes you feel like you're bleeding to death.

—Page 48 of Tessa Waye's diary

Bren's singing about how the hills are alive with the sound of music again. In between verses, she explains to me how I can have all the time in the world to think, how we'll talk about everything during a special seafood dinner in San Francisco, how we're going to "celebrate our futures together."

I have no idea what that means, but it involves every suitcase she owns.

I should tell her the Tates celebrate with Ho-Hos and takeout, not fancy restaurants with names I can't spell, but I don't say a word. It occurs to me that she's trying to win me over. I look around her perfect kitchen in her perfect life and think maybe Bren isn't perfect *because* she's perfect. She's putting on a front like everyone else—including me. I'm not the only one pretending to be something I'm not, and oddly, the idea makes me feel a little less alone. I try to smile at her, but Bren won't meet my eyes.

I can't really blame her.

I sit at the breakfast bar, watching Lily and Bren make lists of everything they'll need until I'm boiling inside my own skin. I go upstairs, and I'm alone for maybe two minutes before Lily arrives.

"You need time to *think*?"

"Yeah."

"I'm going to San Francisco with Bren, and I'll do it with or without you, Wick," she warns.

Exactly. That's what I want. Except I still have to wrap my arms around me to keep from doubling over.

"I know my picture showed up because of you."

I go still. "Why's that?"

"Because it's always you. Just like it was always Dad."

"Then why didn't you want me to say anything? Why did you lie?"

"To protect you, to give you the opportunity to say yes. I *knew* what she was going to ask. I *knew* what we could have had." Lily turns for the door. "But you're right, Wick. Everything really is ruined."

It's the first time I've ever seen Bren and Todd fight, but Todd says I can stay home, promises he'll bring me to Bren for the weekend. My foster mom drives away with Lily in tow while I lie on my bed, work my jaw back and forth until I want to scream.

When I finally push myself upright, I see the sketch pinned to my window. I'm ten feet away, but I still recognize Griff's style. He made the girl look fierce, but drew her eyes sad.

Vaguely, I remember the text: *I'm coming over.* He really did, and he left me the sketch so I would know.

On the nightstand, my cell phone buzzes. For a crazy second, I think it's Griff and he knows I've seen his picture. He knows I'm thinking of him.

But it's not Griff. It's Joe.

Meeting 2day.

Again? I'm not eager for a repeat. I put the phone in my pocket, concentrate on nudging open my window. I carefully pull Griff's drawing free.

It isn't some random girl. He drew me.

He's sketched me in blue and green ink. My hair is loose, and I'm pushing it away from my face with both hands. I look like it's all one big joke, like I'm amused and nothing scares me.

And yeah, the eyes are sad, but they're also . . . knowing. There aren't any tears in them even though, right now, I can feel tears pressing against my lashes. Is this how he sees me?

He made me look like I could take on the world.

He made me look beautiful.

Another text:

1 hr

I grimace. Something's up. That barely gives me enough time to sneak away. I grab my bag, shove the window open a little farther, and tuck the sketch as far under my bed as I can reach. It's the loveliest thing I've ever been given.

I scramble out the window and down part of the tree. I fall the rest of the way and end up in the bushes.

I pop back up, scan for any neighbors. Thank God. No one. I set off for the bike paths.

Almost forty-five minutes later, I reach my old subdivision, making the familiar right off the path, and stop dead. From this angle, I can see straight down the street, straight to Joe's . . . straight to the cars parked outside his house.

Cops.

Oh my God. The cops.

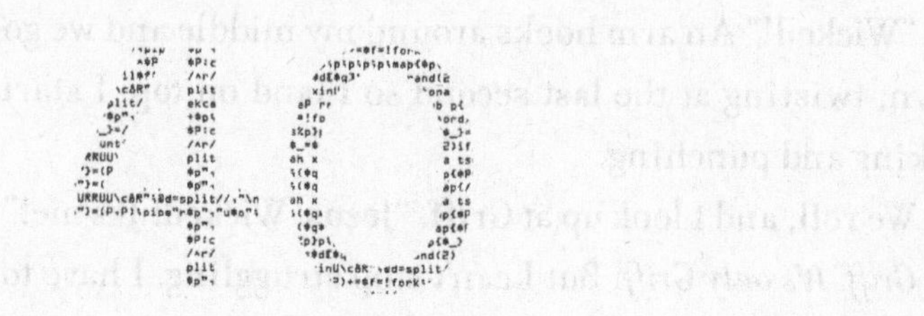

He really does want Lily Tate. She really is next.

I can't help him. Won't help him. I'd rather jump.

—Page 68 of Tessa Waye's diary

They know. It's all over. I want to scream and I want to hide and I cannot look away. Four cop cars are parked on the street and in the yard, lights flashing. There must be ten officers going in and out of the house. They're carrying computers and dragging Joe's gun safe onto the lawn. They're leading my dad to a squad car.

They've caught Dad.

And, like he knows I'm watching, like he knows I'm close, Dad's head swings up, turns toward me. His mouth opens . . . I turn.

And run.

I'm barely on the path before I hear someone coming after me. Just one person? Or is it more? I pump my arms harder, force my feet to move faster.

It doesn't matter. They're gaining on me.

"Wicked!" An arm hooks around my middle and we go down, twisting at the last second so I land on top. I start kicking and punching.

We roll, and I look up at Griff. "Jesus, Wicked! It's me!"

Griff. It's only Griff. But I can't stop struggling. I have to get away. The cops know. They're making arrests and they have my dad and he saw me. He'll think I betrayed them, and he'll be enraged. They'll never be able to hold him.

He'll come for us—for *both* of us.

"It's okay." Griff pushes me harder into the leaves. He has me pinned, and I still feel like I'm going to rocket off the ground. "It's okay. It's okay."

Except it's not. I try to curl into a ball, hold myself together, but I can't. Griff's in the way and I'm spinning apart and I can't stop shaking.

How long until the cops come for me?

I'm sorry, Lily. I'm sorry. I'm so sorry. Griff presses me to his chest. It isn't until my whole face has gone wet that I realize I'm crying.

We spend another hour waiting in the woods, watching the shadows stretch longer and longer. Waiting for cops to come up the path.

They never do.

I push myself upright, and Griff's hand drags down my arm like he doesn't want to let me go. "How did you know they were coming?"

Griff looks away.

I wipe my sleeve across my eyes once more. "How did you know they were *coming*?"

"Because I was in on it."

41

Sometimes I think I got involved with him because I was bored with boys.

—Page 9 of Tessa Waye's diary

"You were in on it?" This doesn't make any sense. It's like when we repeat those random Spanish phrases in class to improve our accents. Everyone is saying the words, and no one has the faintest idea what they mean. That's what this is like. *No me gusta* bullshit.

I put both hands on my knees and grip. "What. Are you. Talking. About?"

"You're not the only one with secrets, Wick." Griff meets my eyes, and whatever he sees there makes him wince. "My cousin's a cop. I do undercover work for the police every once in a while."

"Because they make you?"

"Because I want to."

"Because they caught you before?"

Griff smiles. "Really blown you away, haven't I?"

No. Yes. "So you're a red hat." It isn't really a question, but he nods anyway. "And you know I'm not."

"Yeah."

I thought we were alike, but we're not. Red hats are good hackers. They protect people, systems, websites. That makes Griff one of the good guys, and I'm still . . . just like my dad.

I swallow hard. "So . . . all those times you kept asking me why I didn't do something else for money, what was that about? Some sort of hint?"

Griff studies the ground. "I wanted you to quit. . . . I also wanted to know the truth about why you were hacking."

"Even though you were lying to me."

"Yeah."

"You said they took you in for questioning, but you were really . . . *informing* on us."

"Not all of you. I didn't tell them anything about you. They don't know about your involvement." Griff's hand shoots forward, grabs mine. I start to pull away, but he holds me like he's drowning and I'm a lifeline. "You didn't want to be there. I had to save you."

Something cold coils in my gut. "I don't want to be saved. I don't *need* to be saved."

"Don't you?"

I don't answer. Griff's seen what I am with my dad. He's seen how I have to act with Joe. He's seen the worst parts of me, the parts that make me the most ashamed.

I look away.

"You weren't supposed to be there when they got busted," Griff says quietly.

"Joe sent me a text. Emergency meeting."

Griff's fingers tangle around mine. "I didn't want you to see it."

Too late for that. A vision of my dad walking down the porch and looking up at me floods my brain. I squeeze my eyes shut. "Did you tell them about Tessa? About *Lily*?"

"No."

"Why not?"

Griff presses his hands over both of mine, rubbing his fingers across my cold skin. "I didn't tell them because I knew it would be the fastest way to lose you."

EXCEPT THAT ISN'T quite right. Griff wants to go to the cops, but he wants me to be the one to do it.

"Not going to happen." We're walking to his bike, and as the evening's last joggers pass us, I duck my face so they can't see how I've been crying. I don't need to, though. Griff puts himself between their stares and me.

He grazes his hand against mine. "Are you sure you want to go home?"

Home? Yeah, I guess he's right. Bren and Todd's house is

home now. If they put away my dad, it could be home for a long time.

Well, it could've been if I hadn't screwed it up by telling Bren I had to think about her offer.

"Yeah, the detectives will come by." I straighten. "I want to be there."

"Wick." Griff tucks me close, and for a moment, I let him. "They can help find Tessa's rapist. They can help *you*."

"You mean like they helped my mom?" Griff sucks air like I punched him. "I gave Carson Tessa's diary, you know. I slipped it into his car when he was at my house the other day. You know what he did?"

"What?"

"Nothing. He showed up at Lauren's house that night instead of investigating the diary. He doesn't care about Tessa. It doesn't matter to him. Not really."

Griff's arm tightens around my shoulders. "You don't have to do this alone."

"I'm always alone." And then, because that sounds like I'm whining, I make myself grin. I am not broken. I do not need to be saved. "I'm alone, and that's the way it needs to be."

Griff scowls. "Why do you have to be like this?"

I refuse to look away. "Because this is who I am."

Griff turns for his bike. "Get on."

I start to object. We shouldn't be seen together. It could be dangerous for Griff, for me.

But my hands reach for him anyway.

I climb behind him, feel all my bravado drain. By the time we get to my neighborhood, I'm cold to the bone. We turn the corner, and I see the cops parked at my house, waiting. Griff's left hand squeezes mine.

It's supposed to be comforting, but I still feel like he's driving me straight into an ambush.

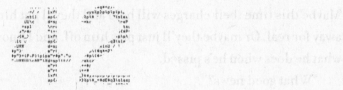

I hated that heroine. You know, the girl from *Twilight*. She just . . . got consumed by Edward. She didn't just fade into him. He devoured her. I said I'd never be like that, and yet . . . here I am. I feel like he's eaten away every part of me.

—Page 31 of Tessa Waye's diary

"Hello, Wicket."

Even though I can't hear Detective Carson over the bike's engine, I can read his lips as he says my name, and I recognize the mocking smile.

I grip Griff's waist a little harder.

Detective Carson is leaning against the trunk of his car, and when Griff kills the bike's engine, he pushes away, comes closer to us. "Hello, Griff," Carson continues.

"Didn't expect to see you here."

Griff pulls off his helmet and reaches around to take mine. "Didn't expect to see you either, Detective. What's up?"

"Thought I would deliver the good news myself."

About my dad. And it is good news. It's wonderful news. Maybe this time their charges will hold and they'll put him away for real. Or maybe they'll just piss him off, and I know what he does when he's pissed.

"What good news?"

"We just arrested your father."

"Oh yeah?" My voice skids high as Lily's, and I have to remind myself these are the people who have let him get away again and again, who let him walk around, destroying anything he wanted, including my mom. Including me. But I still want to do a happy dance. I still want to believe. "You get him on anything that will actually stick?"

"We think so."

"Um, Wick, I have to go." Griff tilts a little so I can see his face. His eyes have gone dark, and his mouth is thin. "You good?"

He says it so flippantly I almost don't catch the undercurrent, the anxiety threading beneath. The way his fingers knot tightly with mine reminds me.

"Yeah, I'm fine." But I know he can feel how my hand is shaking.

"I'll see you around?" Again the squeeze; it's not a question, but a promise.

I shrug. "Okay."

Carson and I watch Griff turn the bike down the driveway. When he hits the road, Carson leans in so close he just has to whisper, "He said you weren't involved, but I don't believe him."

Griff. He really didn't tell.

He said he didn't want to lose me.

"Involved in what?" I manage. The response is slow—too slow—and Carson and I both know it.

He smiles.

"Detective Carson?"

I jump. Todd is standing on the front porch, looking less than amused. Actually, he looks kind of hostile. His tie has been yanked loose from his neck and his shirt is wrinkled, one fist clenched like he's ready to punch something.

"Is there something I can help you with?" Todd asks, not sounding like he wants to help Carson at all.

Briefly, the detective stiffens. Todd's presence doesn't suit him. He wanted more alone time with me.

"Are you all right, Wicket?" Todd's voice grows warm and concerned, like he's worried I'm upset.

I manage a weak smile.

"I just came to give the girls some good news, Mr. Callaway. We've arrested their father. Between the parole violations and the new charges, he won't be seeing daylight anytime soon."

Todd's mouth creases into a smile. "That's wonderful!"

"Yes, sir, we certainly thought so." Todd comes down

the front steps, and Carson angles his body away from him, puts his hands in his jacket pockets *aw-shucks*-style. "But that's only part of the reason why I came by. We believe Mr. Tate was tracking his daughters."

Todd's head cocks and his eyes narrow.

"Considering Mr. Tate's . . . computer expertise, we suspect he was trying to contact them through their various online profiles. If they were helping him in any capacity . . ."

What? I don't know where he's headed with this, but I don't like it.

Neither does Todd. "What are you trying to say, Detective?" he spits. "That they were helping him *elude* you? Are you trying to say my girls were involved in this?"

"Unfortunately, it's an angle we have to consider. Even though I'm sure we won't find anything." Carson retreats a step, but only one. His shoulders square up like he's readying himself for a fight. "It would look better if you helped us build a case against Mr. Tate."

"And how would we do that?"

"Let me have access to Wicket's computer. Let our experts take a crack at it."

Hell no! My coding programs are still safe on my jump drive, but an in-depth search of my erased internet history could screw me.

"We want to make sure they're safe, Mr. Callaway."

"If their father's incarcerated, I'd say they're the safest they could be."

Good, Todd! Fight! If he wants it, he can try for a warrant, but a judge won't give him one. Without Griff putting me at the scene, they can't link me to my dad's plan.

Carson nods. "Except he has numerous friends on the outside, Mr. Callaway, and we both know he wouldn't hesitate to call on them."

Shit. I look at Todd and feel sick. Carson won't need a warrant. Todd's going to give him everything freely.

"I just want them to be safe," Carson continues in an oh-so-reasonable tone. "And I know you want that too."

He wants to make us safe by going through my personal computer? If Bren were here, she'd tell Carson no dice.

But of course, I can't say anything. Not without spilling other stuff.

And Carson knows it.

Todd hooks his arm around my shoulders. "Of course Wicket will give you her laptop."

"It's a desktop," I snap.

"Oh. Well. Then the desktop." Todd looks at Carson. "More than anything, I want her to be safe."

"Naturally," Carson says, but there's something about his tone that doesn't make it sound natural at all.

"But you're wasting your time, Detective. Wicket would never be involved in anything like that."

Todd says it in a way that makes me sound better than a hacker, better than my father.

If he only knew.

"Wicket." Todd nudges me. "Go get your computer."

I open my mouth. Shut it.

Carson grins like he's got me, like he's won.

Like I'm stupid enough to put anything on that computer that could incriminate me.

Bastard. I grin right back. "Sure thing, Detective. Always happy to help."

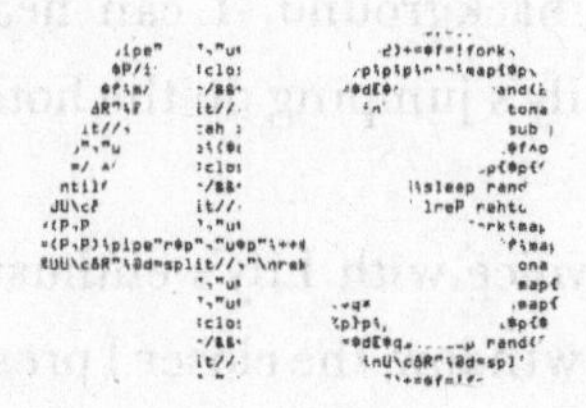

I'm supposed to keep everything perfect—usually I want to keep everything perfect. But I tore apart my first communion dress. Ripped it into a thousand pieces . . . and buried it in the garbage so no one would know. I can't stop thinking about how good it felt, and I have just enough left of me to know that it shouldn't have felt so perfect.

—Page 86 of Tessa Waye's diary

Todd calls Bren immediately, tells her everything before he drives up to the hotel to see them off. After she tells Lily, Lily demands to talk to me. I take the phone up to my room, and as I listen to Lily sing about how we're finally free, I watch a man walk out from our neighbor's tree line again. He stands just beyond the streetlamp's light so I can't see his features, but I know it's not Carson, because Carson never comes on foot, and I know it's not a neighbor, because a neighbor wouldn't stare up at our house. . . .

It's Jim Waye. Again.

"We're free, Wick!" In the background, I can hear something squeaking. I think Lily's jumping on the hotel bed. "Dad's gone! We're free!"

"Yeah," I say, infecting my voice with Lily's enthusiasm. But the closer I press to the window, the closer I press to *him*, the less I can manage it.

He thinks Lily's here. No one knows she's gone yet.

"Wick . . . ? Are you paying attention?"

Waye moves toward our house, and I shoot to my feet. "Yes. No. Sorry. Lil, I—I think someone's here. I need to go—"

"Is it Mr. Waye?"

I stop, put one hand against the windowsill. "Why would you say that?"

"He talks to me sometimes. I've seen him at school when he comes to pick up Tally. He's very sad about Tessa. I think he needs a friend. Maybe he came by to see me."

"Lily, if Tessa's dad ever talks to you again, I want you to go find a teacher right away, do you understand?"

"Why?"

"Just do it. I'll explain late—"

"You can explain now." The squeaking—a rhythmic beat before—stops dead. "Dad's going away for good. Everything's going to be great, and you're being weird. I want you to say yes to Bren. I want you to stop whatever you're doing and say yes."

I stare out the window, watch Waye watch the house, and think about telling Lily what's really going on.

But I don't. I can't.

Lily feels safe now because her own personal big, bad monster has been dragged away. How could I introduce her to another? How could I live with myself?

How could I live with myself if he touches her?

"So are you going to say yes, Wick?"

I look down at Waye, knowing damn well that, even with the lights off in my room, he can still see my shape at the window. "I don't . . . I haven't decided yet. I—"

Click.

She hung up on me. I start to call Lily back and then . . . I don't. When all this is finished, when it's fixed, maybe I'll find a way to tell her what really happened. But for now, I turn to the window, start to give Waye my bird finger, but then I stop. Waye is motioning to me! I step closer to the glass, not believing what I'm seeing.

He wants me to come down?

Hell no! Wait! Hell yes! I spin around, take the stairs two at a time until I rocket onto our front porch. I'm ready to confront him. Ready to tell him I know he did it. I'm ready . . . to see nothing.

The street is empty again.

I look around me. Nothing. I know I saw him. I know—

"Wicket?" Todd appears at my side. He must have come around the side of the house, and he's staring at me like I've lost my freaking mind. "Are you okay?"

"I—I don't know." I try to think of some sort of legitimate excuse for charging out the front door like my hair's on fire.

I don't have one. Maybe it's time for a little bit of truth?

"I thought . . . I thought I saw Tessa's dad staring up at the house."

Todd cocks his head. "Why would Jim come by?"

"I don't—I don't know. Lily says he's been talking to her at school. I just have a bad feeling about it." Lame, but true. I chew my lower lip and try to gauge Todd's response.

He's astonished, worried. *Pissed.*

"Don't worry, Wicket. I'll get to the bottom of it. I'll speak to Lily's teachers as soon as she returns." Todd backs up a step, opens the door a little wider. "Why don't you come inside?"

I nod. *Good. Getting to the bottom of things is good.* And as I watch Todd turn the dead bolt, I think maybe we're finally getting to the end of this.

It's one thirty in the morning, and I can't sleep. Part of me thinks it's because of Lily. Some of me thinks it's because of Griff. Most of me, however, thinks it's the four cups of coffee I've had in the last three hours. With Bren gone, there's no one to stop me, so I've had as much as I want, and now I'm so wired I can feel my fingernails growing.

My cell beeps and the screen flashes. *Griff.*

U still up for getting IP addresses?

Am I still up for it? Hell yes! If we can find who was using that library computer to do the upload, we could catch our guy. My fingers are trembling as I text:

of course.

It's the longest four seconds of my life until he writes:

Meet me at library tomorrow. 2 p.m.

I'm early, but I still don't beat Griff. He's waiting outside for me, slouching against one of the pillars until I get so close that he stiffens.

"You look rough."

My cheeks go nuclear. "Gosh, you're sweet."

"Wait." Griff peels himself off the pillar, rubs the back of his neck. "That's not what I meant."

"Then what did you mean?"

Griff's eyes inch over my face. "That I'm an idiot."

"No, you're not." But I am. Because when he's looking at me, I feel like the only person left in the world, like I'm special just because I'm me. "So. You have a plan for this?"

Griff's gaze sweeps across my face. "Is this what you're like without Lily?"

Yes. No. "He came to my house again last night, Griff. I know it's Waye. This has to end. How are we going to steal this stuff?"

He laughs. "Wicked, we're not going to steal anything. We're going to get them to give it to us."

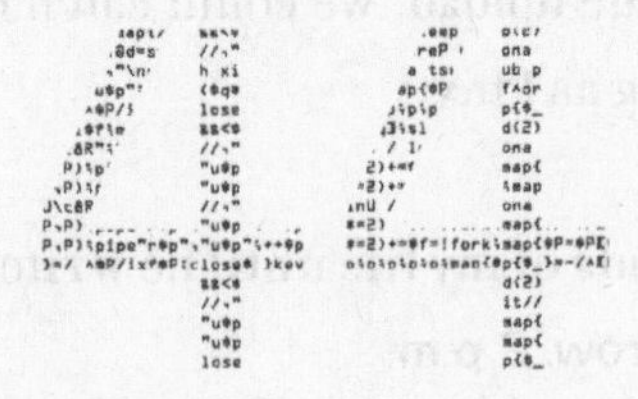

Garbage went out today and no one found my dead dress. I'm more relieved than I would have expected. Everything's still a secret, and I know what I'm going to do is right.

—Page 86 of Tessa Waye's diary

"You can do it," Griff repeats as we make our way down one long row of books. He stays ahead of me, mostly so the two librarians at the reference desk can't see me, but also (probably) to keep me from bolting. I am *so* not on board with this plan.

He leans one hand on a bookshelf above my head, forces me to stop and look up at him. "It'll be easy. Just sniffle. Cry a little. Look pitiful. You're the daughter of a man who has cheated on your mother and you're just asking for a little bit of help."

I chew my lip, think it over. It does sound easy when he

puts it like that. I can do this.

"We're just two poor kids trying to track down whether their father came here."

"That's your plan? Why would they buy it? We look nothing alike."

"Spin the story right, it won't matter."

He sounds cocky, and it should irritate me, but yeah, it kind of makes me want to smile.

Oh my God, he's turning me into a total girl.

"They won't think about details if you sell it right," Griff continues. "We just need to catch her off guard, get her a little confused, get her making decisions from a knee-jerk reaction."

"And that will make her give us the names?"

Griff grins like that's answer enough. He looks so confident, I guess it is.

"Just look pitiful."

I concentrate on Griff, think about being miserable—it's not a hard stretch these days—and try to look suitably sad.

"No, no, no." He shakes his head, but I can tell he's holding back a smile. "That's not pitiful. That's pissed."

I glare at him.

"And that's really pissed." Griff ducks his head and kisses me, hard. My fingers curl around his. "Just let me do the talking, Wicked."

He makes it sound so easy.

We end up waiting in the romance section until the older librarian disappears into the children's section, leaving the younger one running the front.

"Are you sure we shouldn't go for the old one?" I crane my head to see better, but it doesn't do me much good. I'm too short. "Usually, older people are easier to scam, Griff."

"Yeah, but the younger one is recently divorced. She'll be more receptive to letting us peek at the user log."

"How do you know she's divorced?"

Griff points to the fingers on his left hand. "White line where a wedding band would go. You can still see it, and the last time I was here, she was reading a self-help book about restarting life. My money's on divorce."

His money? I start to tell Griff I'm not into betting, I prefer guarantees, when he grabs my hand and hauls me forward. I almost trip. We're walking too fast. We practically charge across the carpeted space and, startled, the librarian looks up.

"Can I help you?"

Griff loops his arm around my shoulders. "I hope so. I have kind of a personal problem I need to ask you about."

Immediately, the woman's eyes shutter. Her defenses go up, and so does my heart rate. I sniffle, round my eyes. Try to look pitiful and forlorn. I have no idea if it's working.

"Our dad left us," Griff says, and it's almost imperceptible, but she winces.

"We think he used the computers here to access

our family's bank accounts. . . ." Griff trails off, glancing around like he's scared someone's going to hear. "He took everything: the savings, the money in the checking account. *Everything.*"

"I don't—"

"Please, just hear me out. I know he used to come here. I was hoping if we could see the user logs and website histories, we could know for sure. It's really for my mom. She doesn't believe he would do it. She keeps coming up with all sorts of reasons why he couldn't." Now Griff is the one who winces. He's talking about his mom, about what it was like to lose his dad. The best lies are the ones with an element of truth. He's the one giving away pieces of himself, pieces he won't get back.

And he's doing it for me.

"She needs closure or whatever, and if she knew he really would stoop this low, it would help her to let go," Griff says. "Please, we all need to know so we can get on with our lives."

The librarian glances behind her where, thankfully, the old lady is still nowhere in sight. When she turns around, her lip is caught between her teeth. "I don't know. We're not supposed to give anyone information on who's been using the computers. It's confidential."

"I know." Griff presses a little closer, and she doesn't back away. "I wouldn't even ask except we're in such a mess now." He fidgets, thins his mouth until he looks like he's holding in all the words he can't—*won't*—say. "We don't know what we're going to do. I'm just trying to help my mom deal."

The librarian's hand goes to her throat, plays with the thin, gold necklace at her collarbone. "I'm sorry."

Sorry because it happened? Sorry because she can't give us the names?

Or sorry because she *won't*?

"Please." I press my hand against the countertop, push down until my veins stand up. Our eyes meet. She's thinking about her husband. I'm thinking about Lily.

And even before she opens her mouth, I know she's going to say yes.

"I can't believe you did that, Griff." We push through the library's double doors and turn the corner. "All the names *and* the website histories!"

"I can't believe you thought I wouldn't."

It does seem crazy now. Totally delusional. I pull Griff close, and he pushes me into the library's brick wall.

"I wanted you to see what I would do for you."

"It's not about what you can do for me. It never was." His fingers are in my hair now, curving around the nape of my neck, pulling me apart. "I wanted your help because I needed *you*."

It slides out of me so fast. Too fast.

"I need you, Griff."

His lips find mine. "You're not alone anymore."

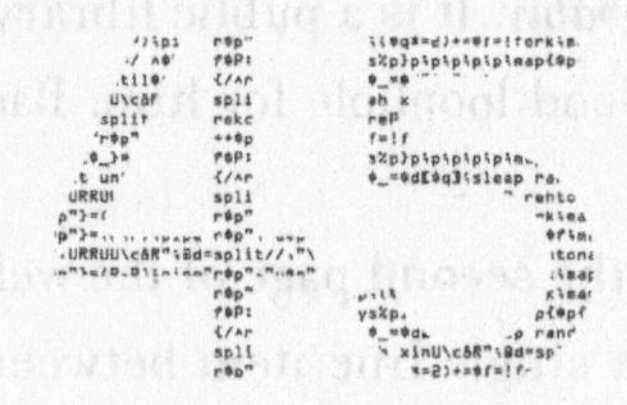

"You're useless to me now, do you know that?"

His lips skid into this secret smile, like it's all been some hilarious joke. But it's not. And that's how I know I'm in trouble. Because what do you do to your toys when you're finished with them?

You throw them away.

—Page 86 of Tessa Waye's diary

The librarian has given us even more than we could have hoped for.

But it doesn't help.

"Someone's definitely logging on to Facebook from this location, and yeah, that could mean anything and anyone, but the time stamps match." Griff turns the pages over and over. Our list of users goes back two weeks, but the website histories are for the past two months. He flips the report to the beginning. "But there are no names associated with the usage. It's like he never signed in."

"Do you think their security is that sloppy?"

Griff shrugs. "Possibly. *Probably.* It is a public library. They're not really equipped. Good loophole for him. Bad for us. It's a dead end."

"Not entirely." I hand him the second page of the web histories report and point to a single line item between icanhaz.cheezburger.com and WebMD. "We do have *this*."

Griff reads the website name, scowls. "LogMeIn? Wick, pursuing that angle will be a royal pain in the ass. If he installed that software so he could use the computer remotely, he could be anywhere. We need a different in."

"No, no, this could work for us." I take the papers, stare at the list some more. LogMeIn is a website service that allows you to remotely access computers. Once you're in, every movement you make is associated with the remote computer's IP address. It's a pretty good cover . . . but I still think I can make it work for us. "Look, we know he's local, because he had repeated access to Tessa, and I'm sure he thinks he's slick, but he's hiding behind store-bought software, and he's not smart enough to switch machines."

"What?"

"The only computer that has usage, but no users, is A5."

"Every time?"

"Every time. We've got him."

"How do you figure?"

Funny how Griff asks the question. I can tell he already knows the answer.

"Because I'll go hunting." I stuff the papers into my

backpack so I don't have to meet his eyes. Somehow we're not the same two people from five minutes ago. Now I'm Wicket Tate, Hacker. Not Wicket Tate, the girl he wanted. It really ought to make me feel stronger, but it doesn't. I feel like I'm draining through my feet, disappearing right in front of him. "I'll do what I always do."

Griff makes a disgusted noise. "With what computer?"

"The library's." I grab my jump drive and start to explain: "Odds are he's going to return to that same IP address. I mean, even after using it to post Lily's picture, he hasn't switched his access up. Look. He's used the LogMeIn service twice after that. It's comfortable for him. He knows it and now we know it. So we'll lay a trap."

A small muscle twitches under Griff's left eye. "Go on."

"I have this neat program. I wrote it to catch porn addicts for my customers. Once you find the target's favorite sites, you piggyback my program onto the website." The muscle's twitching harder now, making my explanations tumble: "When the mark clicks on it, a message pops up about contacting me for further instructions."

Griff goes very, very still. "Contacting *you*?"

"Yeah." I nod. "It'll look like blackmail, like I want money to keep quiet. The link I'll provide is a variation on my Trojan virus, Pandora. It will get me onto his system."

"Hell no."

My chest screws tight. "Griff, it's perfect. I bait him. He follows—"

"And if he's good enough to get this far, he could turn

the tables and come after you. No way."

I look up at him, and yeah, Griff's tall and I'm short, but I feel smaller than ever right now. I feel small and helpless and useless and I *hate* it.

I cross my arms, glare up at Griff. "What else do you want me to do?"

"I don't want you to play bait, Wick."

It sounds like an objection, but it's not. I can hear the resignation in his voice. He knows I'm going to do this and he's scared . . . so am I.

Behind us, the library's double doors swing open, and the young librarian walks toward the parking lot, a brown bag in one hand.

There's only one of them inside. I won't get a better opportunity. I need to go *now!*

I look at Griff, ready to explain, ready to *run*, but he's already moving toward the doors.

The library has a bank of ten computers, and thankfully, only two are in use. There's a harassed-looking mother of two small children trying to email on one end and a senior citizen playing Sudoku on the other. With my luck, I figure A5 has to be one of the computers they're using and I'm going to have to wait.

Then I see the OUT OF ORDER Post-it taped to the screen of one computer. The screen itself is off, but the tower light is still blinking green.

"That one has all sorts of problems," the old lady explains

when she sees me staring at it. "They get it running and then it goes all crazy and they have to call the IT people."

"Crazy how?"

"It won't let you type anything. It's like it just shuts you down."

I smile my thanks and slide into the seat. Shuts you down, huh? More likely it locks up because he's overriding the user so he can use the computer.

I check the ports on the back of the tower. The inputs feel worn, like someone might have been messing with them. I unhook the neighboring computer's monitor cord, re-hook it into the broken computer. Once I get the connector firmly in, the neighboring screen returns to life.

Griff sits down next to me and pretends to search for something on Wikipedia while I do the upload.

"You'll still need a computer for him to contact you," he says, eyes not leaving the remaining librarian. She's refiling books at the moment, but every time she turns in our direction, Griff tenses. "You'll still need a system to hack from so he can't trace you."

Good point. I finish the install, close my program, and pull the jump drive from the USB port. *A very good point. Not that I'm going to admit it.*

"I'll figure something out."

Griff shakes his head once. "No, if you're going to do this, you'll do it with my computer."

"Forget it," I say. And I mean it. You can't just give a hacker any old computer. We have preferences. There are setups.

You don't just start working from someone else's gear.

And you don't involve someone you care about.

"I'll come up with something, Griff. Don't worry." And because that doesn't seem to sway him, I add, "I hunt alone."

Griff tightens like a fist before the punch. "Not anymore." I try to stare him down, but he doesn't soften. "What will it say?"

I hate it, but I hesitate. I'm proud of my Pandora code, but I'm not sure I want him to see it. It's too personal, too abrasive . . . too *me*, but I turn to the computer screen.

"When he accesses this computer, he'll get a message," I explain. "And once he clicks on the message, I'm in. I can get at his information. Here, look."

I tilt the screen a little toward Griff. It says:

Welcome back, pervert. I have you logging in. I have your identity. I have everything I need to go to the cops—unless you contact me first. Find me here.

Find me.

I dare you.

Even though we stop by Griff's house to pick up another laptop, Todd's still at work by the time we return. There's a note on the fridge saying he'll be home after dinner, and the house feels too quiet.

Because Lily is gone?

Best not to think about it. Her absence is a good thing,

and let's be honest, it's good Bren's gone too, because there's no way she would let Griff come up to my room.

He follows me upstairs, spends a few minutes looking around while I set up the laptop. I'm grateful for the space, actually. Right now my skin feels electrified. My vision's going haloed. Oncoming migraine? I'll have to take my pills. Can't afford for this to get worse or it'll slow me down.

I rub my neck where the muscles have curled into rocks. Griff notices. He starts toward me and . . . stops.

"If you pull this off, Wicked, you have to turn in everything you find to Carson. Tomorrow. First thing in the morning."

Turn everything over? So Carson can do *nothing* with it again? Just like he did with the diary?

Then again, if I can get enough evidence, Carson will have to act.

I hesitate. "Yeah. Fine."

Griff closes his hand over mine. I don't even realize I'm leaning into him until my cheek brushes his hoodie's sleeve.

"So what do we do now?" he asks.

"We wait."

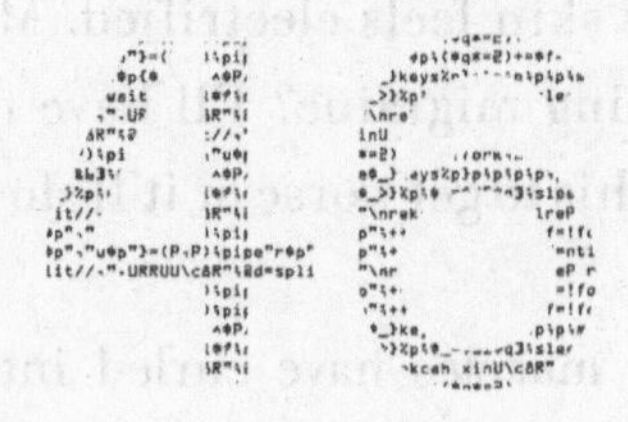

There's no end to this, you know.

—Page 61 of Tessa Waye's diary

Ten hours later, something's ringing.

I roll on my back, blink up at the ceiling.

For three seconds or so, I'm confused. Then everything clicks. My hand shoots across the nightstand, snatches up my cell. "Hello?"

"Wick?"

"Griff!" I sit up straight, press the phone a little closer. At first, I think it's static on the line, but it's not. It's his ragged breathing. "What's wrong?"

"It worked. The Pandora code worked."

Course it did. I push the covers off, wondering why he sounds so freaked. The migraine meds I took are making me feel fuzzy and sluggish. I wrench myself around so my feet hit the floor, and I stand up.

"Wick? Did you hear me?" Griff's voice jumps high. He sounds . . . scared.

And that scares me. "Yeah, I heard you. This is great, Griff. I think—"

"Don't think." Something crashes on his end. I hear a door slam. "Don't think, just run. Get moving."

"Get moving?" *Why? I need to stay put. This is working like we wanted it to work. Why would I screw that up by taking off?*

I lean toward the window, look for Carson's unmarked sedan. He's not here. Yet. "I'm not going anywhere. We've got him."

"Wick, I'm begging you." Griff's breath goes rough-edged, and I can hear his tennis shoes start to slap pavement. "Run. I installed spyware on the laptop I gave you. It notified me as soon as he clicked on your message. The IP address for the computer that took the Trojan matches *your* house's IP address, Wick. Whoever took the bait is inside your house."

I look at the computer, my bed, the open door to my bedroom. I can't make sense of this. It can't be right. *It's not possible.*

Chills push goose bumps through my skin.

"Griff, I have to go." And I hang up while Griff is still yelling. The cell lights up again, but I ignore it and open Griff's laptop instead.

"Work it like any other hack," I whisper, waiting for the computer to return from sleep mode.

Except it's not just any hack, is it? Right now, my head feels filled with ginger ale, and my hands are shaking.

Once the laptop is up, I open Command Prompt. It takes only another moment for me to turn on the remote computer's webcam feed, and this time, it's the sound that comes up first on my machine.

I know the laugh even before I see his face, and when the image pops up on my screen, I want to vomit. I start to scream, but nothing comes out as Todd looks straight into the camera and says, "Hello, Wicket."

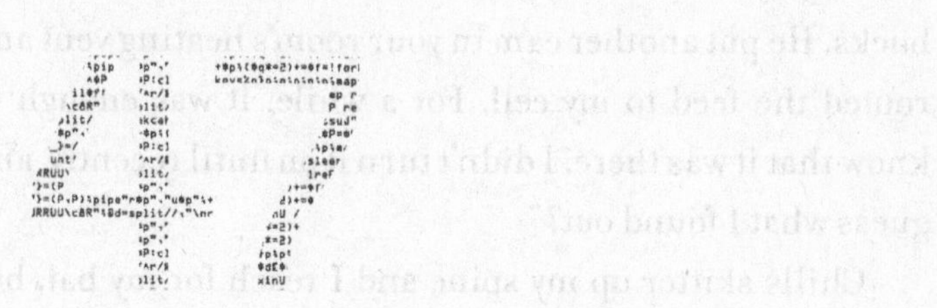

He always hits me where no one can see. The first time it happened, I thought I was seeing him for who he really was. . . . Then I realized I was lying. I've always known who he is—what he is. I was just too afraid to name it.

—Page 79 of Tessa Waye's diary

Todd?! It was Todd? I push back from the desk, feet kicked under me, ready to run. *No, he's been so upset. Her death gutted him. Remember the tears? How he fought her dad? How he was eaten up with guilt? It couldn't be Todd.*

Except he's smiling and nodding like he knows what's tumbling through my head and he likes it. The pieces click into place. Access to Tessa. Access to Lily.

And now we're alone.

"Surprised?"

Todd holds up his cell phone so I can see the screen. It's my bedroom. It's *me*. Right now. "Amazing what those security system install guys will do for an extra hundred bucks. He put another cam in your room's heating vent and routed the feed to my cell. For a while, it was enough to know that it was there. I didn't turn it on until recently, and guess what I found out?"

Chills skitter up my spine and I reach for my bat, but my hand grabs air.

It's gone.

When I turn around, Todd laughs harder. "Missing something?" He holds up my bat so I can see it.

"You said you wanted to protect her," I blurt. "You said you should've done something."

"Protect her from *him*, from that asshole father of hers." Todd's hand grazes the edge of his jaw, as if he's remembering Tessa's touch. "She didn't need protection from me. She seduced me. She *wanted* it. They always want it. I could have had any of them, but I wanted her because she was broken."

Todd's eyes drop to the desktop, where his fingers tap against the wood. "I loved how much Tessa wanted me. She thought I was a god, but it wasn't until she fought me and I forced her anyway that I *felt* like a god. In one afternoon, I finally understood why her father hit her—because nothing tastes better than power over someone else. Made me think about sweet, little Lily . . . and what I could make her do."

My breathing's gone rough and ragged, making me sound like some animal run to ground. I start to grab random objects. Books. Computer cords. A laptop bag. *There's nothing here! How am I going to defend myself?*

"But what I realized is Lily would never be a challenge," Todd continues. "I don't want her anymore. Right now, I want you."

Me? I look back at my computer. The chair is spinning. It's empty. Todd is gone.

He's coming. I run for the door, grabbing the knob with both hands to work the lock except . . . the lock just spins and spins.

"No," I whisper. He must have disabled it. It's useless. "No, no, *no!*"

I hurtle around, launch myself at the window, but when I lift up on the frame, nothing happens. It doesn't budge, and my fingertips graze freshly hammered nail heads.

He's nailed the window shut. There's no escape.

I back away, my eyes darting over the room. I need a barricade, but the bed's too heavy. I'll never be able to move it. My desk? Too light, and it's too small to wedge against the door.

"Oh, Wiiiiccccckkkkeeet." Todd's voice floats from somewhere farther down the hallway. "Are you going to run from me?"

What am I going to do? My eyes fall on my bedside lamp. *I'll fight.*

"I hope you do run." Todd laughs, and I fling myself toward the bed, unplugging the lamp, dipping the room into dark. "I really hope you do. I like it better when I get to chase."

Footsteps. My hands are sweat-slick and sliding along the lamp's metal base. *He's on the stairs.*

I yank the shade off the top, break the cord from the base. Makeshift bat. I hoist it to one shoulder, test the weight. Lighter than I want, but short enough that I'll be able to do some damage. It'll work.

I stand in the dark and wait. When he comes, I'll nail him. Except . . . maybe I shouldn't wait. I shift my weight from foot to foot, trying to ready myself and ignore how my knees want to crumble.

I ease forward, opening my bedroom door so I can see Todd coming—and lights sweep the street outside my window.

"Well, look who's here," I whisper as Detective Carson pulls up.

"Not a runner then." Todd sounds disappointed . . . and intrigued. "Guess you just go for what you know, huh, Wicket? Having that fucking loser for a father, I can't imagine this is the first time you've been chased."

No, it isn't. And you'd think it would make this easier, but it's not. I'm trying not to breathe so hard. I'm trying to be *quiet*, but I can't get enough air.

He's a few feet from me now, just outside the doorway,

and I can't see for shit. After Todd saw my room was dark, he flipped out the hallway lights. Now we're both blind.

Until a dim glow crawls across my floor from Carson's headlights.

Shit! The detective is turning his car around. Is he leaving? For a second, I think about hurling myself into the window, about smashing the glass and screaming for help.

Would I make it?

"I see your hero has arrived."

I stifle a gasp. Todd's closer than I thought, just on the other side of the wall.

"Don't even think about screaming for him," Todd says. "I'll be on you before he ever hears a sound."

There's a creak of floorboard, and blood throbs in my ears. I ram my shoulder against the wall and lift the lamp higher.

"You know he's suspected me all along," he continues, and in the dim light, I see his fingers wrap around the door frame. "That's why he keeps making excuses to come by, why he keeps circling the house."

I hold myself steady even though everything in me is screaming to start swinging. *Careful, you don't want to break his hand, you want to smash his face. You want to get him down so he can't get back up.*

"At first." Todd takes another step, pushing the edge of his profile into reach. He exhales, and I can smell the peppermint he's chewing. "I thought—I hoped—he was after you and your piece-of-shit father. Then I realized it was me and the game was on, but he'll never catch me. Do you know why, Wicket?"

He's trying to get me to talk, get an idea of where I am. I hold my breath.

Todd sighs, disappointed I didn't take the bait. "He won't catch me because after I finish with you there won't be anything left and I'll be gone."

Another step closer and I swing. The lamp base connects with his nose, and there's a sickening crunching noise. Todd screams, lashes out. I duck, but I'm not fast enough, and his hand digs into my hair.

"You little bitch!" he hisses, and yanks me to him. The lamp base's corner has torn his cheek wide open, exposing a seam of teeth. "You will fucking pay for that!"

I kick, connect with his knee, then his shin. He sucks in a hard breath, and I register one horrifying heartbeat before Todd punches me in the face.

Once.

Twice.

Stars explode behind my eyes and warmth courses down my face. Blood. But no pain. Not yet. That will come later. Sticky heat floods my face, the shock making me hesitate.

It's all the opening he needs.

Todd half kicks, half pushes me onto the floor. I fall on my back, rolling even before I fully connect. Surprise is gone and instinct is kicking in. I cannot get pinned. I *must* not get pinned down. He's too heavy. If he gets on top of me, I'm done.

Todd crashes down after me, one hand raised. Something metallic flashes.

Knife!

Todd plunges it downward, aiming at my chest and catching my arm instead. Pain rips through me, shooting all the way down to my fingers.

"When I finish with you, they'll never even find your *pieces*!"

My good hand flails, scrabbles, and connects with a discarded boot. I grab it, smashing it into Todd's broken nose. More blood sprays. He backhands me, and the swing hits me so hard it actually knocks me out of reach. I slide across the floorboards, crash into the dresser, and Todd staggers up, ready to come after me.

He's just not fast enough.

I'm on my feet now, and I plunge into the hallway, into the dark. Todd grabs the edge of my T-shirt. It rips, but it doesn't slow me down. He's right. I do know all about being chased. My dad gave me plenty of practice, and Todd won't catch me now.

I jump the stairs two at a time until I hit the middle landing and my socks slip. I smack into the wall, go down hard on my knees. The pain in my arm streaks tears down my face.

"Got you!"

I look up and see him scrambling down the stairs after

me. I scream even as my feet push me up for one last run that will get me nowhere.

I slam into his stomach, keep pushing until he falls right over me. Todd flips, hits the stairs with wood-splintering force. Something cracks and he slumps. I don't even realize I'm still screaming until he slides to the bottom of the stairs.

Todd lies there, not moving.

Holy shit, I've killed him.

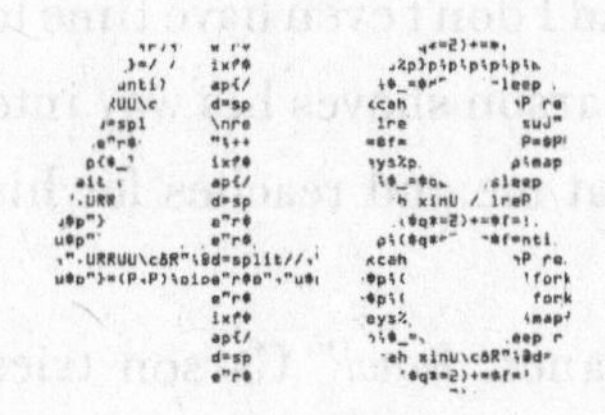

If I do this, what will happen to me afterward?

—Page 82 of Tessa Waye's diary

Carson. I need to get Carson. And like I somehow said the words aloud, I hear the detective bellow my name.

"Wicket!" Something heavy hits the rear door. "Wicket!"

My feet won't move. I can't take my eyes off Todd.

Go. Now. I ease down the stairs, jumping *way* over his chest, and run.

Just like that first night, Carson is on the other side of the French door. This time his pistol butt is raised, ready to break the glass. When he sees me, his hands drop and his head tilts to one side, saying something into the radio pinned to his shoulder holster.

My fingers are blood-slicked and clumsy. They won't work right, so it takes me a second or two with the locks. If I'd tried to escape this way, Todd would've caught me for sure.

The dead bolt slides open, and I don't even have time to reach for the doorknob before Carson shoves his way into the kitchen. He takes one look at me and reaches for his radio again.

"I'm gonna need an ambulance. *Now!*" Carson tries to wrap his arm around me. "Did he get you, too? Wicket, what's going on?"

Get me, too? I don't understand. *Did Todd get me like he did Tessa?*

Carson gives me a little shake. "What happened?"

The detective tugs me down the back steps, snapping more orders into his radio. "Wicket, I need you to come with me. I need you to tell me what happened."

"He attacked me," I manage. My voice sounds too high. I clear my throat, but it only breaks again. "I fought him off."

Carson rounds on me. "He's *here*?"

I nod.

"In the *house*?"

I nod again. Something about Carson's horror is seeping into me. All the hairs on my arms stand up and I know, without a single doubt, something is very, very wrong.

The detective pulls his gun out again, tries to push me

behind him. I won't let him. "Did he say anything about what he did with Lily?"

Lily! "What are you talking about?" Carson starts to back up, and I grab two fistfuls of his shirt. "Lily's with Bren. They're flying to San Francisco. She's safe."

Pity wrinkles Carson's eyes. "Wicket, they never made the plane. He caught them in Atlanta. At the hotel. Bren was tied up for almost twenty-four hours, and we can't find Lily."

Carson tries to untangle my grip. "I have to go inside, Wicket. I need you to stay here."

Stay *here*? Like hell I'm staying here. I glare at Carson, but my brain is filled only with Todd. I will kill him again. I will rip him to pieces. My sister! *Lily!*

I push off Carson's chest so hard he staggers. "Wicket!"

"He's in here!" I spin for the house. Carson makes a grab for me, but I shake him off. Does he really think he can catch me after what I've just been through?

"He's this way!" We're through the kitchen now, into the hallway. "He's—"

Gone. Todd is *gone*.

Twenty minutes later, there must be thirty cops on our front lawn, and not *one* of them will tell me anything more about Lily and what happened. In fact, the only people who will talk to me are the EMTs, but all they want to talk about is how I need to go to the hospital.

"Let go of me!" I hiss at the bigger one. Briefly, we struggle and he does let me go—probably because he doesn't want to hurt my arm any further. The cut's heavy bleeding has stopped, but I'm still slowly soaking through the bandage they wrapped around my arm. The ice pack I'm holding against the wound is doing little to stop the swelling. I'm going to need stitches and antibiotics, but I want my sister first.

Where could Todd have taken her?

It's hard to think with everything going on around us. The front lawn is utter bedlam. Everyone is running around. I rub my hand against my forehead and will my brain to work. Todd couldn't have gotten very far. He's injured, and he hasn't had enough time. He also has Lily, and because he has Lily he would need somewhere quiet, undisturbed . . . convenient.

Carson's thinking Todd would run, but that's not the way my foster dad does things. He hid in plain sight for ages. He knows more about hunkering down than he does about escaping. There's the company office in Atlanta. It would be deserted this time of night. There's their lake house—but it's too far away. . . . There's the church.

"Detective!" I jump off the gurney and ignore the EMTs' swearing. Carson is striding across the front lawn, and I don't want to lose him. This is my chance—and Lily's. I can't screw it up. "Detective Carson!"

He pretends not to hear me, so I grab the hem of his jacket.

"Not now, Wicket. Mrs. Callaway will be here soon."

"But—"

"*Not* now!" He dives into a huddled group of police officers, leaving me on the outside. They mutter among themselves and then, like a pack of cheerleaders, they trudge en masse toward the house.

"He'll be on the road by now, folks," Carson shouts. "I want those roadblocks up yesterday. I want Lily Tate's picture on every news channel. He has at least a twenty-minute head start on us. If we don't close that window, he'll be across state lines."

"Unless he never left!" I shout, and wait for Carson—for *any* of them—to turn around. He has *no* idea where Lily could be.

But I know.

Furious, I twist around, ready to pitch my ice pack across the yard. And that's when I see it. Carson's sedan. With its lights still flashing and its engine still running.

Score.

"Not without me."

Griff comes up so quietly behind me I don't even hear him until his breath melts against the back of my neck.

Maybe that's because, deep down, I was waiting for him.

I turn around, look up at him. "Oh yeah?"

"Not without me," Griff repeats. I can't really see his expression, but then again, I don't have to. I can hear everything he wants to say in his tone. "I can already tell what you're thinking, Wicked, and you're not doing it without me."

Normally, I'd have something to say about Griff's attitude. It's arrogant and demanding, and the way he's pushing even closer into my space should make my hands curve into fists.

"Not without you," I agree.

We make our way to the car. No one notices.

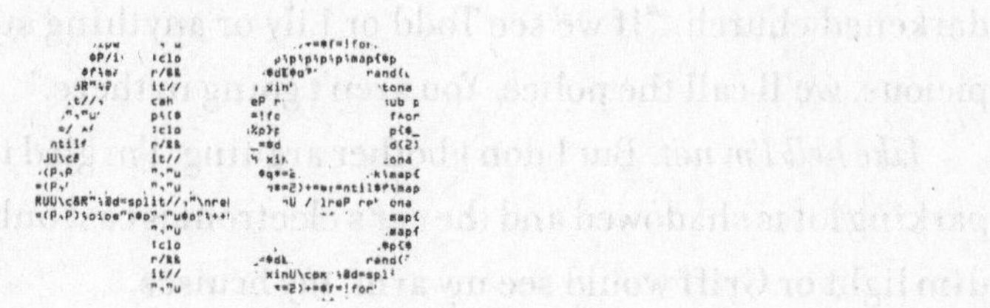

Fairy tales have it right. There are monsters, but in our world the monsters can't be killed.

—Page 67 of Tessa Waye's diary

For the record, driving a stolen cop car in real life isn't like driving a stolen cop car in the Grand Theft Auto video game. For one, I'm better at Grand Theft Auto. For another . . .

I cut a right turn too close, jumping the sedan over the curb. The car heaves and my tires squeal. Half a second later, we're righted and Griff is swearing.

Okay, maybe, it is a little like Grand Theft Auto.

"Seriously?" Griff asks, one hand on the dashboard for support.

I give him my best *What can you do?* expression, even

though I have to clench my teeth to do it. My arm is throbbing now.

"Shut off your headlights and pull around to the side," Griff orders, craning his head to get a better look at the darkened church. "If we see Todd or Lily or anything suspicious, we'll call the police. You aren't going in there."

Like hell I'm not. But I don't bother arguing. I'm glad the parking lot is shadowed and the car's electronics cast only a dim light or Griff would see my arm, my bruises.

He'd also see the blood. I'm pretty sure my bandage is soaked through now, and I feel a little woozy.

We pull into a space near the side entrance, and I shut the car off. There are a few lights on inside, but I can't tell if that's just for security . . . until someone moves. He steps away from the window, backing farther into the building. It's just a flash of movement, a fissure of momentary black in the window's yellow light, but it's enough.

"It's him. He's here." I know it's Todd. It's in the way he hitched as he moved, the way he limped. I hurt him, and he's still feeling it. Good.

I shove open my car door and Griff grabs my bad arm. I nearly buckle.

"What the hell is this?" His fingers move over the bandage, and after examining his fingertips, Griff realizes they're coated in blood. "What. The. Fuck. Wick?"

"He hurt me." I lean against the steering wheel and force myself not to puke. "And if he's willing to hurt me, think about what he'll do to Lily."

I push myself upright, trying to decide what to do. Todd knows we're here now. There's no element of surprise. He has the upper hand. So how do we get it back?

We don't.

"I'm calling the cops, Wick." When Griff stands, he has his cell pinned to one ear. "I told you we're not going in there. He could hurt you worse. I can't let you risk it."

And I can't risk Lily. I need to think. *How am I going to do this?* My eyes skip to the car.

As Griff gives our location to the 911 operator, I paw through the backseat. Empty. . . . But then the parking lot lights catch the edge of something.

I bend down. It's Tessa's diary.

The notebook must have slid right under the seat. It doesn't even look like anyone touched it . . . maybe Carson never even knew it was there. Part of me is horrified by the idea. Another, stronger part thinks . . . it's fitting. Lily was always mine to save. It's what I do. It's what I do for all those women who hire me.

I put the diary up on the car's dash and go around the rear. Inside the trunk, Carson has rain gear, a set of safety vests, and traffic cones. There's nothing useful. Except for the *flares*.

Now *those* we can use.

I collect everything and carry it around to Griff.

"How far away are the police?" I ask.

"Fifteen minutes."

"We don't have that much time. Here, take these." I

tumble the flares into Griff's arms.

"What're you going to do with these?"

"Even our odds against Todd." I point to the church's far end, where a set of shallow stairs descend below the parking lot. "Should be a breaker box over there. Commercial buildings usually keep them on the outside."

"What?"

"Joe taught me. First step of a successful snatch and grab."

"You're going to cut his power?"

"Exactly." I stalk across the parking lot and hustle down the stairs, each step skidding pain up my arm. It's worth the effort, though. A breaker box is tucked just behind some ornamental shrubbery. I flip open the small metal door and squint at my options.

Excellent. I have access to everything. So I start pulling. I shut off every light they have, and the whole building plunges into darkness.

Behind me, a sneaker scrapes against the pavement. It's Griff, and I need to tell him he doesn't have to come, he doesn't have to do this, but the objection dies when I turn around. The parking lot lights are behind him, dipping Griff's face in shadows. I can't see his expression, but I can see he has my flares . . . and he looks like he's not moving anywhere without me.

"Are you ready?" he asks.

Somewhere up above us, there's a solitary scream.

Lily.

It's all the ready I need. I walk up the steps with far more courage than I ever managed when Todd attacked me. I walk straight into the black and feel like our dad prepared me best for this moment in the dark.

"Shit." They're locked. All the doors are *locked*. While Griff shoves his weight against the rear door, I turn right and press between the wall and bushes until my left hand connects with a window ledge.

"Help me with this." It takes both of us, but we manage to pull the sliding window open. I dig my toes into the siding and try to kick my way up. "Boost me."

"Hell no."

"What cop is going to fit?"

"Carson could."

"Carson's not here."

Griff sighs. "Fuck me," he groans, and heaves me up. I catch the window ledge with both hands and ease myself in. Seconds later, Griff lands next to me and starts moving for the church's entrance.

I grab his arm. "Lily first."

We've landed in the kitchen, and briefly, I think we've hit the jackpot. Knives, heavy pans? There has to be *something*.

But no luck.

Hands shaking, I paw through all the cabinets and

come up with nothing, absolutely nothing. The knives are locked up. There are no pots, just an old microwave and a dead walk-in freezer. The only things left in the cabinets are paper plates and cups.

Well, that's no help. I start to slam a cabinet door in frustration and catch myself. The whole church is eerily quiet. Without the white noise of fans and air-conditioning, everything is coming through in surround sound. My breath sounds like a dragon in the dark.

I pull off my new tennis shoes. Another lesson from my dad: Even a squeak can give you away, and I won't risk it.

Thankfully, there's a small amount of light coming in from the windows, courtesy of the parking lot lights. It's not much, but enough for Griff to see what I'm doing. He hesitates, then bends to imitate me. We slide our shoes to the side and stand at the kitchen doorway, hovering like swimmers before the plunge.

"Breathe softly," I whisper, and I guess I'm telling Griff all the ways to stay safe, but I think, deep down, I'm also reminding myself. "And move carefully. You'll have to do it by feel at first, but after a while, your eyes will adjust."

I glance at Griff, expecting to see his profile, but he's staring at me. "I'll go first, Wicked. Stay right behind me."

"I— Yeah, okay, fine." I'm shaking hard now. Worse than ever. I'm not sure if it's nerves or blood loss, but either way, I'm in no shape to lead.

Griff covers my hand with his. "And once we get Lily, you run like hell."

I nod, squeeze his hand tighter. "Running will not be a problem."

"Good," Griff says, and leads me into the dark.

I had forgotten how time stretches when you're panicked. Seconds feel like minutes. Minutes feel like hours. Your flight instinct swears you've hidden long enough and now is the time to run, but that's the fastest way to get caught. You have to take your time. I force myself to think, when all I want to do is scream.

Griff and I break apart, covering the downstairs quickly and quietly. There's no sign of Todd and Lily anywhere. No sniffling from the direction of the pews, no smothered gasps from any of the alcoves. That leaves one alternative: the second-floor offices.

Griff disagrees. "He's too smart to go up there," he whispers. The door leading to the upper floors is at our fingertips, and Griff keeps pulling me back. "There's only one set of stairs, one way to escape. He'd never pin himself down that way."

"Unless he's not planning on escaping." I step forward, resisting Griff. "Suppose Lily and Todd aren't leaving there alive. He has nothing left to lose anymore, Griff. Everyone knows."

Griff's hold slackens and I pitch forward, feeling my way up the staircase as he follows closely behind. We emerge in a small alcove where the choir would sit, and I wait while Griff slides around me, taking the lead. For a moment, it looks like another dead end.

Until we see the catwalk across the first-floor chapel. Bordered by handrails, it leads across the open space below and heads straight to a single door that has the barest hint of light around it.

Flashlight. They're there, inside the office.

My relief tastes like a sob, and I want to shout with joy.

Until I hear Lily. Begging.

I can feel the words, hushed and panicked and pleading, more than I can hear them, and next to me, Griff stiffens.

Oh God, Lily!

If Todd kills her now, it won't matter that the police know. But what do I do? There are two of us, but Todd could still have his knife, and now he has my sister.

"The flares," I hiss, grabbing for Griff. "Throw them over the side."

I can't see Griff's face, but I can hear his breath hitch and hold. He's confused, and I can't speak any louder to explain.

"The flares," I repeat.

Then, suddenly, there's a click and slide. Another rustle, and something passes between us as Griff ignites the first fuse. Light explodes, illuminating us both. We look like we're on fire.

Until Griff pitches it.

The flare arcs in a lazy line across the congregation seats, falling behind the pulpit, into some curtains. Griff adds a second one to it, but this time, he throws long and it strikes the stained-glass windows. Sparks explode, and ahead of us, the door flings open.

A man appears. Somehow, he's darker than the dark, and when he moves forward, he seems to slither. Until his stride catches.

Todd. I'm already flat against the wall, but I press myself even closer. The very sight of him makes me want to crawl out of my skin, start screaming, and never stop.

Todd dashes by without noticing us, his flashlight bouncing light down the stairwell. As soon as I hear him hit the floor below, I fling myself toward the office door.

Inside, there's a little light coming through the window overlooking the parking lot. It's not much, but it gilds a few surfaces. Desk . . . shelves . . . storage boxes . . .

My sister!

"Wick!"

"Lily!"

Griff and I fall on her, hands outstretched and grabbing. My fingers connect with something rough and tight.

Rope. He's tied her up. I wiggle my fingers underneath the knot at Lily's wrists, try to pry it loose. *Have to get her free. Have to get going before he returns.*

"Wick," Lily whispers through tears. "I'm so sorry about everything. I didn't know. I didn't even think—"

"Shh. It's okay."

"It's not okay! It's never going to be okay. I thought—I thought—" Lily gulps, fresh tears staining the backs of my wrists as I yank one knot free. "I believed in him."

I use both hands to frame my sister's face, and for the first time, I'm grateful for the dark because I can feel my blood smear across her cheeks, mingle with her tears. "You were right to believe in him, Lily. Not everyone is a monster. Maybe if I spent less time suspecting everyone, I would be able to see real evil when it's right in front of me."

Lily goes still, and for the time being, her tears stop. I keep working on the ropes. "But none of that matters, Lil, because we're going to escape."

Except we're not, and I know it. The ropes won't budge. After the first knot, the rest won't loosen. My fingers keep fumbling. They're going numb—*most* of me is going numb—the blood loss is slowing me down. I'm not going to save her, and I have to save her.

"Take her." I push Lily toward Griff, tuck his free arm around her shoulders. "She can't run. You'll have to carry her and I can't. I'm not strong enough."

Griff growls. "Not without you."

"Without her, there is no me."

In the half-dead light, I watch Griff's pained expression. "You can't ask me to do this, Wick," he whispers. "You can't ask me to leave you."

"I'm not." An unholy shriek of rage erupts from downstairs. *Todd. He knows. He's coming back.*

And there's only one way out of here.

I shudder. "I'm not asking you to leave me, Griff. I'm

asking you to save my sister." We can't just leave. He'll catch us on the stairs.

Griff looks at me, and even if I don't live to see him ever again, even if Todd cuts me until there is nothing left to cut, I will remember this: Griff didn't hesitate. He pulls Lily close and says, "What do you want me to do?"

"Hide where the choir would stand. I'll draw Todd away." I push myself up. "After we're gone, get Lily out of here."

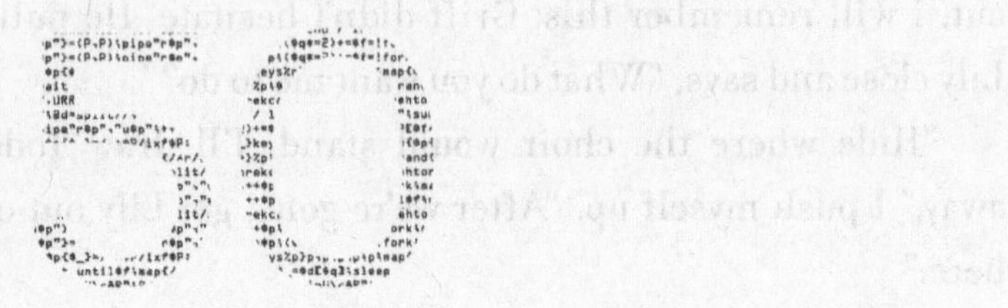

It was never supposed to end like this.

—The last words of Tessa Waye's diary

I wait for Todd in the dark, and when he fills the doorway and his flashlight illuminates his face, I lift my chin, and promise myself I will make sure Todd never hurts anyone ever again.

"You."

"Me," I agree.

Todd lunges forward without checking the room, without lifting his feet high enough to clear the storage boxes I shoved in front of the doorway. He hits them hard, dropping to his knees, hands outstretched to break his fall.

And I smack him in the temple with a paperweight the size of a grapefruit.

He hits the floor hard, writhing in pain, giving me the second I need to duck. I leap over him, my feet churning before they're even near the carpet. When I touch down, I'm gone. I'm running fast, faster than I ever have before. I streak down the catwalk, passing where Griff and Lily are hiding as Todd screams in fury.

And sets off after me.

I can't see the stairs ahead of me, but somehow, I find a rhythm.

I clatter down the steps until I hit the bottom floor—and trip. I stab my good hand into the wall. Right myself. Take off running again.

But the mad dash and stumble make me dizzy. My brain feels turned inside out, and I almost miss my turn. I make a hard left, plunging through a doorway where the Sunday school rooms line each side of the hallway.

Griff and I discovered these during our first-floor search. The rooms open to the hallway, but they also open into one another from the inside. I cut into the first room on the right, and thanks to the moonlight coming in through the windows, I make my way into the third room via the inside doors.

"You bitch!" Todd snarls. He's farther behind me now. By the sound of his voice, he's near the first entrance, the one I took to get into the hallway. That's good. It's where I want him.

Now I just need to draw him closer.

"I know you think you've won, but the police haven't

arrived yet." Judging from Todd's voice, he's coming down the main hallway, so I edge closer to the inside door. He'll check every room, and with this much moonlight, he'll see me for sure. "They'll still have to save *you*, and do you really think I'll let them? Do you really think there will be anything left of you to save?"

Not if you catch me. With a shaking hand, I pull out Griff's cell phone—the one he gave me just before carrying Lily to safety—flip on the iPhone's voice recorder feature, and announce: "Then come and get me, Todd. You want a chase . . . I'll give it to you."

Todd's hand snakes around the door frame and I take off, using the inside set of doors to head back to the hallway entrance. But Todd is just a bit faster and he's on me. His fingers tangle in the tips of my hair, closing in, and I scream in panic. I grab the nearest door with both hands, and as I duck to the left, I slam the door behind me.

It catches Todd's forearm squarely in the jamb. Now he's screaming and I'm away. I race down the hallway, catching the barest hint of flashing blue lights through the windows.

They're almost here. I head for the kitchen, pinwheeling my arms for balance when my socks hit the linoleum. *Please say Griff's got the doors all unlocked by now.*

Somehow it's darker in the kitchen than I remember. I'm groping my way again, and I can't afford to slow down. I can hear Todd's footsteps growing closer.

It takes two hands, but I pry open the dead freezer, pin

back the door, and hit play on the iPhone's recorder before sliding the cell across the floor. It skids under some shelving and smacks against the rear wall as Todd explodes into the kitchen. I drop to the floor and scramble backward until I'm pressed against the cabinets. I can't really see anything now. But I can hear him. The soles of his shoes snap like teeth.

This isn't going to work. He won't fall for it. I shrink down, praying Todd continues straight or else he'll trip right over me. He keeps moving . . . he stops.

Right there in front of me.

I can smell him. Blood and peppermints.

He's going to catch me. I'm screwed!

"Then come and get me." The iPhone finally comes to life, repeating my earlier words. Todd pauses. I still can't see him, but I can feel him panning the dark, searching.

Please move. Please take the bait. If it keeps repeating, he'll know it's a recording. I can hear sirens growing closer, but they won't be close enough if he finds me crouching here. I'll be dead before the police hit the parking lot.

Please. Please. Please.

Todd takes one step . . . then another. He stands at the broken freezer's entrance, and I pull my feet under me. He hesitates, walks over the threshold, and I stand. I count three of Todd's footsteps before I move toward the door. I make myself count two more before I grab the freezer door handle.

"Then come and get me, Todd. You want a chase . . . I'll

give it to you." I hear his shoes scrape as he bends down.

He's found it! I shove the door shut with my shoulder, and Todd shouts. There's a scuffle. *He's coming! Lock it!*

But my fingers feel like overstuffed sausages. I can't see well enough to drive the pin into the lock. I fumble and Todd hits the door, bouncing me hard. I ram my shoulder into the metal, and my vision blurs.

My arm. I can't hold him for another go. The pain is crumbling my knees, driving me to the floor. *Have to get the pin in. Have to.*

Todd pulls back for another leap and—

The pin slides home! He hits the metal door with a resounding slam, but it doesn't move. I've got him.

And just like that, my legs crumple. I slide to the floor and lean my head against my knees as sirens scream and two cops kick through the kitchen door.

In horror movies, you always cut away after the bad guy dies. You don't watch the blood-covered girl let the cops into the church. Which I did. You definitely don't watch her vomit in the kitchen sink. Which I also did.

And you really don't get to see the moment where she realizes nothing will ever be the same now. Her life will be forever divided into Before and After. Her monster may be gone, but in some ways, he'll always live on.

Because she lived on and she will remember.

I'm never going to be free of this. I bend toward the grass, grip the ground until my fingers are buried.

Then I hear my name. I look up and see Griff running toward me. Griff, who saved my sister. Who saved me. He's shouting my name and, I think, something more, but his words are floating away. My ears are ringing. At some point I must have smacked my head. But I do understand this: Griff came back for me.

I blink up at him. Lily and Bren are hot behind him. My sister's hair is a streak of light as she runs toward me. And somehow, that's what undoes me.

I pitch face-first into the grass, grabbing handfuls of dirt to anchor me until Lily kneels down. She's got me by the shoulders now. Everyone's screaming and grabbing at me, but Lily doesn't let go. Somehow we get to our feet, and I walk toward Bren with my sister holding me up.

What Happened After

Because what goes around really goes around.

—A quote from Wicket Tate's blog, KarmaBitchSlap

Yeah, so I guess this is the part where I talk all about how I rode off into the sunset or whatever. Except there is no sunset and there's no riding, unless you count trips on Griff's motorcycle. I'm not going to bother changing any names to protect the innocent. They'd probably be mad if I did.

Lily's started cheerleading. Yeah, exactly. You read that right. *Cheerleading.* I asked her if she was sick. She asked me if I was a bitch. We both about died laughing.

Then I watched Lily do her dance routine, and I understood. She loves the music and the movement. I would never have guessed, and maybe I don't really get it, but I'm glad. She's trying things she would never have dared to try before.

I guess we all are.

My dad's not coming back. Ever. The police caught him with so much evidence he ended up taking a plea deal—not that it's going to do him much good. He's still looking at almost fifty years behind bars. It makes me sound vindictive, but I'm glad. And relieved.

Todd confessed too. Turns out he had been carrying this craving for as long as he could remember, but it wasn't until the past six or seven years that it became unbearable.

He used Bren to fix himself, marrying her because she was successful and couldn't have kids. He thought it would be perfect . . . until Bren wanted children. They moved to a family community, became involved with the church. Suddenly he was surrounded by the very thing he wanted to avoid. He couldn't get away. And then, slowly, he didn't want to get away because there was Tessa.

God, poor Tessa. I don't think he wanted her because she was beautiful, but because she was broken. It drew him, or at least that's what Norcut says. She thinks that in that horrible moment when Tessa found the courage to say no, Todd found himself, his real self. He discovered he enjoyed inflicting pain, and the man he was afraid of becoming was exactly who he wanted to be.

I guess we're all figuring out who we want to be. Bren's dealing by divorcing him and expanding the business. Our adoption papers went through last month, and we're thinking about moving. Turns out the local folks don't really understand how you couldn't know your husband was a psycho. They've been pretty ugly to her—well, everyone except for Mrs. Waye.

We ran into her at the lawyer's office and instead of screaming, instead of melting down, she just touched Bren on the arm and told her how sorry she was, how bad she felt for Bren's loss. I thought that sounded a little Dr. Phil, but she has a point. The girl Mrs. Waye loved is no longer here. The man Bren loved never existed.

I don't know. Maybe Tally just asked Mrs. Waye to be nice. I guess I'll never know, but it meant a lot to Bren, and for that, I'm grateful.

Everyone else in town is blaming her. They think Bren knew and turned a blind eye. But other people's choices—your dad's, your husband's, your sister's—don't make you who you are. You make you. I know Bren still feels guilty, though. She thinks she should've known. Sometimes, late at night, I catch her still awake, still mining little details of their married life, looking for clues.

"It's going to be okay," she tells me. "It will be."

Bren repeats it like she's convincing me, but really she's convincing herself. Usually this kind of panicked positivity makes me nervous, but she looks so lost, I stick around. We sit on the cold kitchen floor with her hand wrapped around mine and I tell her that of course it will be okay.

The lie is so smooth it might have some truth to it. So what else? Oh, turns out Mr. Waye kept coming by our house because he suspected Todd. The night I came down to confront him, he thought he saw Carson's car approaching, panicked because he knew how nuts he'd look, and took off.

He said he suspected Todd because he had "fatherly premonitions." I hate that description. It makes him sound like a good guy. But maybe he isn't entirely bad, because when Waye heard what happened, he came up to the hospital to check on me. Forgiving him didn't feel right, and neither of us knew what to say, but he stayed.

So did Griff. He has to be the only person who can make me grin just by thinking about him, and I'm sure I have stupid cartoon hearts in my eyes every time I look in his direction. It's nauseating . . . and awesome. I'm lucky. It's like I got my very own happy ending.

Or I would, if Carson would let me go. The police chief gave him a promotion—like he did *any* of the work—and now he has his own team. Between his suspicions and what Todd must have told him, Carson knows I hack, and he says he'll devote the rest of his life to proving it . . . unless I help him.

It's been pretty easy stuff so far, but now the detective has a new target he wants me to investigate: a local judge. Carson knows the guy's dirty, and I have my own reasons for agreeing with him, but I don't want any part of it. The judge's assistant was murdered. Stabbed to death. But before the killer dumped her body, he carved:

REMEMBER ME

Acknowledgments

It's weird to see *Find Me* with only my name on it, because, God knows, I didn't get here on my own. I have no idea where to begin, so I'll just dive in.

As always, I would be nowhere without my incredible parents, who didn't even flinch when I told them I wanted to be a writer . . . and wasn't going to law school . . . and "Oh, by the way, it's one of those creepy books so you probably shouldn't tell your friends."

Except they totally did tell their friends . . . and pretty much anyone else who couldn't outrun them. I am beyond lucky to have such support.

In the same way I'm beyond lucky to have Wonder Agent Sarah Davies on my side. Words are supposed to be my thing, but I'm always flat speechless when describing Sarah. She has been my agent, editor, and fairy godmother all rolled into one. Needless to say, I wouldn't be here without her. Every author should be so lucky as to have someone like her in his or her life.

Beyond grateful to my editor, Phoebe Yeh, for taking a chance on me and for not being completely weirded out when I trotted forward all the reasons I wanted HarperCollins to be my publisher. I promise, I'm not a stalker. I just did a lot of research . . . which, come to think about it, is probably exactly what a stalker would say.

A big thank-you to my little sis, Merrill, and her husband, Ricky, for the repeated read-throughs and feedback. Another big thank-you to Alana Whitman, Olivia deLeon, and Jessica MacLeish, who make me look so much cooler and more pulled together than I actually am.

I also want to thank Tanya Michaels, Jana Oliver, Valerie Bowman, and Debby Giusti, who believed in me way before I believed in myself. You ladies rock. I must have been a much nicer person in a former life to have earned such support.

Special thanks to the following teachers and professors I had the pleasure of working with over the years: Priscilla Overstreet, Christopher Craig, Margie Lawson, Dianna Love, Mary Buckham, Dr. Mary Alice Money, Dr. Stephen Dobranski, Dr. Michael Galchinsky, and Dr. Malinda Snow. I so, so, so hope you enjoy *Find Me* as much as I enjoyed your classes. I'm writing today because of you.

And thank you doesn't even begin to cover what I owe my awesome critique partners, Jennifer McQuiston and Sally Kilpatrick. I am amazed that these ladies take my phone calls, let alone read my dreadful first drafts. I am so lucky to have them.

A big shout-out to all my friends at Georgia Romance Writers and, of course, my beloved DoomsDaisies, who will probably end up ruling the world, so everyone better stay on their good side.

Another thank-you to my awesome buddies downtown: Drew Nabbefeldt, who told everyone I was his favorite author before I even had a book out; Abra Schwartz, who encourages my bad behavior; Joann Steele, Kristin Smith, Larry Rodrigues, and Steve Herbein, who always cheer me on; and Alexis Kole and Nichole Pitts, who are pretty much made of awesome.

Particular thanks to Cecily White and Meg Kassel for those lightning reads, as well as to Dr. Patricia Recklet, who not only takes care of Tempi the Wonder Pony but also read *Find Me* and, to my utter delight, asked for more.

And, of course, thank you to my husband, Tony Bernard, who was with me the whole way and who believed in me even when I didn't. Most girls dream about marrying a superhero. I actually did. I love you, sweetheart.

Keep reading for a sneak peek at *Remember Me*, the sequel to *Find Me*!

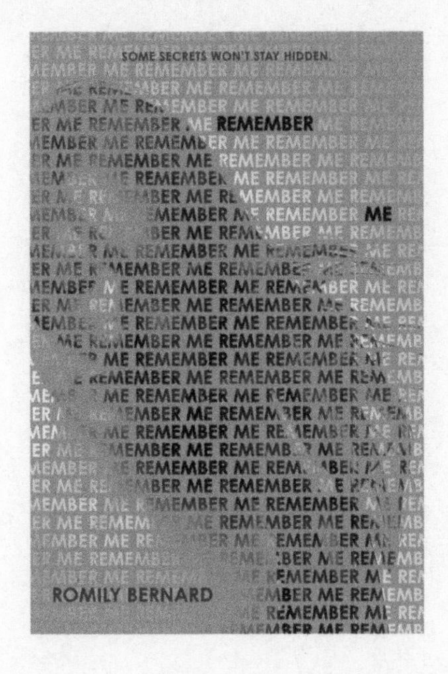

Somehow I think I always knew I'd get arrested. I just never expected it to happen during Home Ec. From the looks of it, Principal Matthews agrees. His face is ham-pink and shiny. He seems angry until I see the grin.

"Miss Tate?" he says. "Could we have a word?"

Love it when they make an order sound like a request. I mutter apologies to my group partners and grab my messenger bag from under the counter, pulling the strap across my shoulder. I've been expecting this moment for almost five months now, and I know I deserve it, but I can't help one last glance at the open window across the room.

If I ran full out, I could escape.

"*Now*, Miss Tate."

Or not.

I walk to the nearest of the two officers and bump up

my chin so I can pretend my joints aren't loosening. The policeman looks me over, scowls. I know what he sees—long, pale blond hair; short, pale blue dress—and what he's thinking: trash. He might even be right.

Nice girls don't write computer viruses.

Let alone use them.

The officer takes my bag and, after he glances through it, all of us tromp into the hallway. Just like I always pictured, Detective Carson is waiting. He looks so happy I start to shake.

"Here she is, Detective." Principal Matthews pats my arm and I have to resist the urge to bite him. "Like I said she'd be."

"Great." Carson jerks his head to the left. "Can we use this classroom?"

Classroom? One of the officers prods me forward and I trip, my feet suddenly useless. If I'm not being arrested, then what—

Shit. It's another job. He's going to make me work for him again.

"Um." Matthews rubs the back of his head, looking dumbfounded, which, to be honest, isn't much of a stretch for him. "It's not really protocol."

"It'll only be for a few minutes, and we'd really appreciate the help." Carson's smile goes crocodile wide. "I'll be sure to remember it."

"Oh, good. That's good." Matthews retreats, refusing to meet my eyes. He pats his pockets like he lost something. "We're always happy to be of assistance."

And, to Matthews's credit, he does sound happy, but when he looks at the floor, the roots of his hair are glittery with sweat.

I can't blame him. The detective has the same effect on me.

I follow Carson into the empty classroom, neither of us saying anything until the door clicks closed.

"Well, well, Wicket Tate." He smiles. "You don't call. You don't write. What am I supposed to think?"

"It's not you. It's me." I tap one finger to my lower lip. "Nah, it's definitely you."

Carson laughs. He sits down on a desktop so we're almost eye to eye, a poster of Spanish verb conjugations above his head as he paws through my bag. "I miss this, Wick. You're always such a smart-ass when you're scared."

"I'm not scared of you."

"You should be." He looks up, the amused smile snapped off. "You're not keeping up with our deal. You do what I want now. Remember? Or else you go to jail."

Carson leans closer and I have to push my feet into the floor to keep from running. "I have evidence you hacked to catch Todd Callaway."

My breath dries up. Stupid how after so many months the name can still make me flinch. Todd. My former foster dad and my former best friend's rapist. He almost killed me. What I did to catch him was justified . . . it just wasn't legal.

"If I can find evidence on what you did to Callaway," Carson says, "imagine what I could find on the work you did for that shitbird father of yours."

Odds are, he could find loads—especially if my father and his partner decide to roll on me. I focus on the Spanish verbs so I don't have to meet Carson's eyes. "What do you want?"

"I have another job. It's perfect for you." When I don't respond, the detective clears his throat and continues, "I want to track Jason Baines and I want you to make it happen. Immediately."

He's right. It is kind of perfect. Baines is a mid-level drug dealer who worked for my father. We have history. If anyone could get close, I could—except this is beyond the type of work I usually do. Before, Carson needed an email track here, a credit card trace there. This is way riskier.

"Find someone else, Carson. I do cyberspace. Tracking that fast would require contact."

"Your *point*? Don't play shy, Wick. Baines specializes in roofies." Carson searches my face and, even though I keep my features disinterested, he still sees something that makes his eyes go plastic bright. "He preys on women. That's not too different from the men you used to catch, right?"

Right. Up until five months ago, I ran an online business specializing in catching cheaters and gold diggers. Most of my targets were guys. Most of my clients were women. And yeah, I did it for money—my sister, Lily, and I needed it—but I also did it because those women needed answers. I made sure the men they loved were really who they said they were. I made sure no one ended up like my mom did.

And later, I used those same skills to bring down Todd and save my sister.

But Carson only knows a little bit about the last part and nothing about the first. He's fishing and I play it blank, realizing too late that I should have played it stupid.

"What are you talking about?" I say, twirling a strand of hair around my finger. Carson's mouth thins and I switch the conversation around. "Look, your best bet for tracking Baines is putting something on his phone, only that's no good because I'd have to get close enough to do it and—"

"And it shouldn't be hard since you two go way back. One of my sources says he'll be selling at Judge Bay's Carnivale party tonight."

"You sure?" Bay is a local luminary: rich, well-connected, the kind of guy who uses *summer* as a verb. I know of him the same way most people like me know of him: He presided over our legal cases. "That's pretty bold."

"My source says your new mommy has accepted an invitation as well."

I go very, very still. "You've been watching Bren?"

"Scared now?"

"No." I'm fucking terrified. I shove suddenly sweating hands into my pockets. "You wouldn't dare touch her."

Only, he would, to get to me. My sister and I were adopted by Bren Callaway two months ago in what the papers are calling a fairy-tale ending. Although the description makes me gag, I can't fault the observation. Lily and I went from foster care rejects to looking like poster children for Ralph Lauren. Yeah, Bren was married to Todd, the psychopath who tried to kill both me and Lily, but aside from Bren's seriously crappy taste in men, she's straight out of Disney casting.

She doesn't deserve what Carson would do to her to get to me.

"I want you there." The detective stands, tosses my bag to me. "Do whatever you have to do. I want to be able to follow Baines's movement by tomorrow."

"Yeah, I'm fresh out of magic wands." Then again, I might not be. Baines isn't the only one who can get roofies. I could knock him out, download a tracking app to his phone. There's a certain poetic justice to it. I'm very capable of this . . . and that fact should scare me.

Actually, it does scare me. Thing is . . . if I tag Baines, Carson will go away. Bren and Lily will be safe. I can go on pretending I'm normal.

For a little while at least.

"Make it happen." The detective stares down at me, and even though it's finally healed, my injured arm starts to burn. "You wouldn't want to ruin that lovely new life you landed, now would you?"

"No." And isn't that just the funniest punch line? Here I am with a new life, new start, and I'm already ruining it. Worse, I'm risking ruining it for my sister—and for

Bren—and they deserve any happily ever after life will give them.

I consider Carson. This is probably where I should cry a bit, but I've swallowed my tears for so long they've turned to bone.

I roll my hands into fists. "Maybe you're the one who should be careful. I brought down a rapist you couldn't. The papers are calling me a hero."

Even if I can barely say the word.

Carson's upper lip wrinkles. "That so?"

Above us, the bell rings. School's finished for the day and the hallway swarms with students, their voices swelling like the growl of distant thunder. How long before the rumor of me getting hauled out of class by the police reaches Bren? Or my best friend, Lauren?

Worse, how long before it reaches Griff?

Is it considerate that I want to be the person who tells him first? Or paranoid? I never told him I was working for Carson. He thinks I'm free.

And just like that, my hands are shaking again. "I'll send you a text when it's finished."

"Good." Carson smacks open the classroom door and motions me forward. I'm almost into the hallway when his fingers sink into my bad arm, pinning me against the lockers to hide his grip. "The next time you think about blowing me off, Wicket, you think about everything I could destroy."

I hold my breath, waiting for Carson to twist my arm

until I want to scream. His hold stays light though. It's not punishment. It's a promise.

"Understand?" he asks, fitting Bren and Lily and everything I want into one word.

I nod, but the detective doesn't let go and I shouldn't look at him. . . . I do, realizing too late he isn't focused on me. He's staring at Griff.

Who's headed straight for us.

"Smile for the boyfriend," Carson says.

Funny how I still can. Smiles are so easy when they're for Griff. I smile. Carson smiles. Griff's too far away, but I know his eyes have narrowed.

The detective snorts. "I'm always amazed at the way he looks at you."

Me too.

Carson leans down, his lips so close to my ear the words escape in a hiss: "Think he'd look at you the same way if he knew what you really are?"

He does know. Griff helped me escape my father and Todd. He knows what I was before and he never wants me to go back.

"Think he'd still want you if he knew you were working for me?"

No. Yes. I don't know and it makes my chest shrink tight. This is what happens when you end up with a hero. He expects you to be just as noble.

And I'm not.

Carson releases my arm, his thumb curving across the

spot where Todd rammed in the knife. "I enjoy our little talks. I like seeing everything you've got now, gives me more I can take away. We understand each other?"

"Perfectly."

"Good," the detective says, and swings away from me, cutting left, cutting right as the students surge around him.

"What was that about?"

It takes me a beat before I can finally turn around, and when I do, Griff cups my jaw. His long fingers reach into my hair, streak chills down my spine.

"Todd," I say. The lie is sluggish. I'm looking at Griff and can see only Carson. I shake myself. Another problem with heroes: If you confess your secrets, they will want to save you.

I want to save myself.

"They found some additional information," I add.

Griff frowns. "Anything we should worry about?"

"No." I smile and it makes him smile. He looks at me like I'm perfect.

What happens if that goes away?

"It's under control," I add, and it *is* under control. That part, at least, isn't a lie. I will fix this. I *will*.

Someone jostles Griff from behind and he steps into me, filling my nose with the smell of grass and gasoline and oil paints from his art class. Griff braces one hand above me, shielding me from the crowd. "We still on for tonight?"

I blink. *Dammit. How could I have forgotten?* "Um, yeah, it's just that I have this thing I need to do. With Bren. Can we meet up later?"

"Of course," he says. And kisses me.

I wrap my arms around his neck and he tugs me close, his hands skating over me, dragging shivers across my skin. I feel my heartbeat . . . *everywhere.* Does it make me pathetic that Griff can burn everything else away?

Everything, but this: Would he want me if he knew?

Yes. Of course. No doubt.

Even though I repeat the words, I don't believe in them any more than I believe in the fairy-tale ending I've been given. There's no such thing. Or there wasn't until I met Griff.

Which side of me is worse: the pathetic girl who wants the boy or the pathetic girl who's afraid of the detective?

I break off our kiss, tell myself I'm breathless from Griff and not because I'm scared. Even though I know that's what lives at the bottom of this: I'm terrified. I don't want to lose everything I've been given.

I curl my hands into Griff's shirt. He grins and my heart stutters.

"So I'll see you later then, Wicked?"

The nickname still makes me blush. "Definitely."

Another kiss. This one's hard and fast. By the time my fingers curl into his chest, it's done. He's turning away.

Gone.

I chew my tingling lips and reach for my phone, dialing

a number I haven't used in ages and should have forgotten. Stringer picks up on the third ring. There's no hello, but I can hear his breathing.

"Hey . . . it's me." I lean against the lockers, cradling my bad arm.

"Been a long time, girlie."

"Yeah, it has." Months and months, actually. Before I went into foster care. When Stringer and I were just good earners for my dad. "I need your help."

"What kind of help?"

"Roofies. By tonight."